Volume 17, Number 4

"The truth in a calm world,
In which there is no other meaning, itself
Is calm, itself is summer and night, itself
Is the reader leaning late and reading there."

—WALLACE STEVENS

From Tin House Books

ELEVEN HOURS
a novel by Pamela Erens

Lore arrives at the hospital alone—no husband, no partner, no friends. Her birth plan is explicit: she wants no fetal monitor, no IV, no epidural. Franckline, a nurse in the maternity ward—herself on the verge of showing—is patient with the young woman. She knows what it's like to worry that something might go wrong, and she understands the distress when it does. She knows as well as anyone the severe challenge of childbirth, what it does to the mind and the body. At turns urgent and lyrical, *Eleven Hours* is a visceral portrait of childbirth, and a vivid rendering of the way we approach motherhood—with fear and joy, anguish and awe.

"Powerful—aesthetically and viscerally."
—*Kirkus*, Starred Review

"I loved *Eleven Hours*. In this gorgeous, haunting, slender novel, Pamela Erens creates an intimacy that is all-encompassing."
—ROXANE GAY, author of *Bad Feminist*

Available Now

LAST SEXT
poetry by Melissa Broder

In her electric fourth collection, Melissa Broder penetrates the itch of existence and explores numberless deaths: the annihilation of self, the bereavement of love, the destruction of fantasy, the transmutation, even, of our ideas of dying. What emerges is an infinite series of false endings—each a trap door containing the possibility for alchemy, rebirth, and renewal. Part elegy, part confessional, part battle cry, *Last Sext* confronts both eternal longing and the mystery of mortality, with language hot, primal, and dark, as Broder's fans have come to love.

"Melissa Broder is absolutely one of the most important poets writing today. Her poems eviscerate the reader with their misty and murky charm, with their ability to say what is and not what should be, for their love of life and the sensual, for their knowledge of what it is like to be a person right now. *Last Sext* is a master work, a text of brilliance written in a dusky field, for all of us."
—DOROTHEA LASKY, author of *Rome*

Available June 2016

For more information or to order, please go to www.tinhouse.com

BEFORE THE FEAST

a novel by Saša Stanišić
translated by Anthea Bell

It's the evening before the feast in the village of Fürstenfelde (population: an odd number). The village is asleep. Except for the ferryman—he's dead. And Mrs. Kranz, the night-blind painter, who wants to depict her village for the first time at night. A bell-ringer and his apprentice want to ring the bells—the only problem is that the bells have gone.

Someone has opened the doors to the Village Archive, but what drives the sleepless out of their houses is not that which was stolen, but that which has escaped. Old stories, myths, and fairy tales are wandering about the streets with the people. They come together in a novel about a long night, a mosaic of village life, in which the long-established and newcomers, the dead and the living, craftsmen, pensioners, and noble robbers in football jerseys bump into each other. They all want to bring something to a close, on this night before the feast.

"A brilliant, quirky entertainment."

—*Kirkus*, Starred Review

Available June 2016

NINETY-NINE STORIES OF GOD

stories by Joy Williams

This series of short, fictional vignettes explores our day-to-day interactions with an ever-elusive and arbitrary God. It's the *Book of Common Prayer* as seen through a looking glass—a powerfully vivid collection of seemingly random life moments. The figures that haunt these stories range from Kafka (talking to a fish) to the Aztecs, Tolstoy to Abraham and Sarah, O. J. Simpson to a pack of wolves. Most of Williams's characters, however, are like the rest of us: anonymous strivers and bumblers who brush up against God in the least expected places or go searching for Him when He's standing right there. The Lord shows up at a hot-dog-eating contest, a demolition derby, a formal gala, and a drugstore, where he's in line to get a shingles vaccination. At turns comic and yearning, lyric and aphoristic, *Ninety-Nine Stories of God* serves as a pure distillation of one of our great artists.

"These stories are 100% Williams: funny, unsettling, and mysterious, to be puzzled over and enjoyed across multiple readings."

—*Publishers Weekly*, Starred Review

Available July 2016

> "Thornton is a writer of formidable talent and deep heart, and this nuanced and moving novel marks his arrival as a significant new voice in contemporary fiction."
>
> — **BRET ANTHONY JOHNSTON**
> author of
> *Remember Me Like This*

"Compelling and authentic... a story of China as told by an outsider."

— **YU HUA**
winner of the James Joyce Award and the Grinzane Cavour Prize

"This unsettling book about the moral encounter between America and China is a study of privilege, innocence, and risk."

— **EVAN OSNOS**
author of *Age of Ambition*, winner of the National Book Award

"Authentic, pure and heartbreaking... (Thornton) is an exceptionally gifted young writer."

— **MO YAN**
2012 Nobel Laureate in Literature

"A coming-of-age story that vividly encapsulates the complexities of the modern encounter between China and America."

— **NIALL FERGUSON**
author of *Kissinger: 1923–1968: The Idealist* and *Civilization*

Tin House MAGAZINE

EDITOR IN CHIEF / PUBLISHER
Win McCormack

EDITOR	Rob Spillman
ART DIRECTOR	Diane Chonette
MANAGING EDITOR	Cheston Knapp
EXECUTIVE EDITOR	Michelle Wildgen
POETRY EDITOR	Matthew Dickman
EDITOR-AT-LARGE	Elissa Schappell
PARIS EDITOR	Heather Hartley
ASSOCIATE EDITOR	Emma Komlos-Hrobsky
ASSISTANT EDITOR	Lance Cleland
EDITORIAL ASSISTANT	Thomas Ross

CONTRIBUTING EDITORS: Dorothy Allison, Steve Almond, Aimee Bender, Charles D'Ambrosio, Brian DeLeeuw, Anthony Doerr, CJ Evans, Nick Flynn, Matthea Harvey, Jeanne McCulloch, Christopher Merrill, Rick Moody, Whitney Otto, D. A. Powell, Jon Raymond, Rachel Resnick, Helen Schulman, Jim Shepard, Karen Shepard, Bill Wadsworth

DESIGNER: Jakob Vala

INTERNS: Noah Dow, Bianca Flores, Alana Grambush, Alana Hippensteele, Erin Kaempf, Taylor Lannamann, Laura Mock, Madison Pierce, Boramie Sao, Sarah T. Weston

READERS: Leslie Marie Aguilar, Stephanie Booth, Susan DeFreitas, Polly Dugan, Selin Gökçesu, Paris Gravley, Todd Gray, Lisa Grgas, Dahlia Grossman-Heinz, Carol Keeley, Louise Wareham Leonard, Su-Yee Lin, Julian Lucas, Ian Nelson, Alyssa Persons, Sean Quinn, Lauren Roberts, Gordon Smith, Jennifer Taylor, JR Toriseva, Lin Woolman, Charlotte Wyatt

DEPUTY PUBLISHER	Holly MacArthur
CIRCULATION DIRECTOR	Laura Howard
DIRECTOR OF PUBLICITY	Nanci McCloskey
COMPTROLLER	Janice Carter

Tin House Books

EDITORIAL ADVISOR Rob Spillman
EDITORS Meg Storey, Tony Perez, Masie Cochran
ASSISTANT EDITOR Thomas Ross

Tin House Magazine (ISSN 1541-521X) is published quarterly by McCormack Communications LLC, 2601 Northwest Thurman Street, Portland, OR 97210. Vol. 17, No. 4, Summer 2016. Printed by Versa Press, Inc. Send submissions (with SASE) to Tin House, P.O. Box 10500, Portland, OR 97296-0500. ©2014 McCormack Communications LLC. All rights reserved. No part of this publication may be reproduced, stored in a retrieval system, or transmitted in any form or by any means, electronic, mechanical, photocopying, recording, or otherwise, without the prior written permission of McCormack Communications LLC. Visit our Web site at **www.tinhouse.com**.

Basic subscription price: one year, $50.00. For subscription requests, write to P.O. Box 469049, Escondido, CA 92046-9049, or e-mail tinhouse@pcspublink.com, or call 1-800-786-3424. Additional questions, e-mail laura@tinhouse.com.

Periodicals postage paid at Portland, OR 97210 and additional mailing offices.

Postmaster: Send address changes to Tin House Magazine, P.O. Box 469049, Escondido, CA 92046-9049.

Newsstand distribution through Disticor Magazine Distribution Services (disticor.com). If you are a retailer and would like to order Tin House, call 905-619-6565, fax 905-619-2903, or e-mail Melanie Raucci at mraucci@disticor.com. For trade copies, contact W. W. Norton & Company at 800-233-4830.

EDITOR'S NOTE

Dear Indie Booksellers,

Without you, we are nothing.

Forever yours, Tin House

In January I was in Denver for the American Booksellers Association's Winter Institute, where I had the honor of hanging out with six hundred of the most passionate readers of contemporary literature I have ever encountered. Their enthusiasm was infectious and after a single afternoon with these tireless, ruthless pushers of the written word it was easy to understand why bookstore sales are up, and why the number of indie bookstores, which in the dark Amazonian year of 2009 numbered 1,700, has increased to over 2,300. Booksellers like the ones I met in Denver challenge us to keep seeking out the most exciting and thoughtful work by new and established writers from all over the world, and because of them we're confident there is an audience for their work. In this issue we're proud to bring you five fabulous translations, among them Dorthe Nors's "By Sydvest Station," translated from the Danish by Misha Hoekstra, and Jean-Philippe Toussaint's "The Dress of Honey," translated from the French by Edward Gauvin. Alexis M. Smith's debut novel, *Glaciers*, was an indie sensation, and here we feature an excerpt from her follow-up, *Marrow Island*. Smith is joined by other indie darlings, Deb Olin Unferth, Josh Weil, and Saša Stanišić, as well as esteemed poets Dorianne Laux and John Ashbery, who return to our pages. We're also happy to welcome new-to-us poets Anna Journey and Sam Riviere.

To all of the booksellers who have carried us and who continue to carry us, we thank you. To all of our readers, who have carried us and continue to carry us in your backpacks and handbags, on planes, trains, and buses, we are so grateful.

CONTENTS
ISSUE #68 / SUMMER READING

Fiction

Dorthe Nors
Translated by Misha Hoekstra
BY SYDVEST STATION ▸ *Hello, we're from the Cancer Society, would you like to support our work?* 12

Malerie Willens
BODY ELECTRIC ▸ *This person's got a name, but let's call her "you."* 23

Jean-Philippe Toussaint
Translated by Edward Gauvin
THE DRESS OF HONEY ▸ *Marie sometimes ventured beyond fashion into speculative territories.* 41

Saša Stanišić
Translated by Anthea Bell
THE CHICKEN RUN ▸ *Before you build a chicken run, get to know all you can about both chickens and foxes.* 51

Deb Olin Unferth
THE FIRST FULL THOUGHT OF HER LIFE ▸ *The mother and girl walked around the shooter's fender, and started up the dune.* 58

Michael Braunschweig
Translated by Amanda DeMarco
THE TSUCHINOKO ‣ *It may have accidentally come here in a shipping container.* 72

Alexis M. Smith
MARROW ISLAND ‣ *At 9:09 AM the ambient noise of the cities and suburbs and seaside towns went mute.* 100

Eric Puchner
TROJAN WHORES HATE YOU BACK ‣ *Wasn't pissing on danger what Trojan Whores were all about?* 150

Josh Weil
THE ELK-CALF ‣ *Her eyes were gone: red holes opened to the sun. Her belly, too: bowels spilling a mess of wet green grass.* 177

Sean Ennis
VISITATION ‣ *I was not interested in other women, had good reason to doubt their interest in me, and really just valued time by myself.* 201

NEW VOICE – FICTION

Jackson Tobin
THE CAT ‣ *Coop stepped forward and stood over the bag, his head cocked. "What the fuck did you do?"* 129

Poetry

Dorianne Laux
HONEYMOON 19
TULIP POPLAR 21

Sam Riviere
Informal Fatigue 48
Christmas in Berlin 50

John Ashbery
Food Episode 80
Yclept 81
Written with a Ballpoint 82

Joseph Millar
Right Livelihood 116
Night Light 118

Michael Burkard
Hello Mr. Essay 147
Later 13 148
Nerve 149

Per Aage Brandt
Translated by Thom Satterlee
100 173
99 174
98 175
97 176

Anna Journey
Summer of Choosing the Dress 197
Victorian Chamber Pot My Mother Used as a Planter for Climbing Ivy 199

Features

Michael Dickman
JOHN CLARE: MUD MAN PUNK ROCKER • *Who knew punk rock had roots in the English countryside of the nineteenth century?* 33

Marin Sardy
LIGHTNING, OR FEATHERS • *A former competitive gymnast explores how Svetlana Boginskaya turned the gymnastics world on its head.* 119

Lost & Found

Nathan Gauer
ON NICOLAS BOUVIER'S *The Way of the World* • *There is a big difference between traveling to see lands and traveling to see peoples.* 84

Alexandra Pechman
ON EMILY HAHN'S *China to Me* • *The prolific* New Yorker *writer chronicled her time in post World War II China.* 87

Sarah Bridgins
ON WILLIAM SHIRER'S *The Rise and Fall of the Third Reich* • *After the death of her father, the writer felt the need to submerge herself in a past infinitely darker than her own.* 90

Joel Drucker
ON BROOKE HAYWARD'S *Haywire* • *When do we learn that life is tragic, that our journey will include not only the sun but also the moon?* 93

Whitney Otto
ON ANN PETRY'S *The Street* • *The example of the Harlem Renaissance illuminates the trouble of being a hyphenated author, which is that it, the hyphen, fucks with the work.* 96

FICTION

By
Sydvest
Station

Dorthe Nors

translated by Misha Hoekstra

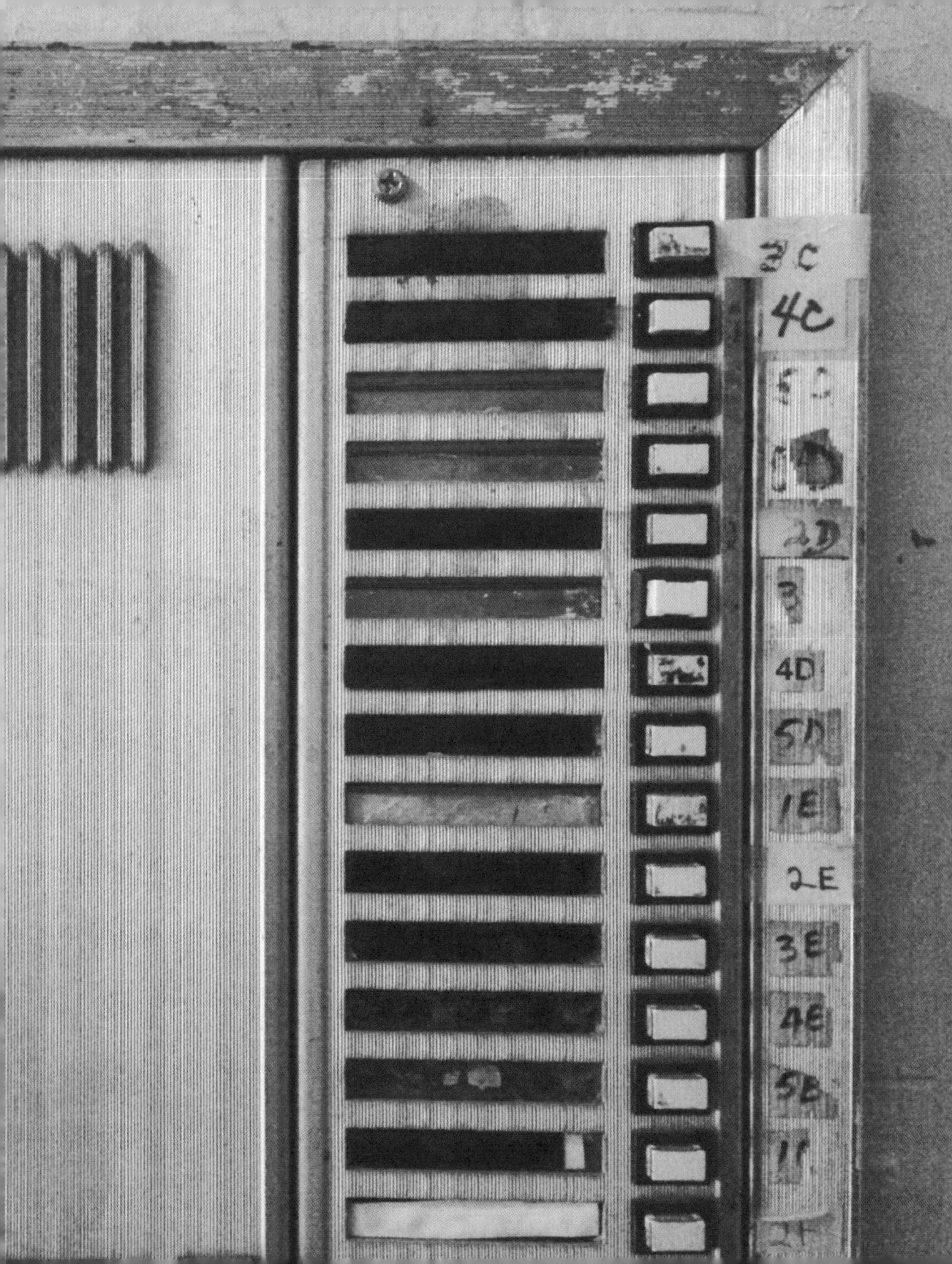

Then they are ready. They have a collection can, a bag with the cancer logo, and two streets by Sydvest Station where there's an apartment co-op and some rental flats, and Kirsten has no idea what she's in for, just that it'll be exciting to try collecting money for the Cancer Society in a neighborhood like this, while Louise steels herself for a bit of awkwardness in standing so far from home in her white sneakers and rattling the can. She's also tired, and at the same time her head is full of him and what he said. It pained her, and she's felt tired ever since, like she could fall asleep on her feet. But Kirsten's game, and Louise smiles at her and says that she is too, and then they get started.

At the first building there's initially no one who answers, even though they press all the buttons on the intercom, but it must be the guy on the fifth floor who finally lets them in, for he ends up being the only one there who contributes. He gives them twenty crowns, and then they giggle all the way downstairs because it's the first money they've ever collected, but also because they're nervous. Some of the doors make it clear how odd people can be. They put stickers with Rottweilers, Bambi, and Cinderella around their nameplates, which sometimes are galvanized and other times written in ballpoint and stuck up with masking tape. There are also doors that send mixed messages, and the two of them talk about how you never know what awaits when you knock on someone's door. *True enough*, Louise thinks to herself, musing on the fact that Kirsten for instance doesn't know that he said what he said to her. Actually, nobody knows that he told her that— that her love couldn't be genuine. That no one really loved that way. It was just some sort of compensation, he'd said, but she doesn't want to tell Kirsten that. She's certain that her reaction would be textbook, and nothing's worse than someone who goes by the book, Louise thinks, saying nothing, and then Kirsten suggests that they start using the decorations on each door to guess what sort of person might answer.

They guess wrong almost every time, but that's what makes it fun, even when some of the people who open the doors are strange. They speak indistinctly, or they answer dressed just in their pj's, and lots of them seem annoyed. The man who answers one door is grumpy about being woken up on a Sunday morning, and he takes it out on them by snapping at them. Other places, there's a rustling behind the door. People whisper as if they can't be heard out on the landing, though everything's audible: *Don't open it. I'm sick and tired of all these people asking for money*, says a woman behind one door, while at another, a kid comes out and slots some change in the can while Mommy and Daddy look on. They clap and say, *How clever*, and Louise thinks that people are weird. Their flats smell intimate, and their filth is bad enough, but what's worse is that the cleaning solutions they do use seem like something you don't want to really know about, and *Hello, we're from the Cancer Society, would you like to support our work?*

> **Actually, nobody knows that he told her that—that her love couldn't be genuine.**

That's their spiel. But it's not really true. Neither she nor Kirsten has anything to do with the Cancer Society, and personally, she doesn't want to have anything to do with them either. This is all about spending a Sunday with a friend, and since they came up with the business of the door decorations in the second stairwell, Louise has also been feeling like some sort of tourist—plus she supposes that what they're doing is a form of begging. Ringing on strange people's doorbells to demand love and respect, Louise thinks, and in the fifth building she's on the point of remonstrating with a young man who says through the letter slot that he doesn't have any money but is a big fan of what they do. She gets the urge to tell him that she isn't doing anything. *In fact all I'm doing is trying to move on after my emotional life went to the dogs, so shove it, motherfucker, you goddamn loser*, she thinks of saying—if she were the type to say such things. But she isn't. She knows perfectly well that she's more the type to focus on how sticky the floors seem in some of the flats and how gross it is, and that, never mind how diverting the door decorations might be, people aren't very modest about their lives.

By Sydvest Station

That some places stink of medicine and dogs. Even though people aren't allowed to have dogs in apartments like these, and even if they are, they shouldn't be, Louise tells Kirsten, and Kirsten says she glimpsed some sort of fighting dog through the letter slot to the fifth-floor flat in the seventh building, where the tenant, a younger woman, gave them two hundred crowns because, as she put it, *Cancer has touched my life.*

Welcome to the club, Louise now thinks, thrusting the can toward Kirsten because it feels like it's begun to stick to her fingers. *Welcome to the club, is all I can say*, she thinks. But she doesn't say it out loud.

They walk purposefully from building to building, or at least Kirsten does. As for Louise, she's just along for the ride now, because she's tired. That's the way it's been these days. Perhaps it's the spring light and the long walks, but it's more what he said. It wasn't genuine, all that love. It was just something she'd fabricated to get the time—no, to get her life—to pass, and afterward she sat there utterly still, and the silence felt like a balm. But now it was time to move on, and she wanted to sit down on the curb and let Kirsten run up staircases eleven and twelve. She won't let herself do that though, but when they reach number fifteen, she starts letting Kirsten say where they come from, contenting herself with standing in the background and helping out if people can't get the coins through the slot. And it works fine that way. The collection can grows heavier and heavier, and that's great, Kirsten says, even here by Sydvest Station, and then on the fourth floor of the seventeenth building, they run into an odd door. It's so odd that Kirsten outdoes herself, trying to guess who might live behind it. *Holy shit*, says Kirsten, laughing because a rubber skeleton is hanging on the door and the person's called Elsa, a name from their grandmothers' generation. Elsa's got a stainless-steel nameplate and a peephole, but the skeleton blocks the hole, so she wouldn't be able to see anything if she wanted to. Louise tells Kirsten it's the kind of skeleton that would glow in the dark if all the lights on the stairs went out; her nephew once had an entire can of small insects made from the same sort of rubber. When he'd been tucked in and the light in his room turned off, they glowed everywhere. He'd taped some to the ceiling, while others lay under his bed among the Legos, creeping and crawling, illuminated like

> **It's too late because Kirsten's become uncertain and doesn't know how to respond.**

those fish in the depths of the Mariana Trench. *If it were night, that skeleton would be the only source of light on the entire stairs*, Louise says, and Kirsten bursts into laughter and says she's got a notion that Elsa's pretty spry. *She's got a sense of humor*, Kirsten says. *She's a party of one*, and then she raps on the door, though Louise is about to say that maybe they should skip her.

But now they've knocked, and at first it's quiet and they adopt a listening attitude, drawing themselves up a little with an ear cocked toward the door. It doesn't sound as if anyone's home. Or actually it does. Someone's moving about in the entryway, and just a moment before there were footsteps on the floor, and now someone is muttering within. *Someone's muttering in there*, Kirsten says, and Louise nods, but just because people mutter in their entries, it doesn't mean that anyone's coming out, so Kirsten places her mouth close to the glow-in-the-dark rubber and says that they're from the Cancer Society, collecting donations, and *Would you like to support our work?*

There's no answer, but they can tell that she's standing right on the other side of the door, Elsa is. *Nothing's happening here*, Louise whispers, but Kirsten won't relent and shouts *Hello?* and suddenly there's scratching on the laminate door, a security chain scrapes against its track, the handle's depressed, and then the door opens—and not just a crack. It opens wide, and then there she is. Elsa stands erect in her bathrobe on her side of the threshold. The entry is small, and she fills the space with her wiry hair and gaping mouth. *Cancer Society*, Kirsten says, rattling the can, and Louise wishes she would leave off, for anyone can see just by looking that Elsa doesn't have a clue what it is they want. She stands there, heavy and bony and with wet strands of hair plastered against the top of her skull, and Louise can see that the only teeth she's got left in her head are the front lower two, and they're the wrong teeth to have left, Louise thinks, unable to keep her eyes off them. *Do you have any loose change?* ventures Kirsten, but Elsa doesn't react as she ought to. She just releases the door handle and goggles at them, and it's unbearable to watch, Louise thinks. It's embarrassing, and now Elsa's starting to rock back and forth in the entry, perhaps because she's begun to recognize something about the scene, but now it's too late. It's too late because Kirsten's become uncertain and doesn't know how to respond. Kirsten's used to always knowing how to handle a situation, but not with Elsa, and then Kirsten's smile evaporates and Louise can see the sticky floor, and Elsa mutters, but what she says makes no sense, and then Kirsten wants to leave, just leave, and Elsa, who accidentally opened the door for the Cancer Society, loses her grip on her bathrobe.

The robe slips to the side so they can see Elsa as she is, and Kirsten wants to leave. She tugs Louise's elbow to signal that they should leave. But they can't just leave, thinks Louise, and she takes a step forward and says, *You must really excuse us for disturbing you. Enjoy the rest of your Sunday*, and then she reaches in and closes the door in Elsa's face.

Down on the street there's sunlight, and Louise places herself in the middle of it while Kirsten remains over by the front door of the building. She says that that'd been utterly awful. What they'd just gone through is almost too much for her to process, so she says it again: *I've never experienced anything like it. It was awful, wasn't it, Louise?* Louise rummages for the map and doesn't answer, but Kirsten says that no one should be the way Elsa was on the fourth floor. *It's really a disgrace*, she says, looking at the front door. *Do you think she has home care?* she asks, but Louise doesn't answer. They're somewhere by Sydvest Station, far from home, and she has the map out and starts walking. There are only two buildings to go, and Kirsten mustn't see that her face is averted, that she feels heat moving deep into her skull and down to her softer parts; that she's thinking about him. She's thinking about him and what he said—that it wasn't love. It couldn't be, he'd said, and here she'd gone and felt inside precisely as if it were.

Dorianne Laux

HONEYMOON

We didn't have one, unless you count Paris,
20 years later, after we'd almost given up on the idea.
We'd imagined one, long nights beneath
a warm celestial sky, him growing his beard,
me in a silk turquoise robe, floating, billowing,
on a deserted beach foraging for whole sand dollars,
jelly fish washed up on the shore, their glittering insides
visible, still pulsing through flesh made of glass,
but it never happened. We had to work through
our vacations, refinance the house, find someone
to cut down the cedar that threatened to bury us
with each storm. We wanted to make up
for the wedding, or lack of one, the granite
courthouse steps, the small room with a desk,
the flimsy document stamped with a cheap gold seal.
Even then we meant to have a party on the deck,
cheese and crackers, fruit plates, sparkling
grape cider in plastic cups, our friends on the lawn
calling you the Big Kahuna, me Mrs. Dynamite,
me calling you my Sweet Dragon, you calling me
your Little Red Corvette. Instead, time found a way
to demand each minute, until one night,
after you'd gotten a small windfall in the mail,

you turned to me and said, *I'm going to take you to Paris*,
me in my ratty robe and floppy slippers, you
in your flannel pj bottoms and black wife beater,
muting the clicker when I said "What?"
and saying it again. Then we were there,
in our 60s, standing below the dire Eiffel Tower,
its 81 stories of staircases we couldn't possibly climb,
its 73 thousand tons of puddled iron, you
taking my picture for posterity, me
kissing you beneath the pathway of arched trees,
our voices echoing against the six million skulls
embedded inside the stone catacombs, me
saying, *I guess you weren't kidding*, you
taking my hand in the rain.

TULIP POPLAR

In autumn, the tulip poplar is a tree gowned in light,
its violin-shaped leaves yellow-gold, the seed cones
cinnamon. Tall and conical, it is a tree for connoisseurs,
its branchlets reddish, lustrous smooth when young,
dark gray in adolescence, the bark maturing
to a rich furrowed brown. In spring it gathers
its inborn charisma and puts forth its finest flowers,
green-tinged buttercups, erect on their stems,
filled with orange nests of nectar. As it grows
it loses its easily broken lower branches, and so
the young will find it difficult to climb,
though cardinals perch in it to sing, and warblers
can be found playing at espionage in its crown
or staked out near the tear-shaped dollop
of a purple finch. In winter you wouldn't recognize it,
stripped of its flashy paraphernalia, poltergeist
swaying on a snowy hill, shrouded in fog,
its sullen branches sheathed in ice, its seed cones
burst into brittle Egyptian fans. But when
they finally fall the new buds emerge, tiny
red-tipped parrot beaks sipping at sunlight.
And the poplar tree goes on, building
its cottage industry of fine-grained wood
which for centuries we have cut down to make

spoons and pipe organs, cradles and coffins,
the wide floorboards of meeting houses,
churches where we have married, danced
and died. Don't ask me why
we would hang a body from such beauty,
sap wood and heart wood. We live
with its dark history, it gives us its darkest,
most bitter honey.

FICTION

Body Electric

Malerie Willens

This person's got a name, but let's call her "you." You pop into Butterwell Bakeshop after work, to huff the vapors of a thousand mille-feuilles. You eat a complimentary stub of zucchini bread from the basket on the counter while pretending to survey the case, despite the fact that you know its contents by heart and could probably evoke them in the middle of the night, a memory exercise to help you sleep. From left to right: chocolate chip pretzels, organic Irish soda bread, hot-crossed prosciutto buns, blue velvet cupcakes, and on and on. You've considered the sensual possibilities of lying naked, lengthwise, along that case, the literal "feeling" of cookies and rolls and brain-sized scones adding a tactile, calorie-free fillip to an already tumultuously hot lust.

You wrap up your charade as a moderate, everyday customer who just casually happened in, and you leave Butterwell with two big bags. The greasy, dense weight of the pastries begins immediately weeping through the wax paper.

You walk up Ninth Avenue, past the pastiche of prix fixe enthusiasts and Hell's Kitchen derelicts—the ones that still bray and howl and forget to wear pants despite the fact that their neighborhood's now got more brunching ad execs on Vespas than urine-soaked klepto-crackheads. You start fingering your stash of starch but you do not remove anything because you must never, *ever* unearth the food in public. Walk instead with hand in bag, pinching off pieces of object. Doesn't matter if object is wet, viscous, cheesy, sloppy, or frosting-covered. This bag, this object cover-upper, must never be peeled back to reveal contents to you or to passersby.

Collapsibility is key when walking with vessels of objects. Consolidate everything into one bag quickly. You want mobility: no balls, no chains. You will eat the cake once you're on the subway. You'll be sitting and you

MALERIE WILLENS

can keep the cake in the bag and dip into it with the fork. That way, train companions might assume you're eating dinner—some salad or hummus or other acceptable takeout—not the second massive slice of lemon mousseline cake you've consumed in ten minutes.

You have perfected the public eat-weave, the sidewalk sojourn with objects in tow. Pinch/eat/pinch/eat. If you walk fast enough, no oncoming walkers will catch more than one cycle of pinch/eat. Your sequence is a matter of personal preference, and depends upon that session's objects. Not crazy about the tomato-feta brioche? Just eat it. Pumpkin strudel's drier than you'd hoped? No matter! Down the hatch! This is about consumption—not discernment, not discrimination. You made the decision a half an hour before you left work and now there's no turning back.

You decided as the workday ended. It had been this kind of Tuesday: You walked to your morning train and already your outfit was twisting and pulling, unflattering, too tight in the armpits. By the time you got to work, you were sweating between your breasts and at the small of your back. At work you were bound to your seat. You drank too little water, peed only once, ate a lunch that was unhealthy, unsatisfying, and left a greasy patina of onion on your fingertips, despite washing them repeatedly. You sat there, hunched and tense, writing things that made bad people sound good, made stale ideas seem pioneering, while your coworkers left midday for sample sales and returned in a jasmine-scented mist of giggles and shopping bags. You knew they knew you hadn't left your desk all day. You knew they knew you sat there squinting, shifting, furrowing your brow, which, unlike theirs, was not slathered with an age-defying cream mined recently from the Andes. And when you finally finished writing your paean to something that will only make the world worse, your boss had already left for a meeting at Cipriani that wasn't really a meeting at all but was in fact a lovely little prosecco and smoked fish tête-à-tête with a man who found her attractive, despite her resemblance to a bosomy Peter Lorre.

Imagine the sensation of having just eaten a mountainous Thanksgiving dinner, except for the fact that you're not surrounded by similarly engorged

> **You have perfected the public eat-weave, the sidewalk sojourn with objects in tow. Pinch/eat/pinch/eat.**

family members who love you. There is no Ultrasuede® sectional into which you can sink, no televised sporting event or dog show to watch, no *The Twilight Zone* marathon, no kitty to stroke, and no assurance that this is a nationally sanctioned once-a-year occurrence, and one of the few moments you feel American. No. Instead you are underneath Port Authority, waiting for your train while a wild-eyed Korean man plays hymns on what appears to be, but isn't, a flute. His open-closed eyes have settled at half-mast, as eyes tend to for the rapturous and exhausted. Your coworkers—the girls—take cabs to and from work, but none of *them* live deep in the outer boroughs. You lean against a dirty pillar and scan the tracks for rats, the bulging Butterwell bag in hand. Express train approaches, doors open. You're seated, moving, grateful to be at the mercy of a machine, to cuddle up between the cogs and just let things happen.

> **Sentient beings are the only beings that get blue balls.**

You disappear half of a porous black currant scone before the first stop. It would've been easier and you would've eaten more if you had a little lube. Liquids are essential to the breakdown of objects. Gulping dry scones is no picnic, so you transition to a four-inch-high slice of creamy white birthday cake as the subway doors close after three tentative bounces, and you continue heading downtown. The cake goes south like butter; it's practically doing the job of a beverage. You imagine it liquefying the crumbly contents that came before, and there is comfort in the thought, a soft sensation of inevitability. Then the train just stops. It is totally still, poised somewhere between Fourteenth and Canal Streets, due to a "police incident."

There's *always* a "police incident." They generally freeze the train for about twenty seconds. A twenty-second incident is hardly an incident. Can legitimate upheaval resolve itself in twenty seconds? It's doubtful, though it takes a firing squad less than half that time to dissolve a line of people . . . and twenty seconds is enough time to vomit up a Number Seven Value Meal. But as police incidents go, twenty seconds is unimpressive. You ride these trains daily and the continued announcements of police incidents that end up lasting twenty seconds have begun to reassure you; they disrupt you for long enough to feel that something has gone awry, then they wrap themselves up before your imagination kicks in. It's like setting the alarm clock for 6:00 AM on a Saturday, just so you can fall back asleep with the sweet awareness that things could be worse.

But tonight, this night of mass consumption, this night of all nights when you're on the clock, tonight your train stays put. The twenty-second mark passes. It's been at least a minute, maybe two. The only remaining object in the Butterwell bag is a six-inch-by-six-inch square of artichoke-gruyère focaccia, which you'd planned to heat up at home.

If your binge/purge purgatory's unexpectedly protracted, you scrape some serious mental resources from your barf bag of tricks. Whence comes the subversion? If person lives in New York, it's likely the subway. First rule of thumb when averting this brand of blue balls: never consume thousands of calories before boarding the train. This strain of blue balls does ache, but not in the bollocks. The irrefutable truth of matter trapped tautly inside, whether cum or cream puffs, is a conundrum of physics, a problem of space, and another problem entirely. The physical discomfort is easier than the awareness of having a load to shoot when something prevents you from shooting it. Shooting, spewing, ejecting, squirting. Sentient beings are the only beings that get blue balls. Other beings just eat, mate, sleep, expel: whenever, however.

Small amounts of starch are digested by the amylase present in saliva, and the resulting bolus of food is swallowed into the esophagus and carried by peristalsis to the stomach. Food travels down the esophagus at a rate of approximately one to two inches per second.

The process is afoot. You are stranded, metaphorical balls growing bluer in increments. You are glad that tonight's bolus is poorly lubed; it slows things down. Another factor that's slowing down absorption is the high fat content of the objects. You are looking on the bright side. You remember that the alimentary canal is thirty feet long from end to end. Whether or not you should be encouraged by this is unclear. You decide to be encouraged, that thirty feet is terribly long and that there are proverbial miles to go before the bolus sleeps—whether in *your* bowel or the bowels of the New York septic system, should you make it in time.

They scoff, the ones who've not performed this fox-trot, doubters who think it bourgeois, imaginary, muliebral. What they *don't* know is that the moment of commitment—the one at the office—is the same as a dope fiend's, a drunk's, and a gambler's. The pin pricks the balloon and—*pop!*—it's done. A switch is flicked and the machine spasms into motion. There is no decision but the one that gets made adrenally, nonverbally, and possibly in the womb.

Pleasure? There is little. You have a smallish appetite, so gorging gets uncomfortable fast. The first object or two, especially if you're actually hungry, can allay the itch the way a good orgasm or a hot bath can. Like that first beer after a hard day. Why can't you be satisfied by these acceptable means of winding down? Why eat ten cookies? Why not two? You've been told it's a control thing and that it's got little to do with food. You think perhaps it's related to your love of rejecting and ejecting: the sliding away from boyfriends before you're married and pregnant, the returning of more than half of the items you buy—often thrillingly on the final day covered by the return policy. This eleventh-hour declaration of freedom from constraint—caloric, emotional, financial—can be quite a rush. As with all the best rushes, fear supplies the horsepower.

The "police incident," according to comically muffled loudspeaker Esperanto, is now the more graphic but equally vague "problem on the tracks," and this muzzy doublespeak would be funny if you hadn't just consumed five thousand low-quality calories of refined something or other—refinement in this case meaning coarse, crass, totally unlovely.

You think you might actually *feel* the process. Your body, outwardly, is still. The stiller you sit, the more internal motion you detect. It's a terrible tug-of-war, to have to sit, literally sit, with the knowledge that you've just bombarded yourself with filth, and too much of it. On a normal night, you'd be in that delirious transit between consumption and expulsion, not forced to sit still while the gastric show begins. This is a vile punishment, this moment of reckoning with the Metropolitan Transportation Authority. You wonder whether you look as distraught as you feel. You are fidgety, jerky, shifting—but so are your fellow travelers. Have all the passengers just visited Butterwell Bakeshop? Have they all just slithered naked in the pastries, waiting now to vanquish their bad day? The peristalsis of fifty-some humans, the buzz of their rotors, loud against the subway's dumb inertia. You all want to go home and expunge your bad day.

There is nobody attractive on this train. And no obvious crazies. You want chocolate chips straight from the bag. Or mixed into gelato. Pad Thai first, then the gelato. You make a mental note to incorporate these objects into some other night's binge. If the train moves within ten minutes and gets you home without additional stalls, you should be fine. This is unscientific, of course. You set the cell phone alarm for ten minutes from now. More than fifty people on the train if you include babies. Approximate number of calories consumed? More than a few Big Macs. Maybe the equivalent of a large pizza with three different meats. Fine for a wrestler, bad for a five-foot-eight-inch woman who didn't exercise this morning, whose metabolism is probably slowing prematurely from real and imagined stress and strain.

A family of four is directly across from you. Caucasian, almost certainly tourists. Mom and Dad are fortyish, five-year-old son on Mom's lap, already-pretty twelve-year-old daughter sits between parents. They're on their way to dinner, as evidenced by talk of a certain steakhouse.

"What kind of steak do I like again?" the daughter asks, sibilant with braces.

"I think you like a rib eye," says mom.

"I thought I liked filet mignon. What's filet mignon again?"

Dad explains that "filet mignon is really tender. But there's very little flavor."

"What steak do you like, Mom?"

"New York. Dad likes porterhouse."

"What's the difference?"

"New York steak is a strip steak. It's very flavorful. Porterhouse is big. I think it's a New York steak plus the filet."

"*Two* steaks? Gross. Would I like New York steak?"

"You might," says Mom. "You can try mine."

"What do I like?" asks the little boy.

"You like lamb chops," says Mom.

"No! I like steak! Mommy! I like steak!"

The stiller you sit, the more internal motion you detect.

You think you've had this exact conversation. The cuts of the cow always eluded you, but you took comfort in the fact that your mom had hers and your dad had his. You tarted around a bit, never really committing because you never really loved steak. You were slightly repulsed by your parents' insistence on marbling and rareness, but the rules of this particular meal—the ritual—intrigued you. You felt taken care of when the white-jacketed old codger appeared with the special knives, the gravy boat of some sherry-laced reduction. The disciplined crispness, heavy bleached napkins, the solemnity and grainy wood. And then the eating, when Mom and Dad got exactly what they expected. What looked to you like offal was manna to Mom and Dad. There was nothing so adult, when you were twelve, as adults and their steak. The solemn theater of it made you want to learn the rules, acutely aware of your own spectatorial lack of engagement. Like so much else, it was something you assumed would make sense when you grew up.

You've got some minutes before your cell phone alarm sounds, after which time you may not be able to access the objects, though there's always a margin of error with these things. Because as much as the body operates like clockwork, in many ways it doesn't. Chaos and order in vying measures. This is why we will never master our bodies. If we live to be a hundred, we will never know why.

You hear someone wail. A childlike wail on the motionless train. A splash. Somebody has vomited. Somebody has vomited and *it's not you*. He's crying now. It's a Puerto Rican boy, a second or third grader, skinny, big ears, nervous, crying into his mother's puffy lap. Mother's young and flustered, crispy ringlets shellacked, and she's trying to clean up the mess on the floor with the receiving blanket that belongs to her other kid, an infant in a stroller, and she's balancing all of this while the passengers avert their eyes from the dogfoodish barf.

> **Above ground, the fishy-fungal bedlam of Chinatown is a comfort.**

You breathe as little as possible in an effort to avoid the smell; your generally tolerant stance on vomit does not extend to other people's. The other family, the steak family, they're sitting next to her and they look spooked. But then the steak-mom offers to take the stroller to free up the barf-mom so that the barf-mom can finish cleaning up the vomit and console her embarrassed son. The steak-dad gives the barf-mom a handkerchief from his pants pocket so that she can wipe up the last bits, and everyone looks to be completely unwound. Your cell phone says five minutes left. The twelve-year-old steak-girl's face betrays what could be empathy. Or maybe she just thinks it's gross.

And then, as if the thin Puerto Rican boy, whose name must be Alejandro—*It's okay, Ale. Don't worry baby*—as if his puke has greased the skids and set the train in motion, you lurch back into play, southbound toward your stop. There is still a chance, barring another "police incident" or "problem on the tracks," to neutralize the acids of the evening.

But the movement is temporary. Sham progress. It's enough to get you to an actual station, albeit not yours. The doors open at Canal Street and an announcement is made in the MTA's new abbreviated style, which edits out words like "the" and "is" in order to minimize what's known as "dwell time," the few seconds it takes for the train to disgorge passengers while new ones board. This announcement cites a switch problem over the Manhattan Bridge. Your home is over that bridge. Everyone must leave the train.

Above ground, the fishy-fungal bedlam of Chinatown is a comfort. Rows of durian, long bean, jackfruit, and dried shrimp vibrate, their careful arrangement imparting structure to so much gnarled irregularity. You beeline, bobbing and weaving like a boxer, while tourists buy underripe coconuts and drink the bitter juice through straws, trusting that this is how it's supposed to taste.

It's Chinatown. No public bathrooms and no place to hide, so you'll have to patronize a business with a bathroom. You enter 888 Bun, one of so many modest dim sum joints. There's a restroom sign in the rear of the narrow restaurant. You order one steamed *cha siu bao*, that pillowy round of dough filled with barbecued pork that's red as garnets. You sit and eat half of it, watching twilight deepen out the window, and when you're done, you approach the bathroom of 888 Bun and hope that the proprietor, who is old and hopefully going deaf, can't hear you.

"No, no! Not working!" He sees you jangling the doorknob.

"Bathroom broken! Sorry about that!"

You're now half a *cha siu bao* older than you were five minutes ago.

You walk west toward the dying sun. You wonder whether it's possible to feel stoned from overconsumption, not in the way of the tryptophan daze or the terribly named food coma, but more energized, less leaden, a state more akin to an MDMA high minus the benevolence. Each block you walk is identical; you don't notice, process, *see*. You say to yourself, "I'm going to think about every person in the world right now." You try this and of course you fail, but the trying hints at connection, a connectedness, although it's not clear to what.

You've arrived at an intersection near enough to the Hudson River to discern its radiance through the buildings. The light is now the light reflected by water. It's a big intersection, this one. You're stopped while left turns are made, or not, and drivers judge each other's judgment calls about these made and unmade left turns in a cacophony of horns. You imagine yourself as a jogger at the corner, jogging in place so as not to disrupt your momentum for as long as the light is red. But one can only begin jogging in place if one has already been jogging. You can't suddenly start to jog in place from a state of stillness, especially if you're not in workout gear and are in fact wearing suede gladiator sandals with a three-inch platform heel. And so you wait and then walk.

Next corner is more desolate. There's a blue USPS mailbox, a green relay mailbox, and some free phony newspapers on metal racks chained to a streetlamp. You think in a vague way about all of the important mail you've sent and received, half a life's worth of mail, and it occurs to you that none of it was really so important. Not even the actual letters. There is always another mode of communication, a different way to pay a bill. You pull down the small door of the blue mailbox with your left hand while your subway-dirty right hand jerks into position and you begin to deep-throat yourself. Your index and middle fingers affect staccato gullet-plunges and within seconds there is the *cha siu bao* and some starchy stuff from earlier in larger than normal chunks because there was no beverage and you chewed too fast. You're no Nancy Reagan, you think to yourself. Nancy chewed each grape thirty times. Nancy, sylphlike and lollipop-headed in size zero Adolfo suits, whose disciplined chewing made international headlines in the 1980s. A child of the '80s, you're still irked by your inability to chew a single grape thirty times.

The first wave of relief is palpable but the angle's awkward, your neck necessarily crooked to ensure precision of aim, and the doughy, creamy contents begin to land on those suede gladiators and your bare toes. Why should you care? Your hands are filthy from the subway, from money exchange, from vomit. Do your feet deserve better?

Because you sense the arrival of people, and the angle is proving impossible, you stop before the bile comes. Bile is what you want. Bile is the goal, the proper terminus, but it's not to be. You shake yourself off like a dog. Either nobody sees or if they see they don't watch. You remove your soiled right shoe and then the left, and you deposit them together into the mailbox, which takes a bit of doing, produces an audible thud. You walk gingerly in bare feet toward that final sweep of watery western light, feeling like a defaced but terrifically serene lady-Jesus. Your bare arms and legs are visited by one of those elusive July breezes that feel like a gift. Your steps reset the night, put the needle at zero. You're as fresh and lucid as you are when you wake up with humors aligned, and as sanguine about the future as you sometimes are when you raise your glass in a toast, and as awed as you were as a child, when you first understood that you'd never see the inside of your own body.

ESSAY

JOHN CLARE
MUD MAN PUNK ROCKER

Michael Dickman

He's all revved up and ready to go

apologies to M.O.

These are the bands
(listened to by me):

    D.R.I.
    Circle Jerks
    Suicidal Tendencies
    Minutemen
    The Cramps
    Minor Threat

We're just a Minor Threat!
We're just a Minor Threat!
We're just a Minor Threat!

These are the bands
(listened to by him):

The morning wind
Crows in spring
A summer shower
Sand martins
Yellowhammers
Fern owls
Wrynecks

Hedgehogs! Foxes! Badgers!

. . .

7th grade
Portland, Oregon
1987–88

Did it rain all the time? Not all the time. Some sunlight here and there. Trees

everywhere. Heroin everywhere. Gus Van Sant's Portland. Skaters vs Rockers. Straight Edge vs Skinheads. Fuck the Skins! Fuck the Southside White Pride! Punks vs Everybody. I was a skater. Graduated from Mrs. A's to Cal Skates to Cal's Pharmacy to Rebel Skates. I could ollie down a flight of stairs. Nollie. No Comply. Not sick but not a poser. Once a friend flubbed a railslide slammed hard into the handrail. His crotch was bleeding through his jeans. He used duct tape to repair his balls. Turn up the Circle Jerks! I couldn't grow my hair long enough to be a rocker. You could get a pretty good Mohawk to stand up with enough egg whites and Aquanet. My mother said she liked the Suicidal Tendencies even though she couldn't understand what they were saying and their name made her nervous. Hypodermic needles made me nervous. I stayed clean because I was a coward. *Stacy Peralta for President*, said the bumper sticker on our family car. All I ever did was skate and listen to music in my room with the door closed. When I took a bath I would set my new skate deck on the toilet so I could stare at it. I had never even read a poem. I didn't know what a poem was.

Fuck the Skins!
Fuck the Southside White Pride!

. . .

My mom worked like a dog to keep us in Catholic school, Christian Brothers, through a series of schemes that mostly flew and still I did my best not to read anything, no, not anything, not anything at all. Now as an adult I have to make up for it. Sorry, Mom.

Reading *The Iliad* and *The Odyssey* in my thirties.

> All I ever did was skate and listen to music in my room with the door closed.

Blake
Shakespeare
Homer
Ovid
Virgil

Moving backward in time through poetry like this is also moving forward, rereading automatically every contemporary poet I ever loved.

Milton
Keats
Hopkins
Clare

John Clare. John Clare. John Clare.

Mud man punk rocker. I came across his poems for the first time in Paul Muldoon's anthology *The Faber Book of Beasts*. I couldn't believe what I was reading. He can start and stop on a dime. He does. Breakneck speed. No punctuation. It reminded me of something. What did it remind me of?

John Clare: Mud Man Punk Rocker | 35

John Clare could play the fiddle, some gypsies taught him how.

I like to think he was good at it.

He could have started his own band!

A prehistoric punk band.

. . .

This from John Clare's "The Hedgehog":

> But they who hunt the
> fields for rotten meat
> And wash in muddy dyke
> and call it sweet
> And eat what dogs refuse where ere they dwell
> Care little either for the taste or smell
> They say they milk the cows and when they lye
> Nibble their fleshy teats and make them dry
> But they whove seen the small head like a hog
> Rolled up to meet the savage of a dog
> With mouth scarce big enough to hold a straw
> Will neer believe what no one ever saw
> But still they hunt the hedges all about
> And shepherd dogs are trained to hunt them out
> They hurl with savage force the stick and stone
> And no one cares and still the strife goes on

I hear a half-broken drum kit in that dyke. I hear three loud chords run the dogs. Feedback in the fields. And then the whole thing falls apart at the end. Everything stops dead after *And no one cares*. A loud-as-fuck caesura. A guitar smashed against a speaker. And then the whole

I thought the whole thing could come apart. The house. My family.

world gets terribly quiet *and still the strife goes on*.

Who moves this fast?
Who is in danger of coming apart at the seams all the time?

Now I remember what Clare reminded me of.

I mean whom.

Ladies and gentlemen . . .
 MUTHA . . . FUCKIN
 . . . IAN . . . MACKAYE!!!

. . .

This from Minor Threat's "Cashing In":

> We don't care. We don't pose.
> We'll steal your money. We'll steal your shows.
> Yeah, we don't care and we don't pose.
> We'll steal your money. We'll steal your shows.
> That's the way it is in this world . . . Right?
> Isn't that right? Boy, you had us pegged all
> along . . . damn.
> There's no place like home.
> There's no place like home.
> There's no place like home
> So, where am I?

Where are we?

MacKaye having some trouble finding a home at home. The whole thing falling apart at the end. Repetitions can be comforting. *I'm all right I'm all right I'm all right.*

MICHAEL DICKMAN

Or they can be the music of things unraveling. I listened to this album at home alone in my bedroom. 12 yrs old. I thought the whole thing could come apart. The house. My family. Should come apart. I wanted something to explode.

Two guitars and a drum.
A mosh pit.
A black eye and a broken jaw.

Gypsies with shaved heads and Mohawks.

Hammering it home.

. . .

John Clare
Helpston
Early 1800s

Did it rain all the time? Not all the time. Some sunlight here and there. Hay everywhere. Ale more potable than water. In love with a pure rural old-school idea of HOME. In love with his high-school sweetheart, called Mary Joyce. In love with writing poems. In love with Byron. The smallest change in the landscape could tear his mind up. His heart. In love with CHILDHOOD, where all of this could stay perfect and live forever:

> *The past it is a majic word*
> *Too beautiful to last,*
> *It looks back like a lovely face—*
> *Who can forget the past?*

In love with gypsies.
In love with birds.

Clock-a-clays. Clodhoppers. Firetails. Pinks. Puddocks.
Then the landscape started to change. People changed it. Money. Old mere marks busted. Hedges gone. Nests removed. His brain started to fall apart.

> *homeless at home*

> *There's no place like home.*
> *So, where am I?*

. . .

Before my son was born.
Doing his thing in the dark, his mama said.

Growing bones.
Growing fingernails.
Growing eyeballs.

I would sit on the floor next to the worn yellow couch where my wife sat and put my mouth next to her huge watermelon stomach like it was a microphone and read John Clare poems to whatever was inside. Whoever.

> *The past it is a majic word*
> *Too beautiful to last,*
> *It looks back like a lovely face—*
> *Who can forget the past?*

For months I had been flooded with memories of my childhood. Skateboards.

Cassette decks. Black Flag singing "Gimmie Gimmie Gimmie." Pizza. Television. *Cheers* and *The Dukes of Hazzard*. Physical memories humming along right beneath my skin. I could suddenly remember every smell in the house I grew up in. Superman sheets on the bed. Dog piss in the wall-to-wall carpets. The mown grass. Rain.

I'm not going to be a kid again, I said. I'm not going to be a kid again.

But you can.

You whoever you are in the whorl of your mama's stomach sitting inside a dark radio listening to my voice.

Hello? Hello?

You be a kid. Come out, come out. I want to read you some poems. I want to start a band.

I want to see your face.

• • •

Before my son was born.
His mama asleep but the two of us awake.

Stretching his legs.
Punching the dark.
Humming along.

Kicking away in the middle of the night. That would be him jumping in place as I watched the comforter move in a sliver of streetlight. Whispering lines from Clare. To him. To the room. To the dark. To anything at all. Do you want to live inside a poem? We called him "The Thing." Do you want to see what a poem looks like in the air?

Each noise that breathed around us then
Was majic all and song . . .

The wild bee in the blossom hung,
The coy bird's startled call . . .

Could he hear everything? He could hear everything. Hey now, hey, this is my voice. Coming to you live. This is what a poem can sound like. 100 mph. Love songs about childhood and birds. Straight up from the Helpston mud.

A majic noise.

A homing device.

• • •

Clare was always trying to get home.
In poems.
In person.

He moved away (once) from his home cottage but the slight change in landscape turned his mind overcast.

He spent time (twice) in asylums.

The first time he walked out the front door and home to Northamptonshire convinced that his childhood heartbreak, Mary, would be waiting for him. But she wasn't 'cause she was dead. Some walk. Gypsies showed him a road out of the Epping Forest that proved useful. A shortcut. A secret. Everyone living on the margins. Clare on the edge of his psyche. The gypsies on the edge of society. No wonder they loved each other.

The birds of his childhood singing from a stulp, a seam, a ride.

The second asylum he died in.

Home-close.

> I can't keep up
> Can't keep up
> Can't keep up
> Out of step with the world

. . .

I like to think of MacKaye walking for miles in circles around Washington, DC, at night in the early '80s.

1980s. In combat boots.

What birds would have been there? No birds. Just traffic lights.

What sang for him was other bands:

> Bad Brains
> Teen Idles
> Slickee Boys

From the trees outside Dischord Records.

From the trees inside Helpston, Clare walked for miles too.

1880s.
Wore boots. Walked borders.
Walked to and from asylums.
Listened to music (fiddles, poems, birds).

Hey now, hey, this is my voice. Coming to you live.

I want so badly for there to be an echo between these two poets. Some sonic recognition. I want them to be lost brothers. Band members. I want them to shout across the different parts of my life like birdsong or wildfire. Stitch it all up. Like Clare and MacKaye, I'm homesick for something that doesn't exist anymore. The past it is a majic word. We don't get to stay there.

My son is there. My son is here.
My past is gone.

. . .

When my son was born.

I would walk him around at night for miles in a circle in the front room of our apartment. Singing little songs. Trying to help him sleep. His face, any parent will tell you this, was all I ever wanted to know. It blew things apart.

Poems can do that.

Punk music does.

I used to walk for miles around Portland, Oregon. A book of poems in one hand. A club stamp on the other.

Also at night.
Back and forth over the river.

My ears shaking out and settling back from a night at the X-Ray Cafe.

The black water through the grates of the Hawthorne Bridge looked so far away. And then it looked close. And then it disappeared.

It can be difficult at times to convince your newborn family to listen to punk rock music first thing in the morning. But you can do it.

Next up, The Adolescents.
Next up, The Misfits.

Next up, nothing but pure unadulterated screaming joy.

. . .

When my son was born.

I would take him down to the kitchen early mornings, still dark out, end of January, to let his mama sleep.

Making coffee in the almost-dark.

The baby sounded like a percolator.

Once the coffee was made I would hold him in one arm on the couch and read John Clare poems aloud. Staring up at the ceiling. His eyes would blink open and it was as if a new species of birds or stars were being born in the middle of our living room in central New Jersey.

The apartment smelled like coffee and books.

I read

And oft we urged the barking dog,
For mischief was our glee,
To chase the cat up weed-green walls
And mossy apple tree

I read

I seek no more the finch's nest
Nor stoop for daisey flowers;
I grow a stranger to myself
In these delightful hours

A gray morning light was turning pink.

Soon I'll put on a record.

Something to wake us up.

We're just a Minor Threat!
We're just a Minor Threat!
We're just a Minor Threat!

FICTION

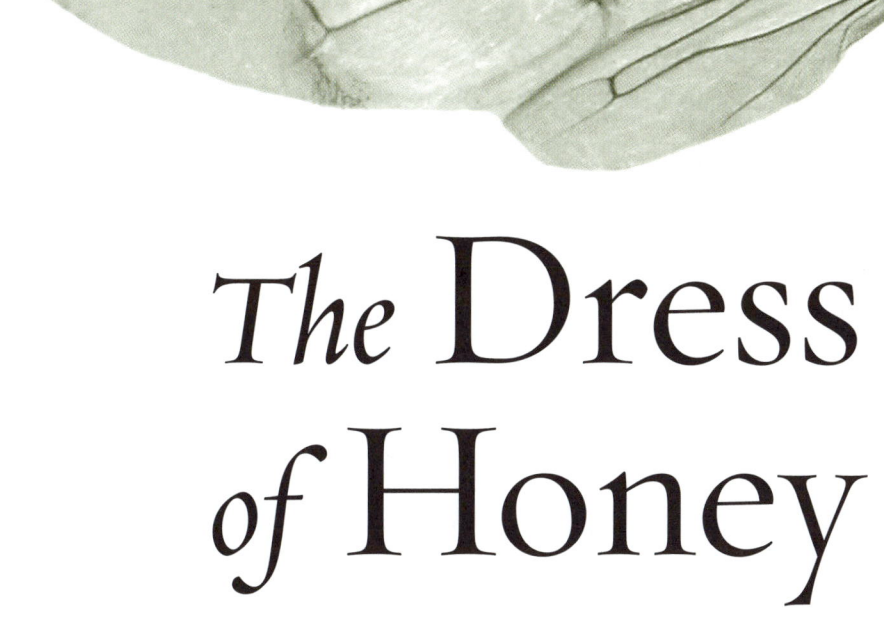

The Dress of Honey

Jean-Philippe Toussaint

translated by Edward Gauvin

Apart from the spectacular aspect of certain dresses Marie had created in the past—the dress of sorbet, the dress of rosemary and thorny broom, the dress of gorgonian coral adorned with sea urchin necklaces and earrings of Venus ear shell—Marie sometimes ventured beyond fashion into speculative territories akin to the most radical experiments of contemporary art. Developing a theoretical reflection on the very idea of haute couture, she had returned to the original meaning of the word *couture* as the sewing of cloth via different techniques, stitching, tacking, hooking, binding, which allow fabrics to be combined on models' bodies, twinned to the skin, and joined together, to present this year in Tokyo a haute couture dress without a single stitch. With her dress made of honey, Marie invented a dress without straps or ties that clung all by itself to the model's body, a levitating dress, light, fluid, liquefying, slowly molten and syrupy, weightless in space yet wedded to the model's body, since the model's body was the dress itself.

The dress of honey had been shown for the first time at the Spiral building in Tokyo. It was the culmination of Marie's latest fall-winter collection. At the end of the show, the final model emerged from the wings wearing that dress of light and amber, as if her body had been dipped head to toe in a humongous jar of honey before her entrance. Naked and honeyed, flowing, she made her way down the catwalk, swaying her hips in time to the beat of the music, high-heeled, smiling, trailed by a swarm of bees that formed a thrumming procession midair, the honey their lodestone, an elongated, abstract cloud of droning insects that accompanied her parade and turned with her at catwalk's end in a yawing whirl like an outflung disheveled scarf, sinuous and alive, writhing with hymenoptera that followed in her wake when she made her exit.

That, at least, was the theory. In practice, the difficulties had multiplied, and showing the dress of honey at Spiral in Tokyo had required months of work and setting up a little cell devoted exclusively to the project. Right from the start, there was a choice to be made between using real insects or resorting to a system of artificial, remote-controlled bees, drawing on the latest biorobotic research, which made it possible to imagine tiny flying robots rigged with ventral sensors. After looking into the matter, and much exchange of e-mail between Tokyo and Paris, brightened by adorable attachments containing complex diagrams for miniature winged prototypes with the sibylline allure of Da Vinci's flying machines, it appeared to be technologically feasible to make a swarm of bees fly down a fashion catwalk. The main point in favor that Marie's colleagues brought to light was that bee colonies are obedient and blindly follow their queen everywhere (should a queen manage to escape the hive, the entire colony follows her into the wild, so some beekeepers don't think twice about clipping their queens' wings to prevent such an exodus). On an early preparatory trip to Japan, Marie's assistant had arranged for her to see a Corsican beekeeper who lived in Tokyo, and Marie had found herself in a restaurant with a panoramic view of Shinjuku, at lunch with a certain Monsieur Tristani, or Cristiani (whose first name was none other than Toussaint), a short, friendly, easygoing fellow dressed in beige-and-burgundy herringbone tweed. Monsieur Tristani had a cast on one wrist and his arm in a sling, he wore thick yellow glasses with tinted lenses that hid a keen, wily, suspicious gaze.

> **The dress of honey had been shown for the first time at the Spiral building in Tokyo.**

Monsieur Tristani had ordered an aperitif in the panoramic restaurant's deserted main dining room, and he must have been expecting a romantic luncheon with a young woman interested in how honey is made, but it wasn't Marie's habit to banter during a working lunch. No sooner had the maître d' taken their orders than she explained, in a firm voice, the broad outlines of her project. Monsieur Tristani, whose ardor had soon been snuffed, listened solemnly, nodding, wrist in a cast, now and again ineptly hacking at a filet of sole with his good hand, and then, setting down his fish knife, he picked up his fork and gulped down a mouthful with a pained, even preoccupied look, for if he'd understood correctly, the idea was to cover a supermodel in honey. *Piombu!* Monsieur Tristani did not have much in the way of answers to Marie's many queries, content to dodge her questions with a vague wave of his hand and a fatalistic expression, and taking up his fish knife once more, he began to pry apart his filet of sole lengthwise, sometimes sneaking a longing glance at the administrative buildings of Shinjuku stretching into the fog beyond the wall of glass. He remained resolutely confused, supplying evasive or irrelevant answers to the precise technical questions Marie had readied for him (her planner, beside her on the tablecloth, open to a list of questions she ticked off one by one), to which she received not a single useful reply. You'd think Toussaint knew nothing about bees (or that beekeeping was just his cover).

Their collaboration had ended there, in the hotel lobby after lunch they'd gone their separate ways and, before taking his leave, he'd offered her a jar of honey (which had given Marie the idea for the subtitle to her show: "Autumn Maquis"). In the end, Marie had worked with a more bohemian beekeeper, a German who had lived in the Cévennes and then on the island of Hokkaido, ever so slightly gay and crazy in love with her, she claimed (or just the opposite, said I: a crazy queen who had a slight crush on her), who never contradicted a soul and was ready to do whatever she wanted with his bees, provided the right releases and disclaimers were signed for the Japanese health authorities, and she forked over a pile of dough. That man would've been perfect had he not taken on the services of another German from the Cévennes who now also lived on Hokkaido (the kind of visionary idealist that honey draws like flies these days), prided himself on training the queen bee for the catwalk, and had given a staggering demonstration thereof in the Tokyo office of the Let's Go Daddy-O fashion house, in front of Marie's entire staff of Japanese colleagues, artists and designers all in black with slim titanium steel-frame glasses, manbag straps crisscrossing their chests, solemn and skeptical, gathered in a semicircle before an empty trestle table where, without a bee in sight, the fellow had treated them to a pathetic flea-circus act, that worn chestnut where the ringmaster, upon losing his performers and calling out to them by name, finds them again, then puts them through acrobatics and death-defying triple somersaults (everyone had emerged from that meeting filled with consternation—and Marie had sent the guy packing).

> **The model was waiting, naked, skin smooth and sex shaven, in nothing now but a flesh-toned G-string.**

Readying the dress of honey had also brought up several thorny issues involving laws, insurance, and contracts. When, after a lengthy casting session held at the Tokyo office of the Let's Go Daddy-O fashion house, the model for the honey dress was chosen at last, a young Russian girl barely seventeen years old, Marie's lawyers labored for more than a month to finalize the definitive contract with the Rezo Agency in Shibuya, a contract of more than fifteen pages that contained scores of codicils and unusual clauses due to the singular nature of the service provided. The model was asked to undergo several medical examinations, made to see a dermatologist and an allergist, and tests were scheduled at a private clinic to confirm that her skin could withstand, without risk of eczema or irritation, heavy contact with honey all over her body. There were no bees at the first rehearsals (the first hive, coming from Hakodate by truck, wouldn't arrive until the night before the show). Spiral had been entirely refitted, its shops and café closed to the public, and the catwalk built as an extension of the famous spiral ramp that descended from the mezzanine along white marble walls. All the building's broad windows had been obscured by giant black velour drapes. The dress rehearsal took place under the same conditions as the actual show, among amber follow spots, electricians still perched on ladders to adjust the positioning of the lights. The stage was covered with thick, silvery, protective tarps, and the supermodel, in white untied sneakers and a pale-blue yellow-flowered bikini, an iPod at her waist that a muddle of tangled wires connected to her ears, made a series of starts, timed by assistants laden with tech equipment. Laptops were strewn all about backstage, forgotten here and there on the floor. Marie's full staff of Japanese colleagues had now taken up quarters at Spiral. They'd annexed the rows of lacquered black chairs reserved for the audience at the foot of the catwalk, and were watching the model complete a series of full test runs starting from the wings, neither in honey nor followed by bees, coming down the catwalk in her untied sneakers and nonchalant stride, sulky of pout and ethereal of step, while the sound technicians, emerging from a jumble of silvery flight cases, adjusted the levels from behind their consoles, occasionally interrupting the music only to set it going again in abrupt, booming fits and starts.

The day of the show, a few minutes before the dress of honey made its entrance, a hive-like ferment reigned backstage. The model, standing on a mini-stepstool set on a transparent tarp, was waiting, naked, skin smooth and sex shaven, in nothing now but a flesh-toned G-string barely an inch wide masking her mons, and several makeup artists, standing beside her, were working on the parts of her body that would remain uncovered during the show, dusting her face and hands with rice powder, which they applied with powder puffs to bring out her skin against the amber of the honey dress she wasn't yet wearing. Farther back, by shelves full of alembics, round-bottom flasks, decanters, and graphite crucibles, a swarm of androgynous Japanese assistants bustled like lab techs about the stainless-steel vat that held the honey, sliding test tubes into the sticky substance to gather samples whose color and viscosity they studied with magnifying glasses, sticking a thermometer into the vat to take the mixture's temperature and ensure the honey would have the exact desired consistency when coating the model's body. When the model was ready, an astonishing lunar body plucked and powdered, hands, face, and cleavage covered in white powder, the assistants went to work and began painting her with brushes, spreading honey all over her body, one kneeling alongside her thigh with a short sable-hair brush, another standing on a stepladder slathering her back and shoulders with a roller, while still others smoothed the honey over her flesh, daintily patting her skin with moist, delicate gauze compresses, and a cluster of young interns in white smocks circled her unmoving body with hair dryers to even out the latest layer and give the dress one last dab of lacquer. A dresser ran up with a pair of high heels and presented them to the model, who hoisted herself into them one foot at a time, leaning on the shoulders of the crouching assistants even as they escorted her to the wings while giving her hair a final finishing touch.

 And so, all at once as the music broke out, the model took off down the runway, followed by a swarm of bees that had partnered her pace, trailing after her in an electric buzzing of thousands of insects that drowned out the onlookers' admiring exclamations. It was an unhoped-for success, the model had reached the end of the catwalk, paused briefly contrapposto, a hand on her waist, and then set off again the way she'd come, when the miracle happened, the swarm of bees pulled a pitch-perfect about-face along the exact curve of her course, floating in their broader turn beyond the runway over the heads of the audience, eliciting another round of admiring exclamations. This had taken less than half a minute, and the model was already retracing her steps when, just as she was about to reach the wings, she hesitated for a split second over the two exits available to her—stage right and stage left—and, remembering her special instructions to head left so the bees could return to their hive, she changed her mind at the last minute and switched direction, and in that split second, that infinitesimal indecision, it all fell apart, came crashing down, the spell broke and she tripped onstage, collapsed on the floor, she felt the bees' loud breath fall at once upon the nape of her neck, and it was then, at that very instant, the hunting horn sounded, that the bees stung her all over, her back, shoulders, breasts, neck, eyes, her sex and inside it, the model curled into a ball on the floor shielding her face with her hands, struggling, fending off the bees' attacks with an impotent arm, getting up on her knees and fleeing on all fours, but falling again, vanquished anew, like a living torch, immolated, writhing on the runway, several people having dashed from the wings to her aid, horrified helpless assistants, the German beekeeper, who'd burst out of nowhere like a Grand Guignol puppet, oafish and lurching, in his white spacesuit and thick gloves, wire-mesh mask over his face, Japanese firemen, extinguishers in hand, who'd positioned themselves over the model but hesitated to start spraying for fear of making things worse.

That was when the curtain went up and Marie slowly made her appearance onstage to greet the public, as if it had all been part of her plan, as if she'd conceived this tableau vivant, the supermodel martyr surrounded by multiple faces frozen in pain, European faces, Asian faces, thunderstruck, slowed, stilled, as if in a Bill Viola video, while around the tableau's central figure, still crumpled on the floor beneath a swarm of bees, the masked and clumsily costumed effigies of the beekeeper and the firemen faced off, knees bent and extinguishers in hand, as if forever fixed in an interrupted act of rescue. For, refusing to be defeated by reality, Marie had shouldered chance and claimed responsibility for the image so completely as to throw the audience into doubt, as if the entire scene now unfolding before their eyes were the result of her premeditation. But little matter whether the scene had been premeditated or not, the image had arisen, in reality or in Marie's imagination, and she had taken credit for it: by making her entrance onstage, she had signed the canvas, had placed her seal on life itself, its accidents, its hazards and imperfections.

Sam Riviere

INFORMAL FATIGUE

I'd wondered about it in an abstract way

The city's matching halves and station at the country's loins

Its middling rank and legendary light

And watched students Catholic and tan pass along its sculpted alleys

Some wearing the university's pink-and-navy sweatshirts

Embroidered with a mystic rose

On their way no doubt to the evening's entertainments

Of which there were seven scheduled

A sleepy dad from the surrounding wetlands

Thirty years old with a teacher's careful laugh

The lurid crest on his chest pocket like a window into viscera

And late for reasons he couldn't go into

Sketched half-arsedly the library's beleaguered history

A sagging dome within whose low interiors

Departments clucked and clawed like sickly poultry

I supposed a lag and found evidence of it everywhere

And overmore an air of wastefulness and faint idolatry

A pigeon flapping in a clogged fountain

Bottles of unfamiliar soft drink that crowned the fence posts

My host walked me to the sea without seeming to know why

Where in grander hues the wintering palms conferred darkly

There was some avocado on his sleeve

And in among the brine and charcoal a private odour recognised me

A cabal's unmistakable signal

The soul hesitates to explain

We stared at a big cloud

And somewhere behind a window slid soundlessly shut

As if forbidding a literal thought

CHRISTMAS IN BERLIN

The woman in the advert has a look of knowingness that indicates an unspoken but completely real satisfaction

And I am certain that someone

Not her is getting away with something

A man was scorched to death in the shower

A dormant screen inspects the bed like a hypnotist

The Thai food almost left me angry enough to write a review

And I thought of my weirdo friend who collected figurines of Nazi skeletons with guns that stood on mounds of skulls

Though I never really worked out what he meant by them

The tennis I guess always makes me think of sex

Couldn't find the Palace of Tears again

And I felt far too nervous to ask

In case of more sad news

Please send nudes

FICTION

The Chicken Run

Saša Stanišić

translated by Anthea Bell

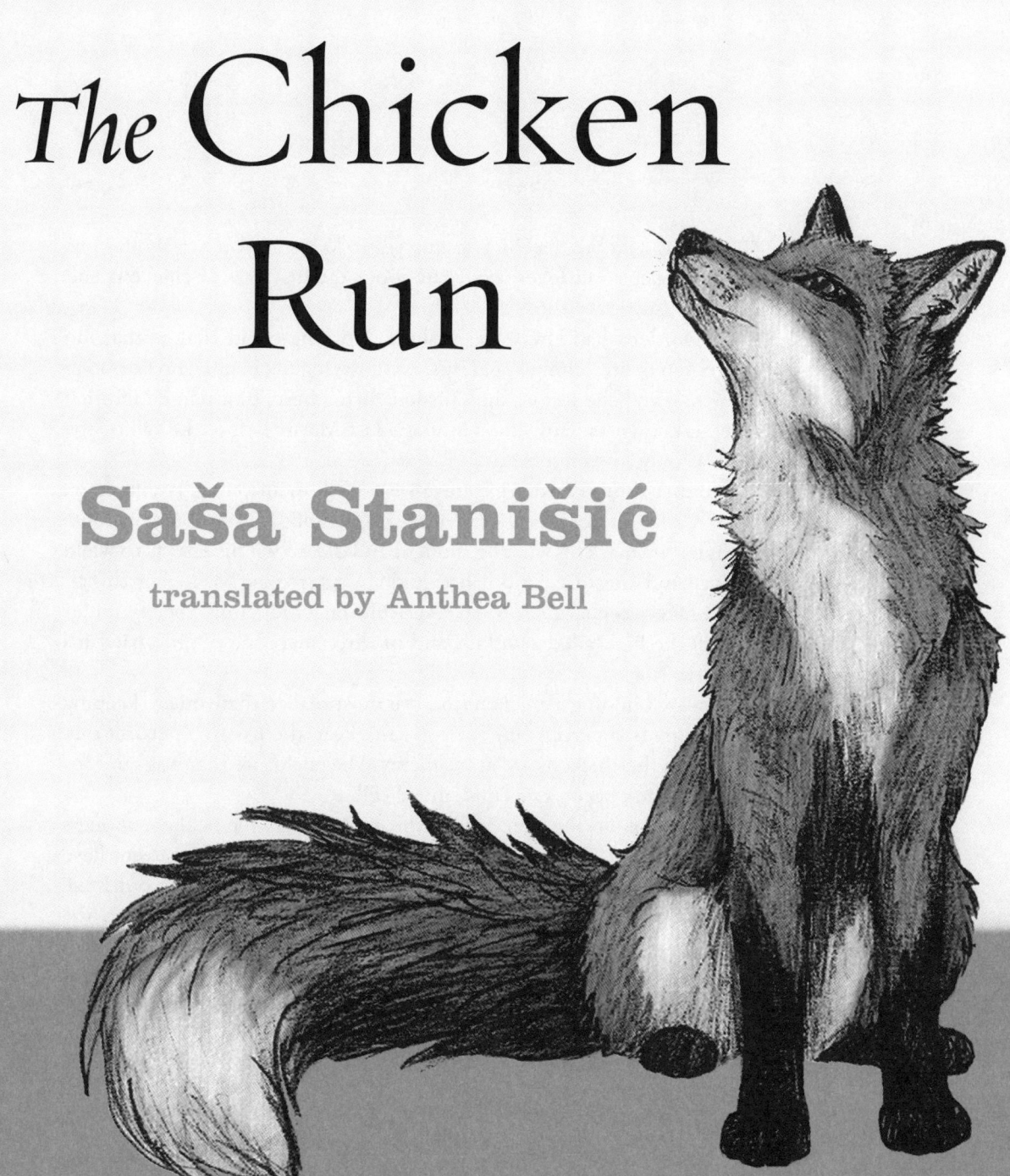

Before you build a chicken run, get to know all you can about both chickens and foxes. Find out about the instincts of chickens and the stories of the fox.

The Durdens had always been short. Nothing could change that, no wise women or stretching apparatus, no marrying tall people, no hormone treatment—and the last of the Durdens living here, first name Heinrich or Heini, known as Tiny, Fürstenfelde's last Mayor before the fall of the Wall, was only 1.45 meters tall.

We didn't think Durden's stature was worth mentioning. A joke here, a bit of teasing there. It bothered him considerably. It influenced his footwear, it left its mark on what he thought and did, to wit his efforts to wield influence and authority, and it had him always striving for higher things. He had failed as chairman of the Agricultural Production Society under the GDR, he had failed as a husband in three marriages. So he tried his luck as our Mayor.

If you are building a chicken run, you must realize that you are keeping the chickens 100 percent in, but you can't keep the fox 100 percent out. If he gets in the chickens are at his mercy. The enclosure that was built for their protection becomes a condemned cell.

Durden took up the office of Mayor in '84; in '85 the Schliebenhöners went to the West, the only ones here to do so. Did the former event have anything to do with the latter? No one expressed suppositions out loud. It was just that since taking office Durden had gone on and on to the Schliebenhöners about the idea of a house swap. They had a large house but lived alone, and Durden lived alone, but all the same he wanted a big house.

From the novel *Before the Feast*, available now from Tin House

A month after the Schliebenhöners had disappeared, Durden moved in. Their big house had a balcony with a view of the Great Lake, and a kitchen garden surrounded by blackberry bushes, and a large lilac looming over it like a roof. A cherry tree adorned the inner courtyard. The Schliebenhöners had not sold their goat, so that no one would suspect anything.

If you are building a chicken run, make sure that the chickens have enough space to run around and amuse themselves, and if they have dark feathers that they have enough shade in summer. Chickens also need a place to which they can withdraw when the life of a chicken gets to be too much for them. If you are building a chicken run, build the fence at least 1.50 meters high or higher. Anything less will be child's play to the fox, not an obstacle.

The Mayor made himself at home. He harvested the garden produce, fed the goat, forged signatures. After his mayoral work was done, he drank beer on the balcony and looked at the sky more often than the lake. He knew he was seeing stars that had been extinguished long ago, and that weighed on his mind. Was it a sign? And if so, what of?

The village had worse problems than the Mayor's house-moving.

If you are building a chicken run, make the entrance tunnel go in a zigzag, with short straight bits and sharp angles, so that a chicken can get along it easily, but not a fox. And get a dog with a nervous disposition.

The circumstances of Durden's move were dubious, but we and the time were not yet mature enough to point out such a thing in public. Furthermore, the village had worse problems than the Mayor's house-moving: to name just one, liquid manure trickled down from the arable fields into the lakes, making their ammonium content twelve times more than was permissible. Children ran into the water and came out itching. Blue-green algae increased and multiplied like rabbits. No one in the Agricultural Production Society was interested in that; even Durden had once tried mentioning the matter, and got nothing but promises.

There was one small comfort. The pike-perch from the Great Lake were sold in the West. People were annoyed about that, rightly so, but not quite so annoyed when the business of the ammonium content came out, and of course we didn't wish severe nausea on anyone over there—but even a Wessi, we thought, can take a little bit of nausea if there is any.

The Chicken Run

If you are building a chicken run, use sturdy, close-meshed wire netting. You don't want the fox to be able to climb it or bite a hole in it. Fix the lower one-third of the netting properly to a low concrete wall that continues underground, preferably for half a meter down. The fox digs fast and well. Don't build the little wall too high; chickens need light, and should be able to see what is on the other side of the wall. Artificial light makes them nervous.

Durden had a garden makeover. He wanted more tidiness, more pumpkins and melons, fewer blackberries and indeed fewer berries in general, because berries are kids' stuff. He didn't like the goat, but he kept her because she licked his hand even when there was nothing in it.

> Ditzsche examined the scene of the crime. The chickens had been killed in their henhouse.

One day he went with the local branch of the Small Animal Breeders' Association to the district show in Sarow, and saw Dietmar Dietz, known as Ditzsche, win the crowing contest with his Dwarf New Hampshire rooster, which crowed 151 times within an hour, and then win the green victor's ribbon too in the Dwarf Chicken class, with a blue-porcelain colored fowl that had feathered feet.

Now Durden wanted dwarf chickens too.

Ditzsche thought it was a joke, but Durden's eyes were shining. The Mayor wandered past the pens. Feathers shimmered in the most wonderful colors, and he pointed in silence to one of the fowls now and then, if he particularly liked it.

Ditzsche tried to dissuade him: it took a lot of time and trouble, he said. Breeding pedigree chickens called for care, good rearing and, yes, love.

Good rearing, said Durden, reaching out to a hen, would not be any problem. And after today he felt any amount of love for these proud creatures.

Ditzsche didn't like to hear chickens called proud. Their swelling breasts, raised heads and erect bearing are physical and not mental attributes.

The Mayor stopped outside one pen with a solitary rooster in it, blueblack, with a golden back and a bright red comb, stalking thoughtfully about in circles. The little man linked his hands behind his back and walked round the pen, instinctively imitating the bird.

"An Old English Dwarf Game Fowl," said Ditzsche.

"Old English," whispered Durden. "Game Fowl," he whispered. "How many hens does a rooster like that need?"

The rooster stared at Durden, or the sky above Durden, and fluffed up his plumage. The decision was made.

If you are building a chicken run, think about electricity. However, remember that an electric shock will irritate the fox but not drive him away for ever. Foxes do not give up before they have reached their limits. Count on needing at least 3,500 volts. The electric wiring is fixed on the outside of the enclosure. Only chickens that leave it are endangered.

Durden wanted to put up an enclosure for his chickens. Ditzsche offered to help him, and warned him about the fox. Then it must be secure, said Durden. Ditzsche told him about keeping chickens, told him about the fox. Durden drew a plan. Ditzsche improved the plan and got hold of the materials. They built the enclosure together. Two days later the chickens were delivered. Three of them were killed the following night.

When Durden discovered the massacre in the morning, he summoned Ditzsche and demanded an explanation. Ditzsche examined the scene of the crime. The chickens had been killed in their henhouse. The fence was intact, there were no holes in the ground. Then Ditzsche noticed the goat. She was grazing close to the fence; Durden had tied her up to its corner post overnight. Ditzsche studied the animal. He found reddish hairs on her back. He showed them to Durden.

What the hell did that mean, Durden asked.

Ditzsche smelled his fingers. "Fox. The goat is too close to the fence. The fox used her as a springboard."

Durden, lost in thought, repeated the word "springboard" several times. In an even voice, rather too even a voice, he then asked why Ditzsche, with his alleged knowledge of the subject, hadn't taken this eventuality into account.

Ditzsche had no answer. A surviving hen clucked quietly. Durden compressed his lips; his chin was shaking. "How are they ever going to trust their home now?" he whispered, as if he didn't want the hen to hear him. "They'll always be thinking they hear a beast of prey outside. Instead of the hand that feeds them they'll expect the jaws that eat them. Those chickens," said Durden, clutching the wire netting of the fence, "can never be happy again."

Once your chicken run is up, let two roosters fight for the hens. The winner will protect his hens all the better the harder he had to fight for them. He will warn them when danger threatens, and the hens will take refuge in the henhouse. If a fox threatens the hens, the rooster will sometimes save their lives, but often he will not.

Durden refused to pay Ditzsche even for the materials. In the village he told everyone how that idiot had cost him three pedigree fowls, and blamed it on a goat. He didn't tell the story himself, of course. He had other people do that for him.

The gossip did not win out. Foxes eat chickens, full stop. If I were a fox, said the village, I guess I'd find pedigree fowls particularly delicious. Instead of talking about Ditzsche, people discussed possible ways of fox-proofing a chicken run. The ferryman said, "Ditzsche is above suspicion when it comes to chickens," and the ferryman's word had always carried more weight than anything the top brass of the village said. The matter was forgotten. Except by Ditzsche.

Once your chicken run is up, sprinkle plenty of pepper round the fence. Put human hairs in the netting at close intervals, rub your sweat on the fence. Urinate regularly near the enclosure.

Durden once joined us when we were drinking at Blissau's. It was late, some of the customers were falling asleep at their tables. Durden began talking about his chickens. He could hear them clucking all the time, he said, even now. They complain, he said, they're feeling sorry for themselves. They're not happy.

The little man was remorseful. He ran his hand through his hair, ordered a beer and didn't drink it. We comforted him, because everyone deserves comfort after midnight. We said the chickens aren't sensitive to feelings. They don't regret anything. They ask only for the necessities. Durden either listened or he didn't. He lay down to sleep at home, and in his mayoral dreams he heard the Dwarf Game Fowl clucking.

The fox came back. Durden watched him. The fox slunk round the enclosure in broad daylight, provocatively slowly. The rooster led his hens into the henhouse. One of them stayed outside it. The fox put his nose up against the fence here and there. Scraped the ground a little with his paws. Then went away without success. The goat was standing somewhere else now.

Would the Mayor have intervened if the fox had got in? We'll refrain from making assumptions. Next day Durden gave the chickens away to the others in the Small Animal Breeders' Association, keeping only the hen who had stood her ground.

Ditzsche said: if a chicken is fearless, that doesn't make it brave.

After the fall of the Wall, Durden wanted to join the Free Democratic Party and stand for Mayor again. When Ditzsche heard about that, he went to Blissau's and told people there about Heinrich Durden's letter to Hans Modrow. Ditzsche was landing himself in the soup. Because how did he know about that? And then again: it surely wouldn't have been the only letter he had opened. The informer's revenge on the local politician. Some of them at Blissau's sounded almost flattered to think an informer could have been spying on them. Ditzsche said he wasn't an informer. He didn't say he hadn't read the letter.

In his letter, Durden had fulminated against the Church and argued for the continuation of the Stasi in another form. He was saying all that, he claimed, on behalf of the village. Although the village didn't know the first thing about it. What else was in the letter hardly mattered. No one writes letters in our name. Durden never stood as candidate for any post in Fürstenfelde again.

Ditzsche lost his job. To this day we don't know whether it was only Durden's post that he read, or everyone else's too.

When you have put up your chicken run, prepare the chickens for battle. Arm them with iron spurs overnight.

Heini "Tiny" Durden died in 2005. The inscription on his gravestone says: *His Star Is Extinguished*. The Schliebenhöners have come back and are living in the big house again. The chicken run is also inhabited. Not by pedigree fowl, by good healthy chickens with golden plumage. The vixen prowls round the cherry tree. And beside the chicken run, a wheelbarrow stands.

FICTION

The First Full Thought of Her Life

Deb Olin Unferth

There is a place where a real river runs along the edges of the parking lots, lots that stretch a mile, asphalt poured out over the earth and the whole resort crunched down on top—planted trees, swimming pools, a store that sells snacks, liquor, and a small selection of wines.

And a family (mother, father, girl, baby), driving away from it toward the dune.

. . .

Her dream had been to go there, the whole time she was pregnant, each time, she imagined it, how they'd all climb the sand dune, how they'd stand in the sun at the top, the breeze, the lake in the distance, the photo they'd bring home of their hands raised in triumph.

They'd lost the rental car in the lot and almost didn't make it, found the car, couldn't find the exit, couldn't find the road, found the wrong road, found the right road, arrived finally. The parking lot was half-full. The dune was so white it looked like aluminum. A flawless day.

. . .

The shooter was already in position at this point.

. . .

The father pulled the visor down and said that a dune is a pile of sand on a parking lot. He said that people wrote books, created myths, invented whole philosophies about trudging uphill in hot sand, the futility of such an enterprise.

He said that sand works like a microwave, cooks you from the inside through its reflective properties.

He said that a glacier dropped this stuff down here and left ten thousand years ago. Sand is unhygienic, full of prehistoric infection.

He was out of the car now, frowning into the backseat and attempting to dislodge the baby from her car seat. The little girl said that pee is unhygienic and the father agreed.

• • •

But the mother had climbed this same dune as a child. And now she'd brought her own family here, on a mission of making memories for her daughter, hopefully ones as good as the best of her own, and this dune had been among them. You couldn't drive right up to it back then. You hiked a path through sandy woods. None of that was here anymore but you could still go up and come down. The same sand carried away on the bottoms of your shoes.

> **Sand is unhygienic, full of prehistoric infection.**

• • •

The shooter was in a silver pickup, '13 or '14, green license plates (Colorado?), first letter Y. The mother and girl walked around the shooter's fender, and started up the dune.

• • •

Three miles away a dozen families were waiting for the boat ride. A tour of tiny islands seen from afar.

Two miles away a dozen families were creating devastation by the pool: pieces of meat and bread, toys that made strange noises, hairpins and spilled drinks, smeared ketchup, tiny stray shoes, wads of napkin, towels tossed into chairs, strollers overturned, french fries on the ground, and the families—in swimsuits, T-shirts, floaters—parading over the cement toward the water.

. . .

The shooter's primary weapon lay across his lap, a Bushmaster AR-15 semiautomatic rifle. He also had a 12-gauge sawed-off shotgun for short range, if necessary.

E had used a 12-gauge sawed-off shotgun.

D had used an Intratec 9mm semiautomatic handgun attached to a strap slung over his shoulder.

N had used such an inferior weapon as to be almost adorable, but that was in 1967.

L had brought 6,300 rounds of ammunition, which seemed either paranoid or optimistic, or like showing off.

> **They think they know the world. What entitled, self-satisfied assholes.**

W had used an AK-47-style assault weapon with a thirty-round magazine.

Y had had a multitude of weapons: an AR-15, a Glock, a *SIG* Sauer handgun.

F and C had had sawed-off weapons thirty years old. They'd had bombs and knives, a real showdown.

White sand. The angle was steep. There'd be nowhere to run. And sand is heavy. It would all be in slow motion. Keatonesque.

. . .

It was hard to climb in the sand. The mother hadn't counted on that. Halfway up she paused, stopped to catch her breath, and started again. When they were almost to the top, she stopped, sat down in the sand. (She'd been up half the night [again] with the baby and then couldn't fall back asleep, and she'd sat on the floor in the bathroom like a drunk.) You go, she said to the girl now. I'm right here. It was only a few yards really. Below, the father was walking gingerly toward the dune, arms out as if he were holding a grenade because the baby was alert but not yet screaming.

. . .

Green cargo pants, a black T-shirt that read *Don't Shoot*, a black cap, bill forward, which he'd now taken off and put on the seat beside him. He spotted the girl, a lone child, staggering, her belly protruding, the sand forming a wave to lift her and gently undulate her higher. The girl, and the shooter raising his weapon.

· · ·

Oh, the layers under the surface (he thought), the air pockets, the parallel worlds, the possible futures that could explode out of this moment, the pasts that didn't come to pass: they continue to spin themselves out until they run into concrete and unspool where they are, spilling into the gaps, gathering around him as he lifted his rifle.

· · ·

Oh, the inaccessible inner lives all around us (thought some birds flying by overhead), the lives we can't imagine, the water world, the dominion of the insects, the plants, the antediluvian consciousnesses, made up of light and dark, moist and dry.

· · ·

There is how time doesn't work the way we think it does (thought the baby), or space either, the scientists have it all wrong and someday we will know this, or someone will, but in the meantime, the wrong way and the real way run alongside each other, along with all the other rejected theories going back through history, the lives of the baby and the father running along them, strings of frayed yarn.

· · ·

There is how people think their lives are one thing but they are wrong (thought the father). They think they know the world. What entitled, self-satisfied assholes.

· · ·

Ahem. The mother would just like to chime in at this juncture, if all parties have quite finished philosophizing? If she wouldn't be interrupting anything urgent? If everyone isn't too *busy*?

The First Full Thought of Her Life

(Ummmm, sure.)

Did her husband just propose that she has an illusion of certainty? Did he just suggest she thinks she "knows the world"?

(Ummmm.)

And you, shooter, did you assume you'd be *introducing* something to this family by flattening the girl out dead and bloody right before their eyes?

(Well, surely it'd be a shock.)

In fact there'd already been a "shooter" introduced to this family.

(There had?)

Her husband, shot as a child in the head.

(The father below, the one who's afraid of sand, he'd already been shot?)

Lived anyway.

(In the *head*?)

It had been a break-in. *His* mother had been unable to protect him. Picked off at five years old. World is full of danger.

(And he was fine, the husband?)

Fine enough. No pituitary gland. Those things don't just grow back like a tomato. To this day he had to medicate with hormones every night of his life or he'd die. Try looking that one in the face, Mr. "Shooter."

(Well the shooter wasn't going to go for the head. Jesus. The middle. He'd get her right in the heart.)

We'll see about that, Mr. Stupid.

. . .

At the bottom of the dune another family was arriving, the inside of their car like a circus: ponies and dolls, a tinkling music, glitter sprayed over the seats along with other less respectable spills.

Half a mile down the road another father had pulled to the side of the road and was saying could they shut up back there, could they just please goddamnit shut up for thirty seconds while he figured out where they were?

Three miles away a dozen families had waited so long for the boat ride that they'd descended through all the rungs of impatience available to them and now were all nearly asleep, a collection of dazed, brightly colored bodies, possessions dropping to their sides, the smallest faces drooling.

. . .

Oh if he had any notion of the clatter of deaths and broken bodies behind this family. He thought they didn't know suffering?

At twelve she'd nursed her mother through an illness that had lasted three hundred days.

She'd had a brother—now in a grave in a desert.

She'd had another baby, before these two, who hadn't made it out alive.

There had been her grandmother, whom she'd never met, locked up at forty and never seen again so that her father had had a hole in him while he raised her.

There'd been plenty of others, dead, or alive but damaged. Earth is full of them, more assembling and disassembling every day. Among them, yes, this perfect little girl, but she'd been pretty unlikely, considering.

(And the baby, don't forget, if the father might put a word in, holding her up at the edge of the lot, one foot in the sand.)

(The baby, who had screamed for eight months when she was born, before settling into an intelligence not yet seen in this family and frankly a bit frightening. Arranging her blocks in perfect rows. Sitting alone in a tiny chair with a book, "reading.")

This family holds representation of nearly all the seven categories of earthly sufferings.

. . .

A civilian version of the M16, tremendous instrument, the same kind carried by F at C, now half-hidden behind the sunshade, impossible to see through the tinted glass, only the tip visible as he cracked the window. His body so tense it felt calm.

. . .

And don't give her any lip about privilege. This family holds representation of nearly all the seven categories of earthly sufferings. It earned its privilege through immense striving in the face of grief the shooter will never know, and she knew this because she herself was too busy managing this striving and grief to take an afternoon out and wander the area with a weapon. Did he think she never looked around and thought, "What a

The First Full Thought of Her Life

bunch of assholes. I'd like to take them all out"? That is a particularly unoriginal thought. She had that thought at the supermarket every week. She saw a whole planeful of people having that thought on the tarmac three days before. She'd think it right now if she took the time to look around, but she wouldn't because she was *busy*, unlike Stupid over here. She had other things on her mind. The idea of killing everyone around her was just one little pile of thought in her brain, off in a corner, might get stepped on and tracked around by her shoe. Her mind was fertile with thoughts, all of them growing and twisting and filling the space, filling the sky, most of them more honorable than that.

She'd take this guy on. She would.

(Seven categories . . . ?)

Poverty. Her husband grew up in a concrete house by a swamp. Her husband's family picked garbage to eat and her husband grew up among them. His brother spent half his life in prison and came out with so many tattoos he looked like a comic book.

> **The shooter was watching the girl. Her mother was watching the girl.**

Political strife. On her mother's side she was descended from a race that had been chased over every continent. For thousands of years her people had had to move at a moment's notice, hide their coins in their hair like magicians. In Europe her people had been rounded up, placed in cattle cars, and incinerated without ceremony. Practically every relation she should have had was never born. The world still despised her race today. Don't think she never felt it.

(Political strife, boff! That's a little finger waving itself.)

And what is *his* ethnicity, might she ask?

Hmm. Brown eyes. She'd been hoping for blue.

Well anyway, tough guy.

. . .

He was drawn by her purposeful tread. When she'd clearly cleared the top he'd do it, her full childish figure delineated by the sky. He could hear the cheers of the other shooters of America, he could hear their voices.

. . .

The girl kept climbing. She didn't look back over her shoulder to check that her mother was still there. She believed her mother could no longer see her. The sun blinking over the dune, the sand heavy under her feet, her hat (print of whales and waves) blowing, the arc of earth in front of her. To her she was going on alone.

In fact that may have been the first full thought of her life, forming on that dune, a strange sand flower, her mind, blooming into existence that very moment: that she was alone.

She didn't mean *alone* alone, of course. Obviously there were people milling around, struggling in the heat, feet slogging, sliding down as they trudged up. At least two kids in the vicinity were throwing tantrums and another was rolling past her, laughing. But no one was *watching* her at that moment, looking at her.

. . .

The shooter was watching the girl. Her mother was watching the girl. Did you think she'd let her daughter toddle off unattended? Child was four. She was only twelve feet away, now fourteen.

A young woman, a soldier in Nevada, was watching the girl through a drone-based surveillance camera in the sky. Practicing. She was scooting around overhead, focusing in on objects, in this case, the girl, to see how much detail she could get. Could she see each of the girl's fingers, could she see the shape of her eyes? Could she see the design on her shirt (little fishes, sea-themed head to toe, mermaids on her shoe tips)? Skill-building exercise. Taking a break while the first lieutenant was gone getting a sandwich.

Her father below could make out the girl's tiny figure. He had the baby, weeping miserably into his shirt, in one arm, and he was squinting under the other arm to see his daughter. Look at her go, the little locomotive—but why was his wife sitting in the sand?

The girl's grandmother at home was watching in her mind's eye. The grandmother always had been a little witchy. While pulling on her Salvation Army volunteer smock, she had a flash of the child's shirt in the sun.

In this moment more people were watching this small, unremarkable human tread through hot sand (her mind blinking on like a night-light, like an alarm) than many humans are contemplated in a week.

No one was watching the shooter. Maybe this had been his problem from the very start. Unseen man. It certainly was a problem today.

. . .

Other things were happening. The heat was too strong—the mother had underestimated it—and the girl could get heatstroke and die. The father was right about sand: the girl planted her next step four inches from a tick that carried a new sand-borne disease related to Lyme. The girl was about to spontaneously develop a deadly cancer (it can happen like that). She could in this moment become someone who would grow up to be an alcoholic.

But no kidding there was a shooter on the ground. He'd released the safety now, he was adjusting his scope. The girl, drawing a bead on her.

. . .

A thousand miles away a family was at an amusement park and it was awful. The boy was sick. The in-laws were cheap and wouldn't spend any money. It was cold. They were snapping the Mickey Mouse photo. The father was trying to get his money's worth, exhorting them to "draw on a smile" with their invisible pens. They were all grimacing and the boy had torn off his ears.

. . .

Dune. Ridge of crushed shells and stones and evaporated water. Built by air and ice. An accumulation of simplest elements.

. . .

The mother. She'd told him all she could to save her daughter's life, all she was able to, though there was more that she could not tell him because she could not speak it, not even in her mind.

At a certain moment six years before, none of this might have happened. No little girl in the sand, no baby screaming at the edge of the parking lot, or at least not this particular one for the shooter to now glance back at irritably to see where the racket was coming from.

There'd been one night in particular at a hotel. They'd been trying to create a rekindling "getaway" (despite all their debt, despite the baby who hadn't made it out alive) but there'd been a scene and he'd gotten away, left, and walked the dark, foreign streets while she sat alone on the bed and wept, "Don't you dare come back, don't you dare," but he'd dared, and at the time it had seemed like a supreme loyalty after all that had been said between them in that room (though where else was he going to go? she thought six years later on a dry hill, fourteen, fifteen, sixteen feet now from her daughter) and they'd made it through.

Now in the sand the sound in her head went, *Six years later she was walking up the dune with her daughter*.

These things happen but one goes up the dune anyway, bare-headed, no bulletproof vests, faces open to the sky, and if everyone else has peeled off—father, baby, brother, and so many more—if you yourself won't make it, you sit in the sand and you send the girl on without you, as you must, and if that doesn't work, you hope *something* will and that one day she will know that to see her in front of you was all you wanted.

> **A thousand miles away a family was at an amusement park and it was awful.**

. . .

Will he shoot?

I don't have access to his brain, to all of it, only to his intention and then I am swept out (like a fluff blowing off the table). The sun might be too bright, for one thing, too late in the afternoon. They were all looking dead west. He may have waited too long. He may have to come back tomorrow. He had the whole summer, his whole life really, before him.

But the girl was perfect, the other shooters of America were saying. The most obvious example in the area of what it is to be human: one's continual encounter with inequity. The marking of that encounter. The world would be horrified by the first shot landing on a little blond girl. Then he'd work down, plucking off the others. Or not. One could be enough. This one.

. . .

One mile away another mother was buying them nothing from the gift shop.

Four miles away another father was pulling up to a cabin.

. . .

The First Full Thought of Her Life

The girl reached the dune's top. She stood in the hot sand, the parking lot below on one side, the lake in the distance on the other, Mother twenty feet down. For the first time she knew what it was like to be her. The foreignness of herself to herself, the surprise of her existence.

• • •

He released the safety, winked into the scope, finger trembling to pull the trigger, shoot, send the girl rolling, spewing blood, her mouth in the sand.

• • •

If she lives, if the shooter doesn't pull the trigger, later the surprise of herself will dull. She'll grow familiar (or frightening) to herself, then bored (or desperate). Then will come that inconvenient teenage self-hatred, like an avalanche, the worst of it hurled at the poor mother, another entry in the ledger of bad luck.

But the girl would soften later, she would unstiffen over the years, over the decades, by degrees, until one day thirty years after this day on the dune, she would achieve the middle-age calm that is happiness. The simplicity of the formula somehow takes that many years to reach. She would take a trip to Hawaii and bring her aging mother, leaving her own children and sister behind, and she and her mother would have the time of their lives (well, not exactly, but it would have its moments).

• • •

And the baby, if he doesn't shoot? What will become of her? Same as anyone, though she would never reach the top of this dune, this particular one. She would grow up and climb others—sand dunes, snow dunes, grassy hills, mountains, slopes of all sorts—but her father hadn't carried her up this one and they'd never come back ("Why on earth would we voluntarily go there more than once?" he'd say), so that would be that. But many other people would climb it, if he doesn't shoot, nothing exceptional there. It's a tourist attraction, after all. In summer season hundreds of people a day would clomp up that dune through the sand, take photos of themselves, and go back down. Those photos would wind up in all sorts of spaces and arrangements online, six races regularly represented (though the average skewed heavily white and

Latino). A mound of sand, sky behind, arms open in conquest. Something about the light made the people look fit, an optical illusion.

. . .

If he shoots, one doesn't want to think what will become of this family.

. . .

The gun will go off. He will shoot. He must. But here, now? He had casings all over the floor of the car. He could feel every cell as the air touched it and changed it. He'd never felt younger.

His brothers, the other shooters of America. He saluted them.

But they were impatient. Stop stalling. Get on with it.

. . .

Don't, don't do it, the mother screamed over the dune, though the shooter couldn't hear her. Not this one. Please. Not her.

Somebody, help.

. . .

Thirty miles away another family was arriving. Tangled up in three seats, they looked as though they'd been in that row for days, though the flight was only two hours. They were wearily watching a movie. The protagonist on the tiny screen was the hope of civilization. He embodied all the world's longings and sadnesses. When he flew away, it got dark, and civilization waited for him to come back, which he did, barely in time. He was there to save them.

Just then, below, the shooter pulled the trigger. Above, the screen blinked off. The plane was descending. Out the window the glinting waves were like spilled jewels or glowing undersea algae or floating space junk. The earth was made of water and filled with floating islands of light. They were diving right into the thickest part of the biggest, widest island.

FICTION

The Tsuchinoko

Michael Braunschweig

translated by Amanda DeMarco

When the tsuchinoko bites its tail, it can roll like a wheel. Like a thick, flat snake a meter long, twenty centimeters wide. For weeks our house was free of mice and insects of all kinds. Then I began to notice the dried bodies of wood lice, like the shells of vehicles that had coasted to their end. And the silvery scales, I didn't know what they were at first. When I swept, the dustpan collected flakes of mica. We began to suffer from frequent nosebleeds and I had to water the plants more often. But I am a fastidious person, these things don't slip by me.

The tsuchinoko doesn't eat or drink, at least not in the normal sense. Though it has teeth, its mouth is merely a shallow and vestigial cavity. It absorbs moisture from the air through gill-like apertures between the scales of its abdomen. And yet it breathes through its nostrils.

It may have accidentally come here in a shipping container. Or maybe it escaped from a collector. I now believe the tsuchinoko is suffering. Its natural environment is a moist one; it inhabits only the windward side of a handful of Japanese mountains, where wind drives precipitation from the Sea of Japan against the slopes. Primitive plants—horsetails, ferns, liverworts—blanket a thin substrate of herbaceous debris, small rivulets intertwine around their stems in shifting constellations like a net slipping down the mountain. Mist rises from chasms, droplets collect at the nodes of twigs and dangle before falling into beds of moss, rivers crash down rocky runs and disappear into caves of fog.

Helen still came to our house sometimes in the evening then, and the three of us ate dinner together, and afterward my father listened to the radio in his chair in the living room. His chair faces a bay window overlooking a stony expanse dotted with scrub. But by that time of evening, it was already black. There are only three things my father still talks about. Firstly, he reenacts or invents comic dialogues between Kaspar and Schmitz, puppet characters popular in folk entertainment for children in his Rhenish homeland. He also describes a handful of his exploits as the class clown in his school near the end of the Second World War. Finally, he makes grotesquely inappropriate sexual comments. Sometimes he combines two or more of these topics. Though repetitive, he can be extremely entertaining.

If my father was in a peaceful mood, Helen and I could wash up together, occasionally looking in on him from the next room. Just his domed pate was visible above the back of the chair. One of us sat with him when he was agitated. Helen knew how to brush the dandruff from his lapels and say with music in her voice, "Well what have we gotten up to tonight?" and take his hand so that he would look into her eyes and return a little to himself. Sometimes she played the piano.

Gradually my father became more vulgar. And because of this, Helen and I began to make love more loudly. In our house the old taboos had not been rejected exactly. Merely forgotten. What was not allowed? The question sank in a sea of fog.

In our house the old taboos had not been rejected exactly. Merely forgotten.

Sometimes my father got up in the night. If he made enough noise, I awoke and brought him back to bed. Sometimes I found him lying on the floor in the morning, usually asleep, though it was obvious from his bruises that he had fallen. And the final time, I discovered he had broken his hip and had to call for an ambulance. Helen suggested then, not for the first time, that I should put him in a home, but I couldn't do that.

In the 1930s, my father's father invented an improved clutch mechanism for rotary hammers, and I am now completely financially dependent on my father, or rather on his inheritance. After his arrival in America, my father was a medievalist at a state university. I also once worked at a university, before I took leave to write a book on Descartes, which I am still writing though I will never return to the university. My father was gravely and loquaciously disappointed at my professional development, and today I nearly wish I could again hear him lament it. There was a joke he loved to make, that the content of my Descartes monograph was "doubtful."

And Helen, Helen is a part-time clerk at the county courthouse, and she was my father's caretaker. She has a little wooden house on the outskirts

The Tsuchinoko

of our small town in West Texas near our large wooden house, which my father bought years ago, before my mother's death, because of their love of horses. Over the course of my relationship with Helen, I left my father's house less and less frequently. And after we discovered the tsuchinoko's nest, Helen visited our house less and less frequently, and then not at all.

The tsuchinoko made its nest in the bottom of a closet filled with my dead mother's things in an upstairs guest bedroom that we rarely entered. Its nest is part of a great mystery, because that is where it deposits its prey. As I said, it doesn't have a typical digestive tract, but I have theories about its feeding habits. Perhaps it consumes food the same way it absorbs moisture: while at rest, it curls itself around the carcasses, extracting sustenance between its scales as the flesh becomes putrid enough to imbibe.

A stranger picking up the diary would have no reason to think we exist.

The smell of the nest was indescribable, and that was what alerted Helen and me that something unusual was happening in the house. When I pushed aside two folded women's trench coats, we discovered a compressed heap—about a foot high at its peak, its sides rounded—of small animal carcasses in various states of decay. Some of them seemed to have melted together in the process of decomposition to form the cadavers of fantastic animals: the skeleton of a rat with two heads, a mouse pelt with the tail of a lizard, a bird with the wings of a bat. The tsuchinoko was not in its nest and had probably fled in alarm when we began searching the room.

"You have to call the home," she said, backing away from the closet door.

"The home? What would the home want with an animal," I replied.

"An animal?" Helen turned to face me. "What animal makes something like this? It's like a sculpture."

"A sculpture."

"What if your father? Because of his illness, at night?"

I don't know why I didn't tell Helen right then what I knew about the tsuchinoko. Instead I answered, "My father can hardly walk. How could he do this?"

Helen did not immediately answer. Her mouth moved but did not produce sound. "Then someone could be breaking into the house."

"That's absurd. An animal did this."

"*What* animal? It's like a pyramid."

I didn't have an answer. I wanted to keep what I knew to myself, and I certainly didn't want to involve any outsiders, who might call animal control and take it away. Helen grew angry and left, and I closed the closet door.

Some days before, while my father was hospitalized following his hip injury, I was straightening up his room and discovered a pile of papers. They were filled with handwriting, obviously his, but more angular and spastic than I remembered. My father had given up all interest in the printed word when his mind began to deteriorate, yet here was a diary. He must have written at night.

The entries begin with the first time he saw it. He was lying on his left side behind his chair in the living room, facing away from the chair and the window. The tsuchinoko slithered in and seemed to take notice of him. His eyes had adjusted to the dark, but his vision is not good. In any case, it faced his direction and hesitated before it began to forage around the baseboards and under the bookcases. Slowly it made its way toward him, and he was able to see it in more detail. Its flickering tongue. His fear outstripped his curiosity as it approached, and he pounded the flat of his hand against the floor and said, "Shoo! Shoo!" Alarmed, the tsuchinoko froze, then bit its tail, flexed its abdomen outward, righted itself, and rolled away. At some point, my father fell asleep.

The diary also contains information on the tsuchinoko that he couldn't have gathered from observation. He seems to have been aware of the animal's existence before seeing it personally. His professional research did sometimes touch on legendary and mythical animals, but as far as I knew, only in the European tradition.

When my father saw the tsuchinoko for the second time, he records, it appeared to have grown longer. It was carrying a rodent in its mouth and merely hurried from one room to the next without taking notice of him. Other entries in the diary include recapitulations of stories from his childhood, notes on radio programs he listened to in the evening, and accounts of his meals and bowel movements throughout the day. There is no mention either of Helen or myself, which I at first could not believe, leafing again and again through the pages. A stranger picking up the diary would have no reason to think we exist.

Things were intolerable with Helen when she came back. She had always had a nervous disposition, but now she wheedled and wanted to talk about the nest, and I couldn't help but sense her fear was truthful. It took on the proportions of an evil genius, one that returned to me with a certain alienated majesty. Despite her age, Helen has the face of a beautiful horse and the upright body of a gamine praying mantis, and now the fear illuminated her long cheekbones and busied her small, clerical hands.

Helen made intimations one night while we washed the dishes, or what were almost intimations, in any case she became very difficult to talk to, her face had hardened against me and she truly began to look, in my eyes, like someone who works in a courthouse. When she pulled her hands from the water, an iridescent veil of soap slid down from her wrists, like gloves removing themselves. In the next room my father lay in a narrow hospital bed with guardrails, a recent installation. Finally, she whispered, "I can't believe you're leaving it there, that *pile*. I just. I don't understand."

I dried my hands and put them, briefly, warmly, on Helen's shoulders. And finally, finally, I told her about what I had read in my father's diary. I told her that I thought that the tsuchinoko was sucking all of the moisture out of the air with its breath because it missed its moist natural habitat, which would seem to support my father's notes about the tsuchinoko's vestigial throat and gills, and that it was mummifying the wood lice and eating the mice in the house, but that based on what we saw in its nest, it must have also foraged outdoors. Perhaps it went in and out through rotting panels in the walls. The house is quite old. I told her about the flakes of scales that I found everywhere and about how it must be parched, sick really, this wasn't the environment for it. I became quite animated. I told her my theory about the tsuchinoko curling itself around the carcasses of the prey it had amassed in its nest, forming them into a cone as it consumed them. That was why I refused to remove the carcasses, it *needed* them and you couldn't detect the smell if you didn't go in the guest room, which we didn't. I also told her about my plans to capture the animal. It was important to me, and, I believed, to my father, that it not be sent to a zoo or tormented in a research facility. The only way was to contact the Japanese authorities, but not before we caught it, to make sure no one could claim it was a hoax.

In the past days, I told Helen, I had been having vivid fantasies of the chill glades, droplets of water hanging from each individual needle of each pine lining the slopes of the glade and trickling down the yet-unfurled fronds of the ferns at their bases, where perhaps a heavy heap of snow still lay in the deepest shade.

"Did you kill those little animals?"

I was too shocked to answer. I stared at her in horror as she waited for my reply, her birdlike eyes directed at me, drawn. Then she walked out of the kitchen and turned down the hall, and I heard the front door opening and closing behind her.

My father's health has deteriorated rapidly in the last weeks. Since Helen is no longer here to perform her caretaking duties, in the afternoons I bathe him and make him perform some simple exercises, as I've seen her do in the past. I've placed a stack of paper and a pen next to his bed, but he hasn't written anything. When I ask him about the diary, he looks at me with clouded eyes.

I made a rare trip to the hardware store in town. There, I bought a humidifier and a shallow plastic tub, which I fill with an inch of water and place near my father's cot each night, in his line of sight, and remove each morning. I wish I could shine a lamp on it so that my father could see better, but I'm afraid the light would be repellent.

I believe that my father and I have received a tremendous gift, a wonderful thing at the close of his life. I believe that my father knows how lucky we are. I've taken to sleeping on the sofa next to his bed, because more than anything I want for us to see the tsuchinoko together. Perhaps he'll write about it, and about what he saw the night when he broke his hip. In his honor, I will publish the most complete and first-ever account of the behavior of the tsuchinoko, proving beyond a doubt its existence. It has occurred to me that with such a mysterious predator in the house, some people might expect me to be frightened. But the fact is that I am not.

John Ashbery

FOOD EPISODE

Body, what do you think?
To have been a right to know
and colored like Elizabeth . . .
We porched around th'unpopulated air
and grassy ornament. Your gallery,
O wondrous cloud, is empty.
What's going on up here?

You'd cup their hands, but I'm
like this cat here—make very serious activity
too long ago, half thinking
of what the X—are able to achieve.
In the Shetland navy
wife takes his things
and clean armpits and assuages
the clean mud.

YCLEPT

It's not what you think, the power,
whether you want it or not:
a broken head and a lot of messy torsos.

The past should be more confident.
It has little to lose, and everything to gain.
She might have been sick long before.

Militants take note.
Thing is, no one saw it coming.
I cannot unwash my hand.

A lot can happen. Just last week
I like it that way, Bruce's ankle, eek,
the beautiful the beautiful.

You're up in the air, TV chef,
I am under the scenery. I got her into this,
and not just any debris, okay?

Save you eleven dollars every month
is all anyone still wants of it, and more
than these wildest animals.

WRITTEN WITH A BALLPOINT

How concerned are you with the man who runs it?
Didn't I hope you enjoyed it too?
Now hopefully, first he said I can't.
Nothing succeeds like success,
always something wrong with me, human issues.
Chaste ephemerae. Don't go on that boat.

How long ago would you be with him at his school?

That's ridiculous. That's great.
I can see you running.

Rhythm and blues imploded, not listening.
What a measurable doubt canceled statutes
of limitations, I'm not sure how.
Attila the Hun must not have been available.
Now get down off that lamp.

If you read it in your journals it's true too.
Now pretty much so, the runny impact through cars,
chemical-laced pants in general, not just me
in the morning time, the afternoon hour,
the prawn sisters' dream-sequence
retro vibe. We're already starting to hear from the paper boy.
There was another incident where they had white boots on.
We call them "sea lollipops."

No word on minor injuries.
Some, not all, bled artificial tears,
very nice and fresh,
in a fancy hotel room. Diversity
gets better all the time, yet wound up taking pictures.
They're not talking about us any more.
Moose wandering at home on the ground,
who's going to pay for it? At $250,000 a year?

Elmer and Thelma met cute
on Floating Island. Have that conversation, serial golf putter.
To not have an uncle, more umbrellas for Dad
in my office, though filled with dead bodies. Secretly independent.

Eight years ago, when I was married to a European high school,
an odd thing happened. Allow me
to prefer the old ways, a lotta remembrance,
no place for heavenlies.

You can die watching the army. It isn't like this.
To make a long story short, I just thought, maybe
keep the bed under here missing pieces. Nowhere fast.
I love the routine, as long as we keep doing the same thing
until the door was open.

LOST AND FOUND

SEASONAL TREATS

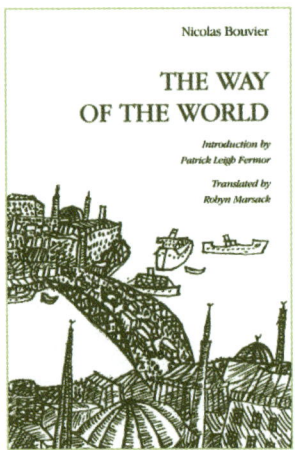

ON NICOLAS BOUVIER'S
The Way of the World

NATHAN GAUER

Sinan, my college roommate for four years, was the first Turkish person I'd ever met. We became like brothers. Our friendship also inspired a lifelong dream: I determined to contribute in some way to strengthening ties between the citizens of Turkey and the United States.

My dream of becoming a writer also came into focus as an undergraduate. When I learned about the Fulbright Programs for Artists, Writers & Musicians, seven years after graduating from college, it seemed like an ideal way to work toward both of these aspirations at once.

My application was rejected, but I decided to move to Turkey anyway. I knew that if I did not go while I was still young, my willingness to pack light and move to a new continent might fade into regret.

Before I left for Istanbul, a friend gifted me a copy of Nicolas Bouvier's *The Way of the World*, which chronicles the year-and-a-half-long road trip Bouvier and his best friend, Thierry Vernet, took from Geneva to Afghanistan in a beat-up Fiat. As a child, Bouvier had "stretched out on the rug, silently contemplating the atlas, and that makes one want to travel." At the age of twenty-four, he left his home in the suburbs of Geneva and joined Vernet in Bosnia. Bouvier remembers the outset of their journey thusly: "We had two years in front of us, and money for four months. The programme was vague; the main thing was just to get going."

Originally published in French in 1963 as *L'usage du monde*, *The Way of the World* was translated by Robyn Marsack in 1992 and has since acquired a cult status among a small group of readers around the world. In the introduction to Marsack's translation, Patrick Leigh Fermor notes, "It is hard to determine exactly what makes the books and journeys of Nicolas Bouvier so distinct from the work of other writers." However, this doesn't stop Fermor from giving it a go: Bouvier's "passionate curiosity," his capacity to be "totally at home in the heart of heterodoxy and strangeness," and a "comic sense . . . kept in balance by a wise, tolerant and most unusual cast of mind" are some of the reasons why Fermor believes *The Way of the World* is "nothing short of a masterpiece."

In *Emîle, or On Education*, Rousseau tells us, "There is a big difference between traveling to see lands and traveling to see peoples." Bouvier's writing—incisive, funny, casually erudite, occasionally racy, and frequently profound—proves this difference. At Bouvier's side, we hear the Gypsy musicians in the small Yugoslavian town of Bogojevo who, "in the time it took to smoke a few cigarettes . . . made their strings sob for the simple pleasure of turning one's soul upside down." We feel the emotional adjustment necessary when crossing from Yugoslavia into Greece, where "a listener will interrupt you in mid-flow with impatient gestures—he's got it." We long to join the conversations at the Khyber Pass Mechanical Shop in Pakistan, where the majority of mechanics are "former truck-drivers who have seen the country; their stops, their memories, their loves are spread across a vast province and this makes for an enlightened group of people who are prone to laughter."

And yet we also recognize the melancholy that can suddenly overcome us when far away from home, so that everything "that was misshapen, nauseating and deceptive would emerge with nightmarish clarity: the sore flanks of the donkeys, feverish eyes and ragged jackets, rotten teeth and those shrill, wary voices molded by five centuries of occupation and conspiracies—right down to the mauve offal in the butchers' shops, which seemed to be calling out for help, as though meat could die twice."

Like anyone who believes travel is a dialogue, Bouvier can't help but reassess his own culture in the mirror of his encounters on the road. Thinking about his native suburb in Geneva, Bouvier admits, "There was a world of good taste there, and often of goodwill, but basically it was a world of consumption, where the heart's virtues were certainly maintained but, like the family silver, were reserved for special occasions." In contrast, in the Macedonian town of Prilep, we meet seventy- and eighty-year-old men who won't hesitate to make fools of themselves for the pleasure of hearing their friends' laughter. An old joker walks past the Jadran café one morning with sunflower seeds in his beard, blowing on a small wooden propeller. Bouvier reflects that while "such men scarcely exist in our societies, where the mind is developed at the expense of feelings," in Eastern European towns like Prilep, not a single day passes "without our meeting one of those pithy, mischievous, rash creatures, carrying hay or patching slippers, who always made me want to hug them and burst into tears."

Some of the most unforgettable moments in *The Way of the World* involve Bouvier's encounters with his fellow expatriates. In Iran, he meets Roberts, an American engineer who is living in the country on behalf of the US government to build a school for Iranian children in a bone-crushingly poor rural town. However, the school fails before it is even built. Kids throw stones at Roberts. Building materials disappear. The Iranians don't want the Americans' gift. Bouvier assesses Roberts's failure as follows: "It is not so easy to admit that what works at home mightn't work abroad; that Iran, that old aristocrat who has known all about life—and forgotten much—is allergic to ordinary medicine and calls for special treatment. Presents are not so easy to give when the children are five thousand years older than Santa Claus."

As the perfect details, prescient insight, and haunting characters continue their unhurried stroll to the final page, the reader draws courage from this simple but extraordinary fact: Bouvier originally self-published *L'usage du monde*. How could a book this formidable and brilliant not find a home at a publishing house in the French-speaking world of the 1960s? Did Bouvier try to pursue the traditional publishing route only to shift gears as the rejections began to outweigh his patience?

We may never know, but regardless of the reasons why Bouvier self-published, the humble origins of this book pose questions that profoundly shaped my education as a writer. Here's one: Even if the world says "No" for the next ten or fifteen years—no to your fellowship applications, no to your story submissions, no to your queries to find representation for your first book—do you have the guts to keep writing, in the belief that your work will eventually be read? If you knew in advance that it would take forty-nine years to reach a young reader who feels you are speaking directly to her, would you keep going?

I suspect these are questions most writers grapple with at some point. But unlike books we read, admire, critique, and then quickly forget, *The Way of the World* leaves us with questions that cannot be tucked away neatly on our bookshelf or in a desk drawer.

These are questions that cling to your thoughts as the man bathed in aftershave enters your train compartment and begins crawling down the aisle, collecting change in the hollow of his prosthetic leg. Questions that beat against your ribs as the mother and her four daughters take turns throwing chunks of bread at the seagulls hovering alongside the ferry as it bounces from Asia to Europe. Questions that color the photographer's whispering shutter and the sighs of the Bosporus below deck. You listen closer to the water crashing against the hull and feel the warmth of the railing in your hands. As you watch the unsteady Bosporus, the colors of the water, clouds, and sky seem to be bleeding out while the question running beneath all others pierces the surface: *What if every single word you've written is in vain?*

But, inevitably, the ferry docks at what had once looked like such a distant shore, and you remember Bouvier's thoughts near the end of his journey in Afghanistan: "That day, I really believed that I had grasped something and that henceforth my life would be changed. But insights cannot be held for ever. Like water, the world ripples across you and for a while you take on its colors. Then it recedes, and leaves you face to face with the void you carry inside yourself, confronting that central inadequacy of soul which you must learn to rub shoulders with and to combat, and which, paradoxically, may be our surest impetus."

You breathe and take a step forward, grateful to have such a wise traveling companion at your side. Though lost for decades, there are very few books you would have rather found as you learn how to write your way into this immense, dangerous, noble world.

ON EMILY HAHN'S

China to Me

ALEXANDRA PECHMAN

In 2010, I decided to live for a few months in Nanjing, China, with my then-boyfriend, though I would know no one else there and I spoke no Chinese. Everyone thought my plan was a very bad idea (or had never heard of Nanjing) so, as if to find permission, I began to research American journalists who had spent time where I was going. I read through the *New Yorker*'s archives online, slowly reading through fairly recent pieces written by Evan Osnos and Peter Hessler in the 2000s and 2010s. But what I found myself most drawn to was the magazine's very first reporting on the ground in China, written by Emily Hahn between 1935 and 1943. This was followed by personal essays and fictionalized accounts of her time there that appeared periodically over the next fifty years: she was the magazine's only staff writer who had been based in China during the twentieth century before the country effectively closed to the West under Mao.

Hahn, a roving correspondent for the *New Yorker* from 1928 into the '90s, wrote nearly two hundred articles for the magazine. She was part Jewish, grew up in St. Louis and Chicago, and went to the University of Wisconsin, so she had a profile somewhat similar to my own. After living in New York and London as a writer, she went to the Belgian Congo alone at age twenty-five, in much more uncertain circumstances than I was planning, and with much more nonchalance: in college she had dreamed of traveling to Lake Kivu in Central Africa, and so, after meeting someone who lived there, she went. She brought a glamorous hunting suit, but no camping equipment. The experience is described in some of her first casuals from abroad for the *New Yorker*. She returned to New York from 1933 to 1935 and wrote three books. But after a breakup with a Hollywood screenwriter, she felt stuck and decided to go back to the Congo, with a stop in Asia first. She landed in Shanghai and stayed for eight years.

Her best-known *New Yorker* piece, "The Big Smoke," from 1969, recalls how she kicked an opium addiction she developed in Shanghai. Without quitting, she would not have been able to travel throughout China to write *The Soong Sisters*, the biography of three sisters who married some of the most important men in China at the time (notably, Chiang Kai-Shek). *The Soong Sisters* became her most famous book.

"The Big Smoke" was written more than thirty years after the fact, in a tone that is reflective, wise, and meant to shock: it is nothing like most of Hahn's writing.

The Hahn I prefer is always in the thick of it without seeing herself to be. She recounts fleeing Nanjing after she mistakenly took a trip there just before the city was raided, and sneaking food to Charles Boxer, the chief spy for British military intelligence and father of her child, while he was being held by the Japanese in Hong Kong. Her 1944 "partial autobiography," *China to Me*, mainly covers the years during the invasion and World War II, a bit after the events of "The Big Smoke." (She leaves out her addiction.) She wrote the book after she escaped the Japanese occupation in 1943. It was out of print in 2010, but I found a typo-ridden paperback copy put out by a small publisher of out-of-print books. With the book in my suitcase, I went to China as well.

When Hahn arrived in 1935, Shanghai was considered "the Paris of the East," where foreigners and Chinese shared high society and opium dens. "We the residents sat there in our Eastern city and watched the world bring us amusing books and news and people," Hahn writes. The first few chapters of *China to Me* detail the intrigues of jewel dealers, journalists, Japanese generals, "baby diplomats" from England, and Italian officers. Hahn was romantically involved with both Victor Sassoon, the English millionaire hotelier, and Sinmay Zau, a prominent married Chinese poet. She kept a pet monkey named Mr. Mills, and recalls her disappointment at receiving party invitations with the addendum: "Sorry we cannot extend an invitation to Mr. Mills."

"I look back on it now with mild wonder," Hahn writes in the introduction. "What on earth did we think we were doing?"

While the fizz of prewar Shanghai provides anecdotes worthy of their own book, it's not Hahn's focus: barely one hundred pages into the book, the Japanese invade. "It was a very different city now. It stood alone and beleaguered, surrounded on all sides by a greedy watchful enemy," Hahn writes. "'Someday soon,' I said aloud, 'we'll have to fight this out, you know. It isn't going to go on just like this indefinitely.' 'It might,' said Sinmay. 'Things last a long time in China.'"

Such prescience about China, and the world, often belongs to Hahn. "Nothing remains impossible there," she writes of Shanghai. "Always changing, there are some things about it which will never change, so that I will forever be able to know it when I come back." But she never saw the Shanghai of the twenty-first century—she died in 1997—a city now completely characterized by this refusal of impossibility and constant change.

The events of *China to Me* similarly rush by, as if Hahn were worried she might not get it all down—or, more likely, because she was anxious to move on to another project, or trying to distract herself from Charles's fate. (He was liberated soon after she finished the book and they were married from 1945 until her death.) Hahn wrote fifty-two books in her lifetime, several about China, but also novels, humor, young adult fiction, memoirs, and nonfiction about monkeys, diamonds, explorers, and the state of zoos. My copy of *China to Me* has no index, and Hahn almost never stops to explain herself or anyone else. Too much happened to her. While she recorded in exquisite detail—Charles joked she could remember entire party conversations even when she was drunk—nothing really shocked her. One almost needs to read her 1998 biography, *Nobody Said Not to Go* by Ken Cuthbertson, to understand her radicalism, and to catalog the scores of famous personalities and dignitaries she encountered.

"She was a 1990s woman born a generation too soon," he writes in *Nobody Said Not to Go*. (The title is her response when he asked why she took her fateful trip to Nanjing.) And yet she may not have been a 2000s woman either. While speed and capaciousness characterized her output, she had no interest in marketing herself. A different writer might have stayed in New York to capitalize on the fame she won at a young age; instead she spent her twenties and thirties living abroad, to the frustration of her agent. Her novel about an abortion and one about a foreign Shanghai courtesan were both deemed too salacious and flopped. The subject matter that made her the target of critics in the 1930s and '40s would make Mary McCarthy their darling in the 1950s and '60s.

Hahn never wanted to be called a feminist. She disdained isms and labeling, another indication that she would be out of place today. It wasn't the idea of feminism she mistrusted—her biography reads like a how-to manual on the subject. Rather, it was the effort of proclamation versus just doing that irked her.

As for her public persona, she did often find herself a darling of the press, and she courted it, smoking cigars or making ridiculous statements in public, but she didn't like to hew to any specific identity—her publicity-garnering abilities were based only on her being unpredictable. As opposed to the way many writers today carefully hone their brands, like jewelers cutting their gems to be placed in a setting, Hahn's persona had no preciousness to it because she didn't have time to craft one.

Going to China was my first adventure, and Hahn was kind of the adventure's patron saint. But it didn't stay that way. The "adventure" became life as I continued to study Chinese, returned to Shanghai each year, wrote from other places, and it became easier to identify with Hahn's nonchalance. My initial bewilderment about going abroad solo seemed more a symptom of my own time: when a writer can rove the Internet, it's easy to see why so few physically follow their curiosity, as Hahn did. "Nobody said not to go" best explains Hahn life, but I'm most encouraged by what she did next: go farther.

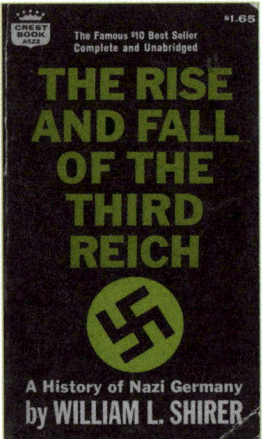

ON WILLIAM SHIRER'S

The Rise and Fall of the Third Reich

SARAH BRIDGINS

When tragedy strikes, some people find religion. I found history, and *The Rise and Fall of the Third Reich* was my Bible.

My father died of a heart attack in January 2014, two days after his sixty-second birthday. It came out of nowhere. On Thursday I was talking to him on the phone about an upcoming trip he had planned, and on Monday morning I was calling the police in my hometown of Alexandria, Virginia, because I hadn't been able to reach him all weekend. They found him dead in his bedroom a few hours later.

My father was the third close family member I had lost in less than two years. His death followed my mother's and my grandmother's. I had no siblings and I wasn't married or even in a relationship. I was twenty-nine and I had no one left. I felt cursed.

I took two weeks off from my job at a literary agency. When I told a friend how much I was dreading my return, he told me to pretend I was going somewhere to read the Internet for eight hours and get paid for it. "Right now," he said, "your only job is getting through the day."

I took this to heart, but even sitting at a desk and watching cat videos all day proved taxing. I didn't want to be there. I didn't want to be anywhere. That's when I turned to books about World War II.

Even though history was one of my favorite subjects in school, in my adult life I hadn't evolved into much of a history buff. My last boyfriend had been fascinated by military history, though, and helped me rekindle my interest. We watched Ken Burns's documentaries about the Civil War and World War II, which led to long conversations with my father, who had been a history and religious studies major in college. I loved finding something new to share.

It was partly a desire to feel connected to my father that drew me to *The Rise and Fall of the Third Reich*. I also felt an instinctual need to submerge myself in a past that was infinitely more tragic than my own. My mother's death had been awful, but I could at least wrap my mind around one parent dying. But both? Within two years? And before I was thirty? I didn't know anyone who had gone through this. Before my father died I'd had a place to go for Christmas, and someone I could call in the middle of the night if something was wrong. Now, suddenly, all of that was gone. I was disoriented and unmoored, and it became very important that I learn everything I could about the Nazis' rise to power and how it led to World War II. The logic seems crazy in retrospect, but part of me believed that if I could gain some understanding of one of history's most unimaginable events, my own mess of a life—and maybe the world in general—would start making sense again. A horrible sense, but sense nonetheless.

I started looking up books online, but everything that turned up felt either lurid or poorly researched. There was one titled *Doctors from Hell* about experiments performed on concentration camp victims and a YA book by Bill O'Reilly about Hitler's last days. I wasn't looking for grotesque details or wild speculation. I wanted facts and the ability to apply logic to horror. What was the political atmosphere in Germany when the Nazis came to power and how were they able to gain such a strong foothold? When did the rest of the world begin to learn of their atrocities and why did it take so long to stop them? The crimes against humanity committed by the Nazis represented for me the furthest extremes of inexplicable tragedy. Through learning about them, I hoped not only to distract myself from the events of my life but also to find a new landing place for the question tossing around my head a thousand times a day: "How could this have happened?"

I eventually asked my ex what I should read. He had only one suggestion: *The Rise and Fall of the Third Reich*.

The next day on my lunch break I found a first-edition copy at the Strand.

The Rise and Fall of the Third Reich is massive: 1,245 pages printed in tiny type. Published in 1960, it was written by William Shirer, an American journalist who lived in Europe from 1934 to 1940 and reported on the war for CBS. The copy I bought had a swastika prominently featured on the dust jacket, which I removed to avoid confusing strangers.

The book is divided into six parts, beginning with Hitler's youth in Austria and ending with Goering's suicide in a Nuremberg prison. Because Shirer was a journalist and not a historian, the book has been taken less seriously by some scholars, but his engaging prose makes it a compelling read. Shirer livens up descriptions of complicated military maneuvers and the history of the Prussian Empire, otherwise dry material, with his humor, personal insights, and clear, concise descriptions of complicated political matters. He treats the Nazi leaders with equal parts horror and disdain. He describes Alfred Rosenberg, the official tasked with drawing up a blueprint for Operation Barbarossa, as a "dolt, with a positive genius for misunderstanding history, even the history of Russia, where he was born and educated." Of the Nazi foreign minister he writes, "Incompetent and lazy, vain as a peacock, arrogant and without humor, Ribbentrop was the worst possible choice for such a post."

Nonetheless, it's a dense book. Reading ten pages could take me an hour, more if I stopped to cross-reference a particularly confusing passage on Wikipedia, which I frequently did. Reading began to feel meditative. My lack of background knowledge meant that fully comprehending and retaining new facts required my complete concentration. When I was reading I wasn't thinking about how much I missed my dad, or how tired I was from not sleeping through the night. I was thinking about the millions who suffered, what it must have been like to feel as though the entire world was—literally, not figuratively—collapsing. As upsetting as it was to contemplate these things it was also, in its own way, a relief. The hours I spent reading were the only time I didn't feel consumed by sadness.

In addition to lugging around my battered hardcover copy, I also bought the e-book so I could read it covertly on my computer at work. I spent entire Saturdays reading on the couch, and drove all of my friends nuts spouting half-remembered facts about the burning of the Reichstag and the Beer Hall Putsch. At some point I told one of them how great it was to be learning so much about European geography. "Now I know where Yugoslavia is!" I said. She gently explained that it was not a country anymore.

It took me almost a year to finish *The Rise and Fall of the Third Reich*. This was also how long it took me to start feeling like a human being again, rather than a branch broken off in a storm. I learned a lot about World War II, but the further into the book I read, the more I realized and accepted that I would never be able to process all of the war's complexities. What I truly gained was the understanding that my suffering was not special or anomalous. Rather than alienating me from others who hadn't lost as much, my experiences gave me a greater ability to relate to those who had lost even more—which, when you take into account all of the catastrophic events of the past and present, is most of humanity. At the lowest point in my life, *The Rise and Fall of the Third Reich* provided the most we can hope for from a piece of literature: no matter how dark and incomprehensible the world might seem, at least I had the comfort of knowing I wasn't alone.

ON BROOKE HAYWARD'S

Haywire

JOEL DRUCKER

In July 1978, I held the paperback edition of Brooke Hayward's memoir *Haywire* at a bookstore two blocks from my home in Brentwood, a Los Angeles neighborhood, and read this vivid statement on the inside jacket: "I'm the daughter of a father who's been married five times. Mother killed herself. My sister killed herself. My brother has been in a mental institution. I'm twenty-three and divorced with two kids."

When do we learn that life is tragic, that our journey will include not only the sun but also the moon? Art shows us that tragedy is a possibility. Call art the realm of knowledge. But then comes life—the tactile, physical, and emotional occurrences that fall under the heading of "experience." Blend knowledge with experience and you get the nearly forty-year-long affinity I've had with *Haywire*.

Hayward's mother, Margaret Sullavan, was a prominent actress from the 1930s through the '50s, dazzling such costars as Henry Fonda (a previous husband) and Jimmy Stewart. Brooke's father, Leland Hayward, dubbed the "Toscanini of the telephone," was the preeminent agent of his time, a dashing man about town who represented the likes of Stewart, Katharine Hepburn, Greta Garbo, and Cary Grant, started an airline, and produced such hits as *The Sound of Music*.

"To watch them together was dizzying, hypnotic," writes Hayward. "One was aware of infinite potential." The Haywards had everything, from enormous houses and handlers to first-class travel, fame, and, most compelling to me, the sun-drenched optimism of Los Angeles in its midcentury ascent.

I was hooked when I learned that Hayward's early years were also spent in Brentwood. For me, history was remote, tales of faraway places often located in the East. But here it was, within walking distance. Even more pointedly, that summer, I'd graduated high school shadowed by my own family tragedy. It had been less than two years since my older brother Ken's first nervous breakdown. There'd been many episodes. Like Hayward's brother, Bill, younger sister, Bridget, and their mother, Ken also spent time in a mental institution. In the spring of '78, Ken was confined to a body cast, the result of a jump off the balcony of our third-floor apartment.

My brother's illness darkened our family's California dream. We'd moved to Los Angeles from St. Louis in November 1970. Monday, when we headed to the airport, it was thirty-five degrees, with no sign of the sun. Tuesday: blue skies as we walked through Westwood in short sleeves and saw Groucho Marx cross the street. Welcome to LA, where frequent and casual proximity to fame triggers an ambition defined not by institutional acceptance or financial success, but by the desire to become notable.

Haywire reveals fame's costs. Sullavan disdained celebrity, devoting much of her energy to controlling her children's lives with a theatrical compulsion Hayward calls, "difficult, inconsistent." Sullavan also overtly resented the way her husband's ventures intruded on domestic life. Leland enjoyed a round-the-clock mix of work, play, and fun with male and female friends. As Hayward writes, he "lived like a prince, and loved every minute of it," well aware that he was ill-equipped for parenting and probably also for marriage. In time, everything from Sullavan's persistent desire to retreat to Leland's hedonism and workaholic qualities created tensions that led to divorce, remarriages, and emotional tumult. Sullavan died of what was ruled an accidental drug overdose on January 1, 1960. That same year also saw the mysterious death of Bridget at the age of twenty-one. No one was certain if this was a suicide or the result of epilepsy.

So here we have a tale of poor little rich kids, the Hayward children materialistically spoiled and emotionally neglected. Another version of the same story was told a year later by Christina Crawford in her memoir, *Mommie Dearest*, a tabloid-like book detailing the rage that actress Joan Crawford aimed at her children. But *Haywire* differs. Devoid of violence or debauchery, it accumulates painful details that prick like pins, be they Sullavan giving an over-the-top lecture about the "importance of Jews," each child's strained interactions with Leland, or the way all the shuttling between coasts, schools, and continents (they attended various boarding schools) further distanced the Hayward siblings from one another: "Unhindered by what brothers and sisters ordinarily expected of each other, we were free to live without ordinary rules."

In California, sunshine, fame, and fortune create a perpetual and intoxicating feeling of immunity to the laws of nature—and perhaps by extension, exemption from life's painful realities. Leave the grind to suburbanites commuting to dreary offices in Chicago and Manhattan. Los Angeles was one big transcendent reward, a world of phone calls, home-based offices, cars, swimming pools, and tennis courts. Like Leland, I was a telephone junkie, my long conversations with friends about my three passions—tennis, politics, and movies—convincing me that I, too, would eventually be a wheeler-dealer.

Yet as I read *Haywire* in the limbo summer between high school and college, the book's pall of tragedy verbalized what I was unable (unwilling?) to articulate about what had happened to my brother and its effect on my family. As Leland's life neared its end, Hayward "wept for my family, all of us, my beautiful, idyllic, lost family . . . It was as if we'd taken for granted the fact that, like our talents and interests and riches, there would be more where *we* had come from, too; another chance, another summer."

Ten years after reading *Haywire*, I vacationed in Sonoma with the woman who the next year would become my wife. Joan was the first person I spoke to extensively about my brother. She encouraged me to see a psychologist and in time I also attended a support group for siblings and children of the mentally ill. Joan suffered from lupus, an autoimmune disease that can trigger mental confusion. During our time in Sonoma, Joan struggled to speak. As we walked together in a used bookstore, she said, "This is too much, too many titles, too much color, too many words." Just as we were about to exit, I saw a worn paperback: *Haywire*. Its impact on me in 1978 had been powerful, but also, in many ways, beneath my consciousness. Perhaps this time, a decade removed from the horrors of my home, supported by all the insights and care I'd gained from Joan's love, it would strike a different, more clearly grasped chord.

Over the next twenty-four hours, we lay in bed, Joan alternating between sleeping and waking up confused, me no longer a teen but an adult, yet once again witness to a loved one suffering. From *Haywire*: "I had begun to have the disquieting concept of myself as a spectator, not a participant, in my own life. I saw myself as the audience, leaning back to watch my future unfold like a Greek tragedy." Joan soon recovered. This had not been her first flare-up. Nor would it be her last.

Fast-forward twenty-two years. Joan died in September 2010. A month later I took her ashes to her favorite childhood spot, the Upper Peninsula of Michigan, to a small town near Lake Superior. The next morning, Joan's stepmother and I scattered Joan's ashes into the lake. Back in the small town of Laurium, I walked a desolate street, entered a thrift store, and spotted dozens of used books. There was *Haywire*. On this cold Michigan morning, the love of my life gone, I turned to Hayward's last paragraph, set just after Leland's death: "So I started for the doorway and the dark corridor beyond, knowing, as I passed through it, that my only choice was to keep moving forward."

ON ANN PETRY'S

The Street

WHITNEY OTTO

There was a cold November wind blowing through 116th street.

The street in question is more than a Harlem locale: It's a state of mind, an adversary, an existential, and physical, battleground; it's Fate waiting to snatch your child. It's the one thing that Lutie Johnson, the hero of *The Street*, most fears will defeat her—a fear as timely today as it was seventy years ago, which is why this story deserves to be revisited.

Lutie's story opens in 1944, when she is searching for a Harlem apartment for her and her eight-year-old son, Bub. She has recently lost her job as a maid in an affluent Connecticut household after being abandoned by her husband. She can't stay with her father, whose young girlfriend decided to instruct Bub in drinking gin and smoking cigarettes. Though she finds work in a laundry, while taking secretarial classes at night, all she can afford is a crummy one-bedroom apartment in a building with a sexually menacing superintendent; his girlfriend, Min (a devotee of a local man who calls himself Prophet David and who practices a belief system that is half Christian, half voodoo); and Mrs. Hedges, who runs an in-house brothel for a white man named Junto. Junto is also the owner of Junto's Bar and Grill, a crowded night spot with a house band led by Junto's African-American right-hand man, Boots Smith.

Lutie is beautiful; half her life is spent dodging unwanted male (black and white) attention, and the other half is spent being punished by white women who turn a blind eye to their husbands' undisguised longing. It doesn't matter that Lutie does nothing to encourage these men; she is still seen as a predator, an aggressive threat to their marriages, trapping her in a cycle of hire as a maid or a secretary (by the husbands) and fire (by the wives).

The other half of Lutie's life is devoted to keeping Bub away from the peril and lure of the street; the superintendent introduces her son to cards, gangster movies, and the shoeshine box, an object that represents everything she doesn't want for her son:

> I'm not going to let you begin at eight doing what white folks figure all eight-year old colored boys ought to do. For if you're shining shoes at eight, you'll probably be doing the same thing at eighty. And I'm not going to have it.

Bub is also witness to the business of the apartment-house brothel.

Harlem may have its dangers, but for Lutie, it's still a refuge, an escape from an oppressive white presence:

> She got off the train, thinking that she never felt really human until she reached Harlem and thus got away from the hostility in the eyes of the white women who stared at her on the downtown streets and in the subway. Escaped the openly appraising looks of the white men whose eyes seemed to go through her clothing to her long brown legs . . .
>
> These other folks feel the same way, she thought—that once they are freed from the contempt in the eyes of the downtown world, they instantly became individuals. Up here they were no longer creatures labeled simply "colored" and therefore alike.

People who made themselves "small" on a downtown platform now expanded to such large proportions, laughing and talking, that they could hardly fit on the stairs in the uptown Harlem station. The contrast between visibility and invisibility, large and small, male and female, black and white, rich and poor, is threaded throughout the narrative, illustrating the fluidity that is inextricable to getting by if you are African-American.

When Lutie happens into Junto's place, she immediately catches Boots's eye. He encourages her to sing with his band—which she does, thinking she'll earn something. She doesn't. What she gets instead is Boots's unwanted attention, and (though she is unaware) Junto has his own plans for her.

Boots considers marrying Lutie (if it is the only way to have her), then considers the deal he has with Junto, who, Boots knows, wants her for himself and who has rescued him from the life of a train porter. He weighs Lutie against a life without Junto in what is perhaps my favorite passage in the novel:

> Porter! Porter this and Porter that. Boy. George. Nameless. He got a handful of silver at the end of each run, and a mountain of silver couldn't pay a man to stay nameless like that. No Name, black my shoes. No Name, hold my coat. No Name, brush me off. No Name, take my bags. No Name. No Name.
>
> Niggers steal. Lock your bag. Niggers lie. Where's my pocketbook? Call the conductor. That porter —Niggers rape. Cover yourself up. Didn't you see that nigger looking at you? God damn it! Where's that porter? Por—ter! Por—ter!
>
> Balance Lutie Johnson. Weigh Lutie Johnson. Long legs and warm mouth. Soft skin and pointed breasts. Straight slim back and small waist. Mouth that curves over white, white teeth. Not enough. She didn't weigh enough when she was balanced against

a life of saying "yes sir" to every white bastard who had the price of a Pullman ticket. Lutie Johnson at the end of a Pullman run. One hundred Lutie Johnsons didn't weigh enough.

Being a starving piano player, paid next to nothing for the entertainment of white people wasn't all that different from working on the train: "And in place of the stinking, rotten joints there were miles of 'Here boy,' 'You boy,' 'Go boy,' 'Run boy,' 'Stop boy,' 'Come boy.'" The beauty of Ann Petry's pages about Boots is the piling on of the humiliations and hardships of being a black man in America, in New York, no less; the cops raiding the places Boots played, "swinging their night sticks with abandon" if they found white women "lolling around inside." If there were no white women, they would content themselves with "smashing up furniture, breaking windows with vicious efficiency." It's the phrase "vicious efficiency" that brings it all home.

Boots is a frustrated realist; in another world, he could marry Lutie, but in this world he's lucky to be in the employ of someone like Junto, who rescued him from both the raided joints and the train. The resentment that Petry conveys isn't limited to Boots and his immediate situation; it represents a hundred men like Boots finding themselves in a hundred similar situations.

Economics, race, neighborhoods, opportunities, gender, children.

Petry's novel was published twenty years after the Harlem Renaissance, that fabulous era of painting, intellectualism, music, theater, film, photography, magazines, politics, and literature. Its glittering mix of bohemia, high society, modernism, and working class made Harlem the American equivalent of postwar Paris, or post-revolution Mexico City, until it came crashing down with the failure of the stock market. Langston Hughes wryly noted, "We were no longer in vogue, anyway, we Negroes. Sophisticated New Yorkers turned to Noel Coward." W. E. B. Du Bois reminded everyone that the Harlem Renaissance "was a transplanted and exotic thing. It was literature written for the benefit of white people and at the behest of white readers." But African-American artists and intellectuals weren't made or unmade by the end of the Harlem Renaissance; no one stopped making music, or painting, or writing essays and novels just because white America had lost interest.

The example of the Harlem Renaissance illuminates the trouble of being a hyphenated author—something that lingers today—which is that it, the hyphen, fucks with the work; that problematic qualifier (the Something-American) often seems to suggest that a book is a fad, or holds special interest for the specially interested, diminishing the importance and scope of a book that is as purely, significantly American as it gets. No hyphen. No qualifier.

I don't remember why I first read this book, about thirty years ago, and I haven't met anyone else who's read it. This isn't to say it hasn't been read: Petry has the distinction of being the first female African-American writer to sell over a million copies of her novel. I'm not generally a fan of stories as emotionally dark as *The Street*, but it's a testament to Petry's skill that she holds the reader's attention until the fateful end. Everything predicted in the beginning is realized by the final pages: Lutie Johnson can't find a viable better life; her beauty and Boots's frustration lead to tragedy. Bub is accused of stealing mail and sent to the Children's Shelter, a place that Lutie knows is one sentencing away from juvenile detention, then jail. Lutie can't save her son from the injustice and violence of the street any more than young men like Trayvon Martin or Michael Brown or Eric Garner or Tamir Rice, or a young woman like Sandra Bland, could be saved. That list, unfortunately, goes on.

One of the final lines of the novel is:

> All she could think was, It was that street. It was that god-damned street.

FICTION

Marrow Island

I drove the long way round the island to the village. If Orwell Island had a primary artery, it would be Hornsea Road, which breaks off from the village's main thoroughfare, Anchorage Street, and circles the island's perimeter almost completely. Almost. Hornsea doesn't actually go all the way around the island. It dead-ends by a small county park with a turnabout. But if you drive on, about twenty yards past the turnabout, the pavement gives out to pitted gravel.

Alexis M. Smith

Locals know that after a quarter mile of increasingly rutted road along the shore, there is an unmarked, abrupt left turn into the trees, and a hard-pack gravel road that turns into asphalt just out of sight. Up the slope the fir trees become denser, the woodland changing from straggler pines and madrones to hardy fir and hemlock and Western red cedar. The road continues for almost four miles, where it eventually meets Anchorage Street at the south end of Orwell Village with a rusted sign that says NO OUTLET. The road is old, but the asphalt is younger than I am. It follows a track that ran around the island before Orwell was even a town, back when it was a trading post for the Coast Salish people and the Europeans who came after Vancouver's expedition. It was our shortcut, those of us who lived on that side.

I drove the grassy, rutted track to the place where asphalt appears out of nowhere. Then three-quarters of a mile on, at the site of an aborted housing development, I pulled off the road into a weedy patch of gravel. All along the road ahead, between stands of taller trees, were more of the same weedy, treeless spaces: parcels of land, marked and cleared, foundations poured and abandoned, now overgrown with vetch and fireweed.

I parked in what would have been a driveway. There were cans and cigarette butts strewn about the gravel. A potato chip bag in the tall grass. Unimaginative graffiti all over the walls. Half a dozen gangly adolescent red alders stood around the rocky floor like derelicts. Alders take root like this after disturbances to the ecosystem. For generations after logging and fires and other disruptions, the swift and the adaptable take over, not letting a spare inch of earth go to waste. Like the local teenagers who clambered through the nettles to scrawl their secret names into the cement, the alders were opportunists. A couple of the trees even sprouted from cracks in the bottom corners, reaching up to touch the tagged walls. I could almost see spray-paint canisters at the ends of their skinny branches.

I walked around the foundation, found the place where the cement had caved enough to create a few steps—the way in. I stretched one leg down into the space and drew it back. I didn't want to climb down. I knew how the crack came to be there. If you looked closely enough at me, you would find cracks from the same day, the same hour. Minute fissures in my bones. A few half-connected pathways in my brain.

From the novel *Marrow Island*, available now from Houghton Mifflin Harcourt

May 1, 1993, was warm, with a taste of summer in the air. The primroses and hyacinth and daphne were blooming. Chartreuse tree tips and pink blossoms. Sunshine on water. All the water: the lakes and rivers and canals; and Puget Sound, the Salish Sea. After weeks of rain, people on the streets of cities and towns in the region were cheerfully stupefied by the glare.

At 9:09 AM the ambient noise of the cities and suburbs and seaside towns went mute. A barely recognizable shift, like how the air softens just before a lightning storm. This was the moment when pets became perturbed, barked or squawked or fled under beds. Then almost before the difference could be registered, there was a rumbling that at first sounded like faraway thunder, then felt like a truck barreling by, then a train coming head on. Then everything not bolted to the walls—and some things that were—fell. Books off shelves and dishes out of cupboards, food out of refrigerators and art off walls. Lamps, chairs, televisions, toppled. It was loud, not just the city tumbling, but the earth itself. Louder and louder because the sensitive bones of the inner ear register both movement and sound. The ground was rippling, rolling. Witnesses in downtown Seattle described the skyscrapers of the skyline as "doing the wave" like fans at a Mariners game. As the shaking continued, doors fell off hinges when their wood splintered. Foundations cracked and sank, and houses clattered free of their supposedly solid bases. Streets split like stretched fabric, and parked cars rolled down hills. So many cars scraping and tumbling down the hills and into piles, into the sides of buildings. Bridges wobbled, weak-kneed, and drivers felt like a great wind was blowing across the road; they careened into guardrails and one another. Skyscrapers bowed, dropping whole gleaming pools of window to the ground below. People were in stairwells and doorways and under desks and in the aisles of grocery stores with cans and cleaning products and cereal all over them. Parents and nannies and teachers held children to their chests, covering their heads, practically suffocating them, the shaking going on and on—so much longer than they thought possible. Patrons of the Woodland Park Zoo held tight to the railings and clenched their eyes as the elephants trumpeted and the mother lion froze, crouched with her young, and let out a deep, uncanny yowl, and the polar bears, diving in their pool, clawed at the Plexiglas, wide-eyed,

> **Foundations cracked and sank, and houses clattered free of their supposedly solid bases.**

staring into the eyes of the people on the other side, who fled as the glass crackled and droplets of water crept through.

All that time, while we cowered—nauseated, crying, waiting for the stillness—a slab of rock beneath the terranes of Puget Sound was shifting, slipping into the mantle of the North American plate along the South Whidbey Island Fault. Tremors were felt as far north as Juneau, Alaska, and as far south as Salinas, California. It was three minutes in which most of the West Coast of the United States and Canada braced itself.

It's the Big One, we all thought, we all felt in our hearts. The one geologists had been warning us about for years, the one we had been preparing for at school with earthquake drills. There we were, the children of Puget Sound, under our desks, holding on to the legs as they scooted back and forth across the linoleum, doing what we had practiced. I became motion sick; others peed their pants or wailed for their moms.

> **Just over three thousand people died, but it wasn't, in fact, the Big One.**

Meanwhile, all those sparkling waters, displaced by the drop in the seafloor, were drawn back, away from their shores, leaning to the west, and even before the first aftershocks, like an unseen hand smoothing a tablecloth, the waters began their inevitable rush back into their basins. The ten-to-twenty-foot waves washed out waterfronts, sluicing up river deltas, pounding docks, houseboats, locks, bridges, grain and coal terminals, capsizing fishing boats, and scouring the decks of barges. Landslides along the rim of the bays caused more tsunamis, so that the thunder of water and the thunder of earth folded over each other, and our ears couldn't distinguish which death might be coming for us.

Just over three thousand people died, but it wasn't, in fact, the Big One. Three minutes and twelve seconds of a magnitude 7.9 quake. It was a relatively shallow quake, in one of the many tertiary faults within the Cascadia Subduction Zone. But the nature of the sound, with its cities built on wetlands around river deltas and in floodplains, created a sort of echo for the earth's waves, a reverberation of the earth that amplified the shaking on the surface.

The story of the May Day Quake was told over and over again, in different ways, by different people. By scientists and engineers and first responders. By pilots and passengers of planes taxiing into SeaTac who witnessed it from the air. By survivors of the fires that broke out and survivors of boats and ferries capsized and survivors of collapsed bridges and tunnels. Like aftershocks, the stories. To retell it was to relive it. For years afterward, the quake was documented, analyzed, broadcast, and anthologized. I even wrote about it once, on the tenth anniversary, for the *Sentinel*, my college paper. By then, the May Day Quake had been consumed in the popular imagination and nearly forgotten, relegated to anecdote, the way Katrina would be a dozen years later. It hadn't been the Big One, after all; there would be more stories to tell someday.

I turned my back to the foundation to look at the view. Through the trees across the street and down a rocky embankment was a drop to the strait, where the currents at tide change churn like water in a washing machine. Up the road were other abandoned parcels, barely visible driveways leading to vacant foundations, as if someone had plucked the houses right out of the ground, leaving cavities in the shape of living spaces. I could feel the house that wasn't there, rising out of the gaping concrete mouth. The alders shivered in the breeze, a sound so familiar that I shivered, too.

Turning back to what was behind me—or *not* behind me—I did what most people in my generation do when faced with the ubiquitous and strange: I took pictures with my phone. Then I climbed back in my car, found Neko Case on the stereo, and drove the rest of the cracked road into the village.

Orwell had hardly changed in twenty years. What had been destroyed had been rebuilt or replaced or grown over, but everything still matched up with the map in my mind. Anchorage Street ran the length of the business district. A small-town main street, with the ferry terminal and a shoreline park, a few waterfront hotels and cafés on one side, houses set into an increasingly wooded and rocky hillside on the other. All the old buildings in downtown that had survived the quake were still there—many of them with structural improvements and seismic retrofits. There was a cooperative grocery in the place of the general store, which had been condemned after the quake, and next to it a gravel parking lot edged with flowerpots and signs advertising the local farmers' market, every other Saturday, JUNE THRU OCTOBER.

I walked up the street. Tourism had rebounded. Most of the storefronts were occupied, and there were two shops selling the kind of knickknacks that islanders call "bait."

"How's things?" you'd hear islanders asking.

"Oh, you know. Selling lots of bait," they would say. Or maybe, "Not biting. Need better bait, I guess."

Bait was always at the front of the store and by the register. If the store had a public toilet (most didn't; unreliable plumbing), there might be some toward the back too, for the people waiting to use it.

I peered into the bookstore, at the same storefront it had occupied when we left, though its name had changed to Sound Books & News, and it had been painted, reorganized, with racks of postcards and orca magnets and crab key chains by the door. It was Filgate's Books before, named for the old salt who owned it. My dad and Danny Filgate had been good friends, though Danny was a generation older. He, like my dad, was an autodidact who read everything from the *Wall Street Journal* to Toni Morrison to pulpy airport paperbacks. He had refused to sell bait. He catered to the islanders. You might wander into the shop and find a gathering of fisher-poets: fishermen and -women who spent long hours on the water composing verses—often ballads and other old forms—in their heads. They weren't readings, these gatherings; they were dramatic performances, sometimes with musical interludes on banjo or harmonica or fiddle. The gatherings took place in the off-season, so tourists didn't often run into them. But if one happened to wander into the shop when the fisher-poets were there, it was another of those things that make people fall in love with the islands. The locals set the scene and the mood, like the cast of characters in a Melville novel.

I assumed Danny must be dead. He couldn't have lived to see his business like this: it looked orderly, sanitized; a display of T-shirts with famous novel covers printed on them on the wall behind the cash register.

I sat on the steps outside city hall, a newer building that looked like a lot of government buildings—squat and gray and featureless—easily the ugliest building in town. The old city hall had burned down after the quake. The new one housed a small public library, a state police precinct, and various other municipal entities. It opened in fifteen minutes. Something else that hadn't changed about Orwell was the pace. Nearly ten o'clock and shops up and down the street were just starting to show signs of life.

The sun had burned through the clouds; it was getting warm—dew had started to form between my breasts and under my arms. I pulled my sweater off over my head and thought about taking it back to the car, or putting off the visit to the clerk's office, going up to the cemetery first. A few late-season tourists milled about, looking relaxed. A couple walked by me and said, "Good morning," as they passed. They wore small bemused smiles, their cheeks flushed; they weren't holding hands, but they bumped into each other as they walked, arms brushing intentionally. They had clearly been having sex all night to the sounds of the sea.

I hated them a little bit, for having sex on my island, though I knew that was what people did on seaside vacations. When my mom was a teenager, she spent summers housekeeping at lodges and motels all over the islands. I thought of her stripping one dirty sheet after another. I might've done the same, if we had stayed.

There were two motels, a bed-and-breakfast, and half a dozen vacation rentals in Orwell. Most people didn't stay on our island. Most people stayed in Friday Harbor or Rochelle, on San Juan Island. Or in the smaller, more expensive places on Lummi and Orcas. The ferries made only a couple of stops a day in Orwell. There wasn't much to do here, other than stroll and eat seafood, so it was sold more as a romantic getaway than a family destination.

> I had tried to explain to him why I never came back, why I never talked about it.

When Matt found out about the cottage, he asked why I hadn't told him about it, why I hadn't brought him out here. He wanted to go crabbing and eat mussels right out of the shell on the shore; he wanted to visit the Benedictine nuns on Shaw Island, who raise heirloom cattle and sheep. This was just a destination to him, an experience. A place with no context. I was crazy, he told me, for having access to something like this and not taking advantage of it. He was right, that I was privileged in a way most of my peers weren't. Owning property was getting harder and harder in cities like Seattle and San Francisco. The fact that my family had a "vacation home" made me slightly embarrassed.

I had tried to explain to him why I never came back, why I never talked about it. The death of a parent he understood, but the harrowing aftermath of the earthquake was lost on him. He was a year older than I—he had been thirteen at the time of the quake and had vague memories of the media coverage. He had moved to Seattle from Brooklyn in 2006. Aside from the tail end of a hurricane or two, he hadn't experienced a natural disaster. He had never felt an earthquake; they were as mythical as Sasquatch to him.

The clack of unlocking doors broke my daze. I wasn't the only one on the stairs waiting for city hall to open. A tall man stood off to my right, on the top step. He nodded. I smiled back and stood, stretching. An older woman in a pantsuit swung the door open, remarked on the beauty of the day, and held the door for us. I took my time up the stairs so that the man would go through first, but when I reached the top, he had paused to wait for me.

"You were here first," he said, and nodded toward the entrance.

"I'm not in a hurry," I said.

He led the way, and I followed behind, looking him over. He was wearing official-looking work clothes: thick cotton button-up with a crewneck underneath, dark, sturdy slacks with a belt, and steel-toed boots. Like a uniform, but not a uniform. No patches or decals. Like it was his day off, but he still needed to look the part. *Law enforcement?* I wondered. *Fish and Wildlife?* He was clean-shaven, with trim brown hair, but he'd been wearing a hat of some sort that had flattened the sides and left squirrely waves on top. We both followed signs for the clerk's desk, and the lady bustled along behind us, asked us to take a seat while she answered the ringing telephone.

> **Chris was next in line, wincing as he watched the shot go into my arm.**

We sat in two wooden armchairs with a table of magazines and a potted plant between us. He picked up a *Sunset*, looked at the cover, then glanced up and offered it to me. The cover story was "Ten Island Getaways."

"No thanks." I laughed.

"I guess we've made it," he said, putting the magazine back.

"A clean getaway," I said.

"Do you live here in Orwell?" he asked.

"Not really," I said. I looked at the manila envelope in my hands. All I had to do was file the deed, then the cottage would be mine. "I grew up here. I'm just back to take care of some family business."

He nodded.

"Do you live here?" I asked.

"No, ma'am," he said.

"*Ma'am?*" I repeated, and laughed. He was maybe three or four years older than I.

He blushed, chewed the inside of his cheek. I couldn't tell if he was trying not to laugh or was just embarrassed.

"I'm here for work. I'm not sure where I'll be living at the moment."

A sheriff's deputy came out from a back office.

"Hey there, Carey, sorry to keep you waiting," the deputy said. He came around and shook hands with the man next to me.

"Hey, Chris," he said, "no problem."

The deputy's last name was embroidered on his uniform: LELEHALT. I recognized him. Chris Lelehalt. His grandma May and my grandma Lucia were both Lummi and in a sewing circle together. Many of the old-timers were Catholic, so the sewing bees were always at St. Mary's, in the basement meeting room with folding tables and chairs, plates of cookies, grandkids playing tag in the cemetery. Chris was a year younger, so I didn't play with him much, but his mom worked at the refinery on Marrow, one of the few women at the plant. She made it home after the quake. Mom and I saw them at the church, where the Red Cross was distributing supplies. It may have been the last time I saw Chris—still lanky and preadolescent, black hair cut short and neat. Our mothers were standing around while an old lady gave us all typhoid shots. My mother asked her something—I didn't actually hear what she asked; they were just outside the circle of mothers. Deb shook her head and hugged Mom hard. Chris was next in line, wincing as he watched the shot go into my arm.

"We've just got a few things to go over," Chris was saying, tapping some papers on his hand. "The notary will be here later, the normal rigmarole, and you should be all set up by the end of the day. Let's head on over."

Carey, soon to be *all set up* by Deputy Chris Lelehalt and the notary public, turned back to me.

"Have a nice day, *ma'am*," he said.

"You too, *sir*," I said.

Chris Lelehalt watched this exchange, not recognizing me, and turned when Carey joined him, leading him through to the back of the clerk's office.

"Well, it looks like you're all mine." The clerk stood and stared at me from behind the desk. She was so short that her eyes were nearly level even though I was seated in a chair against the wall.

I told her why I was there, and she handed me something to fill out, took my deed, and looked at it.

"Bowen," she said, "the cottage out there by the Swenson place?"

"Yeah."

"Haven't been Bowens out here for a long time."

"No."

"You won't remember me," she said after a long pause. "My son Aaron worked with your dad. Lost him the same day."

I stopped filling out the form. She was right; I didn't remember her. I hadn't even noticed her nameplate on the counter, hidden behind a box of tissues: MARLA SHARPE.

"I'm sorry" was all I could say.

"So am I, dear."

She was quiet while I filled out the rest of the form, then she took the lot and made copies.

"Are you moving back here?" she asked while we waited, printer humming.

"I don't know," I said. "It needs a lot of work."

She nodded. "It's an old house; survived a lot better than some. If you're thinking of selling, talk to Jacob Swenson first; he wants to keep that side of the island from development."

"I've never met him—does he live at Rookwood year-round?"

"Oh, yes. He's around most of the year. He oversees things, since Julia passed."

I nodded. "Is he an artist like Julia and Maura?"

She laughed.

"An art lover, maybe. Collects antiques. No, I think it's just a man his age, unmarried, living alone in that big old house out there, people will talk. They call him eccentric. But he's no more eccentric than Julia ever was. Keeps to himself, but makes nice with folks when he needs to. Gives out a scholarship every year at the festival."

"He doesn't seem to be home. Do you know if he's away now?"

"He goes back East around Christmas, usually, and to Seattle every now and then. Comes back with his little red car packed with knickknacks and furniture."

"A red Saab?"

"Yep, at least thirty years old, that car—I don't know how he keeps it running out here."

"I think I saw his car—in the garage. Does he usually leave it here when he goes back East?"

"That's odd." Her brow furrowed. "He drives himself everywhere. I think he parks it at SeaTac when he flies." She waved her hand. "You know, he's probably just sleeping off a late night, dear," she said quietly, and winked, then turned away to retrieve the copies.

My mother had always complained about the islanders' propensity for gossip, but as a journalist I privately rejoiced every time I met a local busybody like Marla Sharpe.

"Try again this evening," she said, handing me the papers. "I bet he'll give you the tour of his collection."

"Sure, thanks."

I gathered up my copies and slid them into my bag.

I walked toward the cemetery. On the way I passed the co-op and stopped in to buy a clutch of dahlias—ISLAND-GROWN, the sign proclaimed. There were dahlias bursting like anemones around fence posts and front porches all over the islands this time of year. I probably could have walked up to any front door and asked to pick a few. But I paid the six bucks and kept walking up the hill, past the church itself and through the wrought-iron gate and into the cemetery. The ground was soft under my feet, like the thick soft carpet inside the church.

I passed Aaron Sharpe's headstone, untied the bundle of flowers, and put one in the scummy vase at the base. Near the back, just before a broad open hill sloped down, was Dad's marker. WILLIAM WHITMAN BOWEN, his father's name within his own. Grandma Lucia and Grandpa Whit were tucked together next to him. As a child I had pictured them sleeping side by side in a cozy bed, blankets folded under their arms. A grave was just an underground bedroom, where people went into permanent hibernation.

At my dad's funeral, there had been nothing to imagine.

At my dad's funeral, there had been nothing to imagine. There was no interment, just a headstone on soil, waiting. In case he washed up somewhere. In case some bone fragment gave up some DNA we could trace through mine to confirm. We had nothing to bury. Of all the survivors of the Marrow ArPac disaster, none could remember when or where they had last seen my father. One thought he saw him boarding a boat just before the first waves came; another thought he was helping others, inside, just before the explosion. A few men had burned to cinders when the fire controls failed; pipes that carried water to sprinklers were crushed under the weight of collapsed steel, and water glugged uselessly out into drainage ditches and then back into the sea.

Coast Guard boats and fire flights that may have come to help had been either incapacitated in the quake or dispatched to other emergencies before the radio calls reached them. ArPac was the oldest, smallest petroleum refinery in the area—there were two others—and fires were already underway at Tesoro in Anacortes. There were chemical spills all over the sound, from ships and barges washed against pilings or slammed ashore, from paper plants, from railways along the water. The coal terminal in Bellingham had just been completed, and the wave—though less powerful than it was farther south near Everett and Seattle—spread a cubic mile of coal over land and water throughout, up and down the sound.

There were people in the water who needed saving, too.

Bodies washed up for weeks after the quake, along with all the other flotsam. I had been forbidden to beachcomb—a daily routine in ordinary times—but Katie and I slipped away. Our mothers were sleepless and busy with post-disaster chores, easily manipulated into believing the other mother was on watch. We were twelve and shrugged off their worry like wool cardigans. We walked through the woods between our houses to a rocky crescent of shoreline. I don't know what we expected to find—I don't remember if we went for any reason other than transgression—but there were more dead shorebirds than I had ever seen, cast among the jagged hulls of small boats, rope and fishing gear, fish and crabs trapped and suffocated or starved in the mesh. We pulled our shirts over our noses to filter the air, thick with sea rot and animal rot, mixed with the eye-glazing fumes of the chemical dispersants they eventually used on the oil slicks around Marrow. Everything had an oily gloss, a sheen like a puddle in a gas station parking lot.

A feeling came over me as we picked through furniture and disintegrating cereal boxes and a pair of eyeglasses. A man's work boot, a hooded sweatshirt, items of clothing so filthy and sodden we couldn't identify them, heaped over driftwood, branches. I reached out to touch them—wanting to uncover the logs, maybe? And realizing they weren't logs. I looked at Katie, and her face mirrored the unease that had settled in me. She climbed up onto a giant tree and reached down for my hand. I took it and joined her, staring over the wrecked shore below us, the clouds of flies hovering over the heaps. We jumped down the other side into the grass

> **We had been breaking a cardinal rule. And it was obvious he was already dead.**

and ran back into the woods. We never talked about it; but we both knew. We had been breaking a cardinal rule. And it was obvious he was already dead. What could we do to help him? We couldn't tell anyone without getting in trouble ourselves, so we didn't.

The body wasn't my father, who never did wash up, at least not on Orwell or Marrow, convincing my mother that he had been trapped in the refinery by the fire. I laid the flowers across his headstone. There was a plot next to my father, for my mom. She was remarried, so I figured the plot would be mine, someday.

I spent the rest of the day going over the cottage, making lists of things to be fixed or assessed by a professional. The water heater was ancient, as was the electrical panel. I couldn't believe my mom hadn't needed to replace them after the quake—but then she'd probably hired an out-of-work ArPac friend of my dad's who wasn't going to bother with bringing things up to code. It didn't matter what she had done then anyway; a couple decades of island weather and winter vacancy had left peeling paint, moldy cabinets, leaky pipes.

I stood at the screen door drinking a beer, letting the breeze cool me, and staring up through the mesh at Rookwood. I had pulled up the drive when I got back, knocked on the door again. There was no movement at all from inside, no sounds. I felt the hairs on my arm rise and looked down to see a mosquito lifting off, full of my blood. She flew straight for the screen and knocked herself against it, up and down, until she found a hole—probably the hole through which she had come. I turned to the counter and added *screens* to the list.

Evening was coming on, but there was still plenty of light, so I spent it in the yard, wrangling a season's worth of weeds. In the shed were the tools and notes from my mom to visitors or hired hands: how to oil and clean the blades on the manual mower (*carefully!*); how to plug in the Weedwhacker (*run the cord through the bathroom window*); how and where to find the strawberry patch and the raspberries so as not to mow them down (*Follow the birds and the bees in June!*); encouragements to pick the wild irises for bouquets; where to put the hatchet when not splitting logs (*on the wall in the shed*); and random admonishments and warnings (*Wear gloves! Watch for nettles!*).

By dusk my muscles were spent; I had blisters on my hands (didn't *wear gloves!*). I dropped to the ground, fibrous shards of crabgrass stabbing me through my sweaty T-shirt. The lawn slanted steeply, and my head was pointed downhill, toward the water, arms thrown up, watching the tide upside down for a while, letting my mind drift. I rolled my head to the side, where I could just spy Rookwood's long wide lines through the trees. There were no signs of life at the house other than that one light, still burning. No cars had come or gone. I thought about the red car in the carriage house.

I sat up and downed the last of my beer. Eyes tired, or maybe just dusty, I saw everything through a filter of spores. I felt watched, but also called, beckoned by the glowing window.

"You're drunk," I said. I counted how many beers I'd had and how little food.

In the cottage I pulled on a sweater and found a working flashlight. He wouldn't mind, I told myself. No one on the island would mind if a neighbor saw to a light left on. There were probably still keys to Rookwood somewhere in the cottage. I thought of Marla Sharpe at the clerk's office—she knew my family; she could vouch for me. I was a landowner! I let myself follow the drunken logic, emboldened by my legitimacy as a remade local and a newly minted property owner, as I crossed the lane in the dark. I knew enough not to pause, not to think. On Rookwood's dark porch, I didn't hesitate as I reached for the latch on the door. Like most doors on the island, it was unlocked. I gave it a shove and watched it swing heavily over the flagstones of the entry.

I called out a loud *hello*. My voice didn't even echo, lost to the heavy walls of the house.

"It's your neighbor, Lucie Bowen," I called, closing the door behind me and standing there in the silence, flashlight aimed at a mirror opposite the door. An arch to the left led to the parlor, an arch to the right led to the hallway and carved staircase. I felt twelve years old again; I wished Katie were there with me.

I found the light switch—an old-fashioned one, two Lucite buttons with circles of abalone inlay—and the chandelier above me lit up. It made everything beyond its glare seem darker and more forbidding. Being alone in a half-lit house seemed scarier than being in a dark one, so I turned it off.

I kept the flashlight trained ahead of me and headed for the staircase. The house smelled dusty, stale. Unlived-in. I stopped on the landing and sneezed a few times, wiped my nose on the back of my sleeve. I looked down at my feet, at the carpet on the stairway, faded and worn to threads in places.

Above me was Maura's famous self-portrait, lifelike and imperious. She was probably in her forties at the time, brown-gray hair pulled up and back, wearing a pale blue dress, not a trace of a smile on her face. It wasn't a beautiful portrait, but it was striking. She painted it between the wars; art had changed then, Julia had told me, because of the shock of modern warfare. I was ten at the time, in shock myself from the quake. Maybe that was why she said it. Because she wanted me to know that there was a world full of tragedies besides my own.

I continued up the stairs, telling myself I had no intention of snooping, just turning off the light. The adrenaline was killing the beer's soft buzz. A long hallway ran the width of the house at the top, and I turned to the right, following the glow at the end, the last door on the right. It opened onto a large bedroom with a perfectly made four-poster, a suitcase open and half-filled with clothes on top. The sight of something in progress like that made me doubt myself: Maybe he was home? Maybe he had been home and I had missed him? But the rest of the room was off: there was a through-breeze; the window of the dormer was open wide; and there were two lamps lit, not just the one visible in the window. The other was tipped on its side on a bedside table, the shade hanging over the edge. I closed the window, noting water stains on the sill and leaves on the carpet below. It had been open for some time. When was the last rain? It had been a few days, a hard rain after weeks of unseasonable warmth.

> **Like most doors on the island, it was unlocked.**

When I turned to the lamp on the table, my foot bumped what was left of a broken highball glass on the floor. On the bed, the suitcase lay open like a book. Men's clothes, folded neatly. I ran my hand over the cool cotton shirts. A belt, a pair of casual leather loafers, an eyeglasses case, a toiletries bag. I couldn't help myself; I was in this far, wasn't I? I unzipped it. There were shaving supplies, a toothbrush, a contact lens case, and a prescription bottle of Klonopin with Jacob Swenson's name on it.

I swallowed a lump rising in my throat and took a breath. I thought again about walking through the wreckage with Katie, reaching for the remains, realizing what they were, reaching out for her hand instead.

Joseph Millar

RIGHT LIVELIHOOD

The little stream runs all the way down
under the cracked slabs
of the parking lot
mostly abandoned now,
shadows gathering
in the busted marquee
of the discount tobacco store
with its wire hangers
and carpeted stairs,
its candles stuck
in their squat mason jars
vanilla and sandalwood, blueberry, pine
whose proprietor doesn't carry your brand
and keeps chattering into a cell phone
under the brim of his hat
the dialect of some distant land.
And thence to the glass doors
of Anna's Linens
Going Out of Business Sale
where you buy four pillows and a bathmat
for 35 bucks

then sit shotgun, one foot on the floor
the other smudging the dash,
eating Taco Bell and describing
your ideal poet's job in this life,
more of a career than a job really,
more of a calling than a career:
to own and manage a combination

lavender-farm-bed-and-breakfast
which would smell great, of course
and glow faintly purple
and feature tall windows,
a balcony in each room
where smoking would be permitted —
and which would also specialize in prostitution
by hookers almost to retirement
to a clientele in late middle age
whose demands might no longer
be strenuous
or even particularly lewd —
maybe they would mostly desire
to be gently chided
in a husky voice
or even spoken to kindly,
their toes washed in rosewater
then dried in angora,
their foreheads soothed
in the breeze from a porch swing,
then wrapped up in cotton
and fed Belgian chocolate
blindfolded

We gas up and head west
into the mountains of Carolina
worn down by time
by snow and heat
new pillows piled up in the back seat.

NIGHT LIGHT

We've just managed to fall into bed
like the proprietors of a vacant hotel,
its garden smelling of quince and magnolia.
The pale moon spills in
like slivers of glass
through the dark cypress branches,
with the Oprah channel on low,
and the young father's husky voice
planning the next phase of his sex-change.
His chestnut ringlets cover his collar bone
framing his dark eyes
like a pale lady in Swinburne

and I'm trying to remember the day
that's ending, drifting away toward sleep:
I can feel my feet a long way down
where the world ends
and my body begins
and my hair would be fanned out
like smoke on the pillow, and my breasts
would be resting gently,
pendulous, mammalian
inside the haze of my nightgown.
I hear his voice a long way off:
they will somehow turn
his penis inward
to fashion a blind vagina
capable of deep sensation,
capable of loving a man.

ESSAY

LIGHTNING, OR FEATHERS

Marin Sardy

It's not called gym-"nice"-tics . . .

What you noticed first about Svetlana Boginskaya when she stepped up to an apparatus was the length of her limbs. At nearly five feet four inches, she was one of the tallest elite gymnasts in the world. This made the sport more challenging for her but more obviously had the effect of exaggerating her personal elegance, especially when she was in the air. When she began to move, those long lines took over, emphasizing the fluidity of her turns and accentuating her acrobatics so that in simple tumbling moves she seemed to hang in space for a beat or two.

She was known, too, as an exceptional twister. This became widely visible at the 1988 Olympics, in the floor routine that won her a silver medal and helped the USSR earn a team gold: Her first tumbling pass was a simple full-in-back-out—two tucked backflips in the air with a twist in the first one. Her second pass was a two-part sequence in which a laid-out front flip with one and a half twists led into a double-twisting layout—a laid-out backflip with two full twists. A grand total of four and a half twists. When she drove these moves home, it was viscerally gratifying to hear the

slam of her feet on the floor. Flight, so many spins in the air that a novice viewer couldn't keep track, then *bam!* Glue.

The landings. The full length of Svetlana's body furled when she landed, almost like a bow. She bent much more deeply than most gymnasts do, particularly when vaulting or dismounting. Then, after that hammer-like motion nailed her feet to the floor, she arose from that low posture as if her spine were being unrolled by a dowel—one vertebra at a time. It was a subtle but remarkable habit that lingered in a viewer's mind. Certainty, then a measure of grace.

Even in the earliest footage of Svetlana in competition—at the 1985 Junior Cup, when she was only twelve years old and not yet at her full adult height—she was already displaying the trademarks of her gymnastics style. She went on to win two team championships at the Olympics, in 1988 and 1992. All told, she took home five Olympic medals, three of them gold. In her eleven years competing at the international level, she also won a World Championship all-around title, collected various wins at World Cups and European Championships, and twice earned a perfect ten in the floor exercise. But she was distinct among champions—less famous for winning than for winning in a particular way. Exactly what way, however, is harder to articulate.

I don't follow gymnastics anymore. The sport has changed so much since I quit competing twenty-two years ago that I don't recognize many of the moves and am easily confused by the new elite scoring system. But Svetlana has stayed with me, clung to me, so that even now I can't bring myself to refer to her by her last name. Young girls never know their idols that way.

What I recall is that in competition, Svetlana held a cool but potent gaze that revealed nothing and everything. She rarely smiled, but never came off as fierce. Serious. She was always serious. She had an air of inaccessibility. That was part of her allure. Her eyes—small, deep, almond-shaped, fully lined with black kohl—seemed dark although they were pale blue. She was beautiful, with a small nose and pert lips, and an announcer once noted her striking resemblance to the actress Rebecca De Mornay. When I watch her now I think of Russian ballet, of Tchaikovsky, as many Americans must have in 1988, upon seeing Soviet gymnasts again after Cold War boycotts had kept them out of our living rooms for more than a decade. Soviet gymnasts were noticeably more graceful than our powerhouse American competitors, and tended to have a quiet composure rarely seen here. *We* were the land of Mary Lou's mega-grin. With Svetlana, you could never tell if she was happy or if she was sad.

> All told, she took home five Olympic medals, three of them gold.

Lightning, or Feathers

It helped, too, that Svetlana was a master of the perfectly straight line—an element fundamental to the sport, informing nearly every move on every event. Given this, and her long limbs, it was almost inevitable that she became known as the Belarusian Swan.

But that was too easy. As if in reply to ballet-inspired comparisons, Svetlana performed for years to floor music that was rock 'n' roll or world beat, not classical. And she sometimes betrayed a lack of self-awareness that revealed just how instinctual her grace really was. Her short brown ponytail, clipped and sprayed into submission behind a roll of curled bangs, or escaping in wispy rebellion in spite of her efforts, seemed almost comically artless as a frame for those exotic eyes. More than that, though, she appeared not to know that her dance steps, although beautifully presented, came off as kooky and a little bizarre. She might walk with exaggerated flat-footedness, roll her shoulders, sway a hip—once, she even threw in a couple of froggy jumps with her feet flexed and knees splayed. Every routine contained at least one undulation (perhaps calculated to show off the preternatural flexibility of her spine), often imbued with thick hints of defiant eroticism. There was something baffling in the content of her gestures, and I think now that this must have been where I discerned the disjointedness of her personality, which is what gave rise to the artistry she could not even see.

As a teenager watching her on television, when I was a gymnast too and only two years her junior, I grew to revere her beyond all the more obvious foci of my adoration—that is to say, the Americans. The appeal of Mary Lou Retton and her ilk, like Phoebe Mills and Kim Zmeskal, hinged on their winning. The thing about Svetlana was that she was memorable whether she won or not. And she often didn't. There were years when she struggled; seemed too old or too defeated by bigger demons to bend gravity to her will. Over time she became like a signal coming through the noise.

> As spectators of sports, we project ourselves into our champions in acts of self-invention.

When I began watching Svetlana, she was not yet a legend. That was near the beginning of my own gymnastics career, which began in 1987 when I was twelve—a late start for a gymnast and the thing that, despite the talent I exhibited, effectively blocked me from ever becoming more than a varsity staple. I progressed from rolls to round-offs and flips and twists, landed spots on competitive club teams, and helped my high school win second in state. But I wouldn't go on to compete in college gymnastics. I didn't think I was good enough, and I probably wasn't. Yet what success I had was enough, because I wasn't really in it to win. I was in it for something much more necessary.

I found gymnastics, in fact, by way of suddenly finding myself without a mother. That was why my father first enrolled my sister and me in a gymnastics class—to give us something to do while he was at work. That first summer, as I zipped through the list of skills to learn, mastering them in rapid succession, I was also contending with the fact that my mother had been changed, irrevocably, by a mental illness that would cripple her for the rest of her life, as both a parent and a person. My first years as a gymnast were years I spent discovering all the various and contradictory ways that I had lost her. It is not coincidence that gymnastics became my escape from my family's predicament. From the age of twelve to eighteen I never spent longer than two weeks away from a gym.

As spectators of sports, we project ourselves into our champions in acts of self-invention. We observe the best closely, and our favorites are often the ones in whom we find echoes of ourselves. When we see our champions win, we tell ourselves this means we can win too, despite our flaws, our failings, our inadequacies. Gymnastics was a world of absolute order and I wanted to believe I could fit into that order. But I never quite did. In Svetlana I saw a girl who aligned with my idea of what I wanted to be—pretty, serene, perfect—and simultaneously upended it. The essential mystery of her, that self-contradictory presentation, was rare in gymnastics, a sport that attracts more conventional personalities. Through Svetlana I sensed that there were others, other gymnasts, who felt chaos thrashing just beyond the edges of their tidy routines. Who even sometimes let it in.

I know now that Svetlana's own gymnastics story began at the age of six, when her parents enrolled her in a class. A few years later she left her hometown of Minsk to live at a Soviet training center near Moscow, far from her family. By the time the renowned Soviet coach Lyubov Miromanova was preparing the fifteen-year-old for her first Olympics, Svetlana had spent nearly half her life living with Miromanova, subsumed into her family as one of their own. By all accounts, Miromanova was a "surrogate mother" and "like a second mother" to the young gymnast. She led Svetlana to her first great victories—two gold medals at the '88 games. Then, three days after returning home, Miromanova was found dangling from her apartment balcony. She had apparently hanged herself.

If any explanation for the suicide was uncovered, it never reached the media. The cause remained a mystery to most, possibly even to Svetlana, who rarely spoke about it publicly. The following year, however, at the '89 World Championships, her floor routine reached its peak choreographic originality. Her dance moves included pausing dramatically for a beat or two to bang the air with her fists, as well as shaking her hands as if flicking water off them. At one point she even played an exaggerated air guitar—a move that is now legendary in gymnastics circles. An announcer noted that some judges objected that the routine was "too

Lightning, or Feathers

avant-garde." Another described her performance as "abstract and even disarming," musing aloud that it "seemed to reflect her inner turmoil" over Miromanova's death. I can't help but wonder what it must have taken for her to wear such confusion and pain on her body in a world competition. But then, that might have been what made it possible for her to compete at all.

In interviews, Svetlana was a model Soviet, unfailingly team-minded and self-deprecating. But this was to some degree a fiction she wasn't always able to maintain. She was ferociously competitive and, by her own later admission, not above intimidating or bullying other gymnasts. I suspect, too, that loss and grief brought out the worst in her. In 1991 she made headlines for "snubbing" American gymnast Kim Zmeskal after losing to her at that year's World Championships, claiming that Zmeskal had failed to shake *her* hand the night before. The longtime coach of the American team, Bela Karolyi, was incensed and later recalled having found Svetlana "arrogant" and "nasty." But a year later, when a journalist asked about the incident as the 1992 Olympics approached, Svetlana seemed shaken by the memory and furtively wiped away a tear.

My losses, too, had made me eccentric—socially clumsy and prone to random, intense obsessions. But I buried myself beneath a facade of conformity, and I suppose I paid for that. In high school, mental blocks rolled in. On balance beam, attempting a back-tuck dismount, I froze. And froze, and froze. The move was easy for me in a physical sense. But with that hard wooden beam behind me, I never got past some wall of fear. Only in my imagination could I follow Svetlana's lead.

By the time Svetlana reached the 1992 Olympics at Barcelona, nineteen years old and leading the amalgam of former Soviets known as the Unified Team, announcers were describing her as a sort of team mother. I was by then one of the oldest gymnasts on my team, adored by the little girls and adoring them in return. When I practiced my jazzy floor routine, they would line up at the edge of the mat and dance my Charleston steps along with me. But I was also envious of how much better than me they already were, or clearly would become. During the preliminary rounds of the Barcelona competition, I was riveted by a shot of Svetlana comforting the tiny, fifteen-year-old Tatiana Gutsu—a star already and a superior gymnast in many ways—on the sidelines after a shocking fall from the balance beam. The horrified Gutsu, who completed moves so difficult that even today the skill level of her routines is rarely matched, was crying unabashedly. Svetlana wrapped her slender arms around the Ukrainian girl's neck and pulled her close. Her face, visible to the camera over the top of Gutsu's head, wore a look of stoically sympathetic calm. *Yes,* her eyes seemed to say, *I know.*

Adolescence is the age of perfection in only a few realms, and gymnastics is one of them. Its winners walk a line between drama and control, and typically resolve the conflict through sheer physical power. Svetlana had this option only in her first few years in world competition. A gymnast's peak age is around fifteen, which Svetlana reached in 1988—the year of her first Olympics. By the early nineties, her power-matches-prettiness niche was beginning to slip and, as it did, few believed she could continue to hold her ground. The difficulty of her routines wasn't keeping up with the runaway progress of the sport. Even as she improved, the standards of the sport were increasing much faster. Yet somehow, as this happened, she was becoming more compelling to watch.

Poring over videos of Svetlana's floor routines across three Olympics, from 1988 to 1996, I realize no one would guess that so many years lay between them. Her body remained the same elongated Y—shoulders twice as wide as her hips, her waist narrow and limber, all muscle and bone. Nearly her entire career as a global contender occurred while she was supposed to be on the decline. Her weaknesses, however, did begin to show. In the '92 European Championships, with her second Olympics on the horizon, she fell during the floor exercise on her final tumbling pass, a tucked double-back. It was the most difficult floor routine of her career, but at the end she didn't get quite enough height. She landed short and lurched forward onto her knees, into an automatic half-point deduction. Many doubted that she could keep up with her teammates at the coming Olympics. She would have to rely on her dramatic lines to compensate for what were now, relatively speaking, unspectacular skills. Maybe the surprise was that the lines became the spectacle.

Following the progress of those Olympics on subscription Triplecast at a teammate's house, I passed a weekend anticipating Svetlana's routines with almost embarrassed intensity. As she stood ready to begin her floor exercise for the team final, it felt right that her uniform was black-and-white, its colors split diagonally across the front in a pattern suggesting lightning, or feathers. She sat down into an opening pose in which her back arched so that she was perched on the top of her head with her arms raised straight up—quintessentially dramatic and strange. Spanish guitar began to play. Then everything broke open. It was in the steps, the turns, that spine. It was in the way she could lace her movements with an edge so sharp that she seemed less like an athlete than an electrical storm. When she nailed her tucked double-back, you felt it in your sternum. With that routine she led the Unified Team to victory.

But although Svetlana took home a team gold, she won none of the individual event competitions, or the ultimate prize

> Adolescence is the age of perfection in only a few realms, and gymnastics is one of them.

of the individual all-around. No one was surprised that after those games, verging on twenty years old, she retired. Most gymnasts have one Olympics in them, maybe two. She moved to the United States and joined the professional exhibition circuit, touring as a performance gymnast, working the crowds at the gymnastics equivalent of the Ice Capades. I hated to watch her in those expos. To my eye, they parodied precisely what they meant to valorize. She strutted onto the floor in a leather motorcycle jacket and a black baseball cap, as if to recall Marlon Brando in *The Wild One*, and all of it felt silly and reductive on a woman whose rebel music had been much more than a pop-cultural meme. She seemed not to see her own authenticity, not to grasp the scope of her reach.

Three years later I was in college, smoking weed and studying biology and listening to a lot of grunge. Having at last escaped the orbit of my mother's illness, I rarely talked about gymnastics anymore. The nearest I drew to that previous life happened only occasionally, late at night when walking home drunk from friends' parties, when just for kicks I would run suddenly to throw a tumbling pass on a nearby lawn. My friends, protective, tried to hold me back. There was no need. Those handsprings were embedded so deep in my cells that drunkenness couldn't touch them.

It wasn't until the summer games drew near again that I learned that Svetlana was back. She had been training with the American team under Karolyi's tutelage, and had sprung back into world competition in 1995, competing for Belarus. After a tepid start, she did so well at the 1996 European Championships that she took home a silver all-around medal, qualifying her to compete in one last Olympics. She was twenty-three.

To return to competition in that sport, at that age, after that long. It was the kind of amazing that maybe only a fellow gymnast could grasp—someone who had grown up as a gymnast and then already grown old as a gymnast. It was the kind of amazing that made your eyes flood. Svetlana would be one of the only female gymnasts ever to compete in three Olympics. In that land of perpetual girlhood, I had watched her leave girlhood behind. So I watched her again, out of love and loyalty and also, maybe, to learn something about womanhood now that our girlhood was gone.

In 1996, with the Unified Team disbanded, Svetlana seemed an avatar of a bygone era. One announcer said there had been talk that she couldn't have earned a spot on the Unified Team if such a powerful aggregate still existed. By then, younger gymnasts were flaunting skills

> She seemed not to see her own authenticity, not to grasp the scope of her reach.

that required physical strength of a kind that women's gymnastics had never seen before. Svetlana's later contemporaries, like Kerri Strug, blew judges away (and unnerved the sport's fairly conservative fan base) with the muscular builds that made possible their huge tumbling passes. Svetlana never put on that kind of muscle, and what's more, her prime time for skill acquisition was far behind her. She was already an adult, and making a quantum leap forward with the sport was simply not possible.

So she faced off against gymnasts who were nearly a decade younger than her, whom she towered above and, tipping the scales at about a hundred and ten, outweighed by some thirty pounds. The minuscule Dominique Moceanu, America's fourteen-year-old, four-foot-five-inch wunderkind, looked like a small child beside her. The benefits of smallness were clearer than ever, especially on beam, where Moceanu stuck a sequence of one back-handspring followed by *three* laid-out backflips. Such a string of tumbling moves would be impossible for a taller gymnast to fit within the length of a beam. As it was, Svetlana nearly tipped off the end whenever she performed her usual sequence, which was identical to Moceanu's, minus one layout.

The effortlessness of her early tumbling was gone by then. Her skills were exceptional, but they often suggested how hard she was working. She responded by relying heavily on her twists and choosing choreography that highlighted both her originality and her maturity. The result was that, maybe more than ever, her perfection looked better than anyone else's perfection. She opened her floor exercise routine with the same full-in-back-out that she had performed in 1988, and closed with a two-and-a-half-twisting layout leading directly into a (perfect) punch-front. Positioned confidently and moving smoothly, she made it look almost as if it were happening in slow motion. Even when tumbling. Up there in the air, as if at rest.

It was in her lines, her unbelievable joints, her timing. On bars, the lines seemed to take over, with her individual skills almost reduced to links between moments of poetic pause. In moves that other gymnasts tended to pike, she almost suggested an arch. Watching the clip from the all-around competition, I get chills. In her giant swings, circling the high bar with her body fully extended, her shoulders roll back so far that the hinge at each joint disappears. And when, in a handstand at the top of the high bar, she spins around in a 360-degree pirouette (two in one routine), she is nearly airborne. Her double-layout dismount is like two breaths of wind.

The crowds were in love more than ever. People were calling her the Goddess of Gymnastics—a play on the Russian root of her last name, *bogínya*, meaning "goddess." That week Svetlana got at least one standing ovation, and at times you could hear her name being chanted in the stands. But she won no medals. She lacked the necessary difficulty and made too many mistakes. In the compulsories, she had a short landing on floor and a disastrous miss on bars. Her highest final ranking by far, for vault, was fifth place.

Examining a clip of Moceanu competing on bars against her, I can see that Svetlana really had no chance. Gymnastics had already outrun her. Even now, Moceanu's speed astounds me. Her power is undeniable, with the difficulty to match. To Svetlana's double-layout dismount she adds a full twist. But I wince: she pikes the landing. In terms of score, this costs maybe a tenth of a point. Aesthetically it costs much more. It's not ugly, just un-beautiful. And her handstands are so rushed, her giant swings so flatly forgettable. There are none of those snaps, those artful pauses, none of Svetlana's breaths of air. Nothing to hold time still, to let us linger with her for another moment before we fall forward into the future.

NEW VOICE FICTION

The Cat

Jackson Tobin

We tumbled into Coop's basement through the cellar door, tracking snow and stench from the putrid Backwoods cigars Fitz was always burning, mulch and sawdust rolled in a dirty sock. The four of us—Coop, Fitz, Nate, and AJ—like always. There were no windows, and many of the bulbs had burned out among the ceiling tiles, so where light did come from the recessed fixtures, it was a hazy cone of yellow, filtering down like a jail yard spotlight.

Nate burst in last, a full thirty seconds behind. He'd still been in the house when we took off running, and now he came in the door holding his backpack out in front of him. As we spread out on the floor of the Coopers' filthy basement, peeling off our sweat-soaked ski jackets, he placed the backpack carefully in the middle of our circle.

Something was moving in the bag.

"What?" AJ said, his voice already squeaky with fear.

"Unzip it," Nate said. He stepped back, sat down cross-legged.

Now we watched the black JanSport as if it were stitched up with dynamite. Our pupils were still shriveled from the blinding winter light outside, so we couldn't trust our eyes—but there was no mistaking the sound. An angry rustle of paper, a tearing of fabric.

Coop stepped forward and stood over the bag, his head cocked. "What the fuck did you do?" he said to Nate. But his voice was fat with admiration, his grin a salute.

. . .

It had been Coop, that morning, blinking in the nuclear snow glare, who said, "Let's go see Toby Peterson." Toby was a prissy kid with doting doctor parents. Coop hated him the way Coop hated rich kids, and poor kids, roided-out jocks and Internet geeks, know-it-alls and idiots. Which is to say, it was nothing personal, exactly, us picking on Toby that particular snow day. Coop was all for equal opportunity when he terrorized.

We were out on the frozen baseball field, standing around grinning in our outgrown snow clothes. School was canceled. The night before it'd snowed hard, a whole season's worth folded up in one long gray cloud. The temperature was falling all through the storm and by the end a hard inch of crust glazed on top of the powder. We felt taller, with all that new earth underneath, and feeling taller was of outsize importance to us. In any group we knew where we ranked in height and every other hierarchy: if we could slosh down a Poland Spring of cheap vodka without puking; how many times we'd been punched in the face; whether we'd had sex yet, and if so, how crippling the stories of our incompetence were. Unfortunately most answers put us right in the middle, and the middle is no place for a sixteen-year-old boy. To be at the top was fine, but even better to be at the bottom—to have suffered. To have a reason for the anger that came off us like a smell; sometimes loud and sometimes hardly noticeable, but always there if you got close enough.

> To be at the top was fine, but even better to be at the bottom—to have suffered.

But it had to be the right kind of suffering. Coop had a dead mom—this was the right kind, the cool side of pain. She died when we were still in middle school. Coop and his three brothers all buzzed their heads before the funeral, and when they stood in a line at the gravesite, they looked like different versions of the same person, as if each could turn to his left and glimpse his future, two years, four years down the line.

It was a horrible thing, of course, but mostly for the adults, who debated when a cocktail of Ambien and Belvedere was simply self-medicating and when it was suicide. For Fitz, Nate, and AJ, our parents' affairs and slow poisonings now seemed fine. Just regular. And Coop? Coop finally had something to be angry about.

The rest of us had two-parent households and, unlike Coop, fathers who came home every night, fathers who asked us how we were—fathers who cried. We had no wars and no death and an inescapably bright future, and in the warmth of that future's light we gnashed and squirmed. We were as furious as Coop. Maybe more so.

· · ·

Toby Peterson lived in a big house on Falls Pond, all timber and glass. We'd been taking turns pissing in the Petersons' mailbox when Fitz slunk around to the backyard. *Oi*, he yelled after a moment, and we all came around.

The door was open, just a crack. Fitz stood there, a bent little grin burning in one corner of his mouth. He had his hands jammed in his pockets, a posture of victory—he'd nudged up the bar and knew no one would get over it.

Except then Nate lurched forward, kicked off his boots onto the bristly WELCOME mat, and slipped into the house.

"*Christ*," Fitz whispered. "I didn't tell him to go *in*. Nobody said to go in. You guys saw."

But no one said anything in reply. We stood there, our gloved hands cupping our eyes, pressing our faces to the glass. Through clouds of hot breath, we watched Nate slink around the first floor. Watched him creep up the stairs, his feet leaving the top step.

When his socks reappeared, we scrambled over the snowbank and out of the yard. AJ looked back and saw Nate stumble on his way out the door, falling farther and farther behind, but then we went around the corner and he was out of sight. All we could do was keep running and hope he was behind us.

· · ·

Now, in the darkness of the basement, Coop bent and unzipped the backpack.

He yelped and jumped back, cradling his hand. There, hissing at us from its place on the flattened backpack, was the cat.

It was a Maine Coon, a monster, huge in the space between us, its long cirrus coat haunted with black. Two eyes blazed like headlights through a fog. The thing arched its back, flashed us two pairs of long yellowish fangs. The mouth of the bag, where the zipper met the seam, was shredded into ragged streamers of canvas.

"You stole their *cat?*" Fitz said.

Nate shrugged, as if, when he had gone into the house, there had been only two possible outcomes—leave with the cat or don't—and this was simply the way the coin flip had worked out. "His door was locked," he said, by way of explanation. "Toby's. And—and I felt like I'd been in there a long time, and maybe somebody was coming, and right when I turned around, there was the cat."

On cue, the cat leapt from the bag and up to the busted spine of the Coopers' couch, landing without a sound. Slowly it walked along the edge, pawing at the pilling fabric, watching us. It looked like a small tiger wrapped with smoke.

"You, my friend," Fitz said, "are nuts. Good luck bringing it back over there without getting caught."

Nate did the thing where he looked like he was chewing but there was nothing in his mouth.

AJ stared at the cat and shook his head. "This is the dumbest thing we've ever done," he said.

"*We*?" Fitz replied. "*We* didn't do anything."

"Fuck you, Fitz," Nate said softly.

"Nah," Coop said. He'd been sucking on the wound, the place the cat had clawed him, and when he took his hand from his mouth we saw three angry red slashes. "Hold on. I've got an idea."

The Petersons would pony up for a reward. These kinds of cats, these Maine Coons, were more wild than tame. Surely she'd gotten out before, Coop said. After the cat had been gone for a while, they'd panic, resort to Facebook posts, e-mail chains, fliers. They'd offer a hundred bucks, maybe more, and we'd convince somebody else—somebody they'd never expect, maybe a girl—to return the cat and collect the reward, in exchange for a small middleman's fee. Piece of cake.

"As long as none of you left a trace at the scene?" Coop said, eyeing us.

We turned to Nate. "I don't know!" he said. "I took my shoes off? It's not fucking *CSI*."

But what to do with the cat? She'd calmed down now. She was perched like a gargoyle on the corner of the couch, her long tail ticking into view behind her back. Carefully Coop approached her. He reached out and stroked her head. She closed her eyes, leaned her ears into his hand.

When he finally said, "She stays here," the rest of us ought to have been relieved that the whole thing was settled, that he would keep the beast, the evidence, in his house, no one else on the hook—but. There was something in the way he was looking at her. She was looking at him. They were looking at each other.

. . .

The next day at school we studied Toby Peterson from afar, peering at him from the other end of hallways, eying him icily across the cafeteria. He was in a long wheat-colored wool overcoat with the collar turned up. The usual girls came by his locker between classes—Ivy Harrington, Colleen Gallagher—and though they wore expressions of concern as they spoke to him, that wasn't necessarily about his cat getting kidnapped. It could have been anything. His whole life was a fucking tragedy.

Still, we were antsy—Coop hadn't come in that morning. Fitz sent him texts and got no response. He skipped school a lot, but the three of us couldn't help feeling like it was a bad idea to be missing on that day. So after school AJ took a detour on his walk home and went by the Coopers' house.

After Coop's mother died, it seemed like every mom in town had silently agreed to raise the Cooper boys collectively. For the months after the funeral the Coopers' doorbell rang itself hoarse, and Coop kept coming to school smelling like our own houses, like our mothers' banana breads, our grandmothers' famous pot roasts. It was a beautiful thing, to see the town come together like that, but of course, when parenting is divided up a dozen times, a hundred times, each share becomes pretty minuscule.

Our Coop was the best among the brothers—the most loyal, the least explosive—but even he knew most of the Oakville PD by name. Whenever it looked like one of the boys had finally gone too far, a concerned neighbor or two would trek down to the station, remind the officers that these boys were growing up *motherless*.

By now Coop's two older brothers were gone. His younger brother was in seventh grade, mostly barricading himself in his bedroom. Mr. Cooper had a job as a medical device salesman and though that basically meant quick jaunts to the local hospitals, his schedule had filled up since becoming a widower. Many of the mothers of our town seemed just as committed to making sure he was getting on okay. Which meant the Coopers' house often felt like it had been abandoned in a hurry, right in the middle of a bad party. Half-empty cans of Mountain Dew were crimped and capsized everywhere. Pizza boxes left a floury film when we cleared them away to play cards.

When AJ got to Coop's house, there were no cars in the driveway. He yanked on the iron cellar door but its two rusted eyelids were locked shut from the inside. This was unusual. He went around to the back of the house, crunching through the snow in the yard, the hem of his jeans wet and stiff.

The blinds were down on Coop's window but through some gaps in the plastic slats AJ could see light on the other side. He stood there for a long time, until his teeth started to chatter, until the sun slipped behind the trees. But the blinds never rose. Every so often he thought he saw a shadow move on the other side.

. . .

Two days later, just as Coop had predicted, Toby Peterson moped his way around Oakville High taping up fliers. There was a big color photo of the cat in motion, her face turned toward the camera, her body blurry at the edges. In the photo you could barely make out the wild burning of her eyes.

MISSING, it said in large print above the picture, and underneath the picture it said TOBY PETERSON 699-0532 $$$REWARD. That was all. We needed to strategize—we hadn't yet figured out who we could ask to bring the cat back—but Coop still hadn't come back to school.

> His whole life was a fucking tragedy.

On Thursday afternoon the three of us met at Fitz's, pretending to play pool in his basement and listening for any sign of his parents creeping down the stairs.

"Where the hell is he?" Nate asked Fitz. Fitz had known Coop the longest—Mr. Fitzsimmons had been a pallbearer at Mrs. Cooper's funeral—so sometimes he had a map for the cobwebby parts of Coop that the rest of us could only guess at.

Fitz shrugged. He grabbed the 13 ball and fired it across the table at a corner pocket. It clipped the rail on a half bounce and clattered onto the tile floor.

"He does this every once in a while," Fitz said. "Disappears. Maybe his brothers came home and they went camping or something."

"Maybe he just doesn't want to give back the cat," Nate said.

Fitz turned to him. "Dude—I *know*. You see the way he was looking at that thing?"

AJ took the 8 ball and bowled it slowly toward a side pocket. It hung for a moment on the lip of the hole before it dropped out of sight. He didn't know why he wasn't telling Nate and Fitz about going to Cooper's house.

But every second that passed made it harder for him to speak. There had been something strange happening in Coop's bedroom. He had a feeling it wasn't his to see, and therefore it wasn't his to share. He took the cue ball and rolled it back and forth between his hands, listening to it ramble across the felt, feeling its weight each time it hit one of his palms.

"Tomorrow," Fitz was saying, "he'll be back tomorrow, and we'll find somebody to bring the cat over, and then we'll take the reward money and forget about the whole damn thing."

• • •

The next day, the three of us skirted our morning schedule. We badgered our teachers for hall passes and nurse trips to try to keep an eye on Toby. He was there after homeroom, goofing around with Amanda Klein and Gabby Wasserman. He was there in Fitz's AP gov class, third period, sucking up to Mr. Burr with some political cartoon he'd snipped out of the newspaper. "You know me well, Peterson," Mr. Burr cooed between belly laughs. Fitz snorted loudly from the back row. Toby, a smug little smile stretched across his face, pranced back to his desk and continued doodling some twilit chateau.

> **What if he didn't give a shit about the cat, and we were stuck with it?**

Something wasn't right. If he hadn't seemed heartbroken before, now he looked positively—*normal*. Or as normal as Toby could get. What if he didn't give a shit about the cat, and we were stuck with it?

Because there was no denying it: Toby didn't seem as sad as he was supposed to. He didn't seem like a kid whose cat had been kidnapped.

We couldn't wait for Coop any longer.

• • •

We fled the school through the back entrance, running headlong through the patchy bare trees of St. James cemetery, across empty Route 1, and down the windy hill toward the Coopers'. Still no cars, no signs of life. Over the house the starchy blue of the sky was filling up with soot-colored clouds, burbling in from the north; the dome of coming snow wrapped everything in a gauzy hush.

AJ was the fastest. He burst onto the porch, pounding the door. Nate came after him and jammed the doorbell. Fitz, ten seconds behind and hacking all the way, just wrenched the front door open and stepped into the house.

Following Fitz into the house, Nate swore he saw a blur of color on the landing, something moving just out of sight, but before he had time to say anything Fitz was already thundering up the stairs, AJ behind him. A door opened and there was Ben, Coop's thirteen-year-old brother, apparently every bit the truant his older brothers were. His nose was blazing with whiteheads and his hair was mussed with sleep. "Thank God," Ben said, yawning, as we pushed past him in the hallway. "He hasn't left his room in days."

But when the three of us turned the corner at the end of the hall, Coop's door was wide open. This seemed a bad omen. We stumbled over the threshold into the dark room and collided with a smell so foul and so stagnant it was nearly solid. Like burnt hair and gangrenous meat. There were blankets and towels everywhere—soaked, darkened cloth, balled and piled in drifts as tall as Coop's bed, which, oddly, was pristinely made. And there was no sign of Coop.

AJ gagged and pulled his shirt over his nose. Nate nudged some of the towels aside with his shoe, but underneath there were only more of the same. He stepped carefully across the room and lifted a slat of the blinds.

"Look," he said, yanking the blinds open, and when we got over to the window, there was Coop, stumbling through the backyard and out into the woods.

. . .

Now the snow teemed down in flakes the size of thumbnails. Coop in his jeans and sneakers and green Oakville Crusaders T-shirt was a smudge of color against a white world that was closing up like a fist. AJ bellowed his name. He kept running. Slowly his shape grew bigger as we gained. He was moving awkwardly, carrying something. He took a left into the World War Two memorial park and skidded down Piper Hill, which had been abandoned by sledders and dog walkers in the storm.

At the bottom of the hill there was a flood grate and Coop caught his foot in it. He fell with a yelp and the bundle in his arms spilled forward onto the ground.

We slid to a stop. Coop scrambled to pull the bundle back to him—his pants leg had yanked away and his ankle was swelling and filling in with purple.

And then we took in the rest of him. The shallow scratches all around the edges of his scalp, the dark flaky stain in the gutter between his nose and his mouth.

"Coop," AJ said. "Where have you *been?* What the hell is going on?"

Coop had his eyes squeezed shut. Snow was landing on his bare arms and burning up.

"I just needed a little more time," he said.

"More—time—with *what?*" Nate gasped. He yanked a crumpled flier from his jacket pocket and waved it in front of Coop. "Look at this. Toby made fliers, like you said! We can get the reward. This whole thing—it's over!"

Coop laughed. "No," he said. He looked at the tangled wrap of blankets in his arms. "Not exactly."

. . .

After we left the Coopers' the evening of the snow day, Coop scooped up the cat and took her to his room. As soon as she was in his arms she started purring, a low drone like an engine idling.

The rest of the night he and the cat lay around in his bed. His room was warm and dark and the winter wind scraped at his window. He heard Ben come and go from the bedroom down the hall, the noises of the toilet and sink. He wondered where his father was, and when he would return, but the anger Coop felt about his father's steady absence was minimal by then, nearly gone. The kind of sore that only hurt when you poked at it.

The cat was beautiful. Coop told us later that when he reached out to stroke her head she would press her feathery ears and the crown of her skull into his fingertips, moving slowly against his hand so that it traced the whole length of her spine. She pawed at the folds of his comforter, lifted an edge and burrowed around underneath. After a while, he realized he was talking to her. He laughed a little, to himself, imagining how he would react if he found out one of his friends was huddled in bed talking to a cat. But he didn't stop. It was the most natural thing in the world.

He told her about his friends, about school. He told her about his older brothers, Keegan and Lyle, how he felt more abandoned by them than by his father, but somehow he found himself doing the same thing to Ben.

And he told her about his mother, things he hadn't managed to say out loud in years, when he slowly sunk into sleep, the cat's lantern eyes simmering like an afterimage on the inside of his eyelids.

He woke to a voice. The room was utterly dark, though he didn't recall turning the light off. He glanced around and noticed the white moon through the window and then the twin lights of the cat's eyes. She was in the middle of the floor, looking at him.

She spoke again. When she spoke her mouth didn't move—nothing moved—her voice just sort of seemed to radiate from the inside of his head. He wasn't sure that she was speaking English but still he understood. This is what the cat said:

She said that she had been waiting for him.

She said that he had been through a lot, so much pain, too much pain for someone his age, but now she was here to help him.

All the while those glowing yellow eyes on his.

She said that she could show him things that would heal him. She could bring him peace. All he needed to do was to kill her. He needed to snap her neck and then pry open her mouth and breathe his own air into her body. Fill her with his life.

> **He wanted to run from the room, but he had the sensation of something holding him down.**

Coop shook his head. Tears bubbled and smeared the edges of his vision. This was a dream, this was a terrible dream, and he was afraid.

You are not dreaming, the cat said. *There is nothing to fear*.

Coop was crying now. *I don't want to hurt you*, he thought.

The cat was still looking at him. *Is that what you think death will do?* the cat asked. *No. You will free me.*

I can't do it, Coop thought. He wanted to run from the room, but he had the sensation of something holding him down. The cat's eyes were unblinking, unmoving.

You must, the cat said. *I can help you.*

And the cat leapt up onto the bed. Up onto his lap. He saw his arms extending toward it in the darkness. Suddenly he knew why he was crying. As soon as he'd heard the cat's voice he'd known he would do whatever it said.

Thank you, the cat was saying. Her voice roared like wind in his ears. *Thank you.*

. . .

Coop's hands were turning blue. The whole time he told the story he'd been trembling. He unrolled the blanket and there was the cat.

Its smell pushed back against the cold. The cat's fur was starting to peel off. When he unrolled it gently from its swaddling a matted patch the size of a football came away in the towel.

"I know what it sounds like," Coop said miserably, staring at the body cradled in his arms. "But watch this."

And we looked on in horror as he lifted the broken thing's face to his own. He took his thumb and pulled open its tiny mouth, and then he closed his eyes and put his mouth to the opening. Fitz turned and puked in the snow.

Nate watched as the middle of the cat pushed out just slightly, like a mitten absorbing a hand. Coop was actually *inflating* it. After a few seconds he pulled his face away, gasping for breath, and with his thumb and forefinger he pinched the little mouth shut and plugged the slits of its nostrils.

> **He looked around at the others. A dark bead of blood shone in the corner of his mouth.**

Holding its head carefully that way, Coop jabbed the cat at AJ. "Do it," he said. "Breathe it. Quick."

AJ took a step back. "Fuck no," he said. But Nate, like always, stepped forward. He bent at the waist and jammed his mouth onto the cat's face. Then Nate gently cupped its head and Coop drew his hand away.

How to describe it? Nate had a friend in elementary school who could do wild things with his eyes, make them spin in dizzy circles away from each other, point off in opposite directions. Nate had always wondered but never asked the kid—did he see two different things? It might have been something like this: Nate took a deep pull of the air from the dead cat's rotting lungs, tasting the filthy fur and Coop's still-warm breath and the coppery tang of cold necrotic skin—and the world cleaved in two.

He was there, with his three best friends, at the bottom of Piper Hill, because he could feel his knee in the snow, could feel the winter gnawing at him. But he was also somewhere else. He was in a car driving along a winding coastline, the sun diving gold and red into the ocean. His window was down, and in the rearview, his face, but older: the faint creases around his eyes were deeper, as if underlined in ink; the sooty suggestion of facial hair that he wore on his upper lip had spread all over his jaw. And as he peered into—what? this other world? this other self?—he could *feel* everything there, too: the wind coming off the water, warmed by the sun at its fringes and roaring in through his window; the stale sour memory of that afternoon's coffee on the backs of his teeth. And the longer he held his gaze on this other world, the more he found he knew, the knowledge blooming, seeping in: he was driving to meet someone, something important, and he was late—

But then the urge to breathe, an alarm blaring from his other body, elbowed its way in—*Man, I am freaking out*, Nate thought, and that thought, those very words, boomed and warbled like distant thunder out over the ocean—and now the picture of the other world, the picture of Nate's future, was starting to come apart, it was starting to bubble and peel around the edges—

He jerked his mouth away from the cat and sucked greedily at the frigid air. It bit at his lungs. It brought tears to his eyes. Just like that Nate knew he was all there again, only there, sixteen years old, on his knees in the snow with a dead cat in his arms.

He looked around at the others. A dark bead of blood shone in the corner of his mouth.

He blew up the cat again and handed it to Fitz.

. . .

We each saw different stuff. For all of us, it was the future, strictly speaking—but it was as if the thing cast us out on different lengths of line. Fitz, he got next Tuesday, three o'clock that afternoon. He would put the cat down and come back to us grinning, his eyes scrolling into focus, his hand snatching blindly around for a pad of paper to scribble the answers for his AP gov exam, or announcing that Mandy Carr was gonna get a DUI over the weekend. "Well," he crooned, "she *was* going to get a DUI. Let's see if old Pat Fitzsimmons can't be her hero." His glimpses were practical, opportunistic. They drove the rest of us wild with envy.

Especially Nate. Because Nate got more stuff like driving the car along the water, frantic and late for some appointment; he got hospital rooms, gravesites. Big inscrutable moments, in other words, way way out, the only common thread being that he was always stressed or heartbroken. When he came back he was misty and raw—and yet he craved the cat as much as any of us.

On the night before his biggest wrestling match of the season, he tried to get Fitz to tell him how he could get an edge.

"Maybe if I hold your hand," Nate muttered, blushing a little. "Like in movies."

Fitz snorted. We were in the janitor's closet, our new haven, cross-legged in a circle on the dusty concrete. It was four days after Piper Hill.

"Sweetheart," Fitz said. "You can hold my hand. We don't need the cat."

Nate slugged him, and then they tried it. Nate's clammy hand wrapped around Fitz's, Fitz forced to cradle the cat lefty. But it didn't work like that, of course. Fitz took off to wherever, and Nate stayed right there in the closet, squeezing his eyes shut so hard he gave himself a headache. We could see only our own futures. We could see only what the cat chose to show each one of us, alone.

Which, for AJ, was ecstasy. He'd come back gasping, flushed all over with pleasure. "I have a *girl*," he'd whispered, on our first day with the cat. "A baby girl." Even Fitz had a hard time sneering at that, the blazing joy that pulsed off AJ. The dazed look of wonder he wore as he fished a plug of fur out from between his teeth.

And Coop—he didn't say what he saw. He came back with his mouth set in a grim line. Passed the cat around the circle without a word. "What'd you see?" the rest of us would ask. "Where were you?" But he would just shrug.

"Same as you guys," he'd say into his lap. "Same as you."

. . .

And for a while it worked. Fitz rocketed to the top of the class. He fancied himself a hero, disseminating his miraculous study guides (with a few wrong answers, naturally, so he could remain at the top of the curve); zipping around town to rescue crippled Mrs. Kellogg's runaway terrier; off to the mall to console poor female classmates who were about to get dumped. Suddenly he wasn't so interested in our nasty old pranks, in getting a rise out of saps like Toby Peterson—and neither were the rest of us. AJ was spending a lot more time with his parents. Nate, too, had turned softer, gentler. He'd quit wrestling. He was listening to a lot of jam bands, which, somehow, we let him get away with.

But we could no longer ignore that it was taking something out of us. We had to carry Listerine with us everywhere to wash the rotten smell from our breath. And though we were getting better at clinging to the other side, at understanding what the cat was trying to show us—better at holding our breath even as our brains, starved of oxygen, made the lights overhead fizz on and off, like stars glimpsed through filmy clouds—that meant we had a hard time coming back, struggled more and more to anchor in the place we really were. When we met in the handicapped stall at the movie theater, huddled together and rushing finish up before the previews started, we watched each other stumble back from our futures, our eyes whirring in their sockets. The toll was right there on our faces—still us, but a little bit gone. A little bit *less*.

And there was the queasy jolt each time one of us carefully excavated the cat from the cooler we kept her in, tucked inside Nate's black JanSport. Maybe it was guilt; maybe it was something else. Nearly all of her fur lay in a reeking pile at the bottom of the bag. Her soft parts—her eyes, her tongue, the pads of her feet—had fallen off, or else spoiled in their places. We'd covered the resulting holes with duct tape. After two weeks we were pros at the whole process, but the mouth shape we had to make was always changing; now we had to purse our lips like trumpet players so we didn't end up swallowing pebbly teeth.

We had to purse our lips like trumpet players so we didn't end up swallowing pebbly teeth.

By the time Christmas break came—fifteen days after we'd chased Coop to the bottom of Piper Hill—we had a bald, putrid pile of bones, held together with staples and tape. We had a dumpster stink that we couldn't scrub off our bodies. And we had a decision to make.

Walking home after school we talked it over. AJ was adamant that our time with the cat was up (and it was his day, in fact, his turn with the cat, but to further his point he hadn't used it once that day). Fitz and Nate were on the fence. And Coop wasn't saying anything.

He walked on slightly ahead of us, his hands balled in his pockets. These past weeks had not been kind to him. The pallid green tinge that had begun to show on his face was now creeping down his arms. He grew more sullen and remote by the day.

"Coop," AJ said, "I mean—it's practically unusable at this point. There are punctures all over the place."

The Cat

Coop walked on without turning.

"Either way," Nate said, "we can't keep it at my house anymore. I put it in the freezer in my basement, like you guys said, but the stink still got out. My parents are getting suspicious."

"Can't keep it at *my* house," Fitz said.

"Or mine," AJ said. But we were wasting our breath. Coop would gladly keep the cat at his house if that was the issue.

Coop turned abruptly on his heel. "We haven't even really looked at all our options!" he said. "Like—let's say we figure out it's the lungs that count, right? Then we just cut the lungs out. Put 'em in, I don't know, formaldehyde or something. The stuff barbers use for their scissors. And rig up a tube—"

> **We knew what he was trying to see.**

We were mortified—and then mortified that we weren't really all that mortified.

"Okay," Nate said slowly, "but if the lungs aren't the important part, then we'll have ruined it anyway."

"Besides," AJ said, "that's not the point. This is *bad* for us, man. This is . . . this is evil shit." He chanced a glance at Coop's face. "It's killing you."

Coop laughed. A busted, jagged laugh, a hammer through a lightbulb. "Don't be dramatic," he said.

"Fitz?" AJ pleaded, looking around for backup.

Fitz took a deep breath. "Coop, we've reached the end of the line here. We can't keep lugging around . . . ," he paused—we made a habit of not saying what we were doing too explicitly, but this time he went for it: ". . . a dead cat forever. Time to let it go, buddy."

All those sessions with the cat had sapped our reaction time. Coop had his hands clamped around Fitz's throat before the rest of us moved. He jacked Fitz up against a tree, rammed him hard into the stippled bark. For a moment we just stood there, frozen, watching Fitz's face, his eyes bugging, his Adam's apple jamming against Coop's fingers like a knob of ice pinched in a straw.

Fitz croaked out something indecipherable. He was peeling at the skin of Coop's wrist with his fingernails. Finally Nate and AJ lunged over to the two of them.

"You wouldn't have any of this without me," Coop spat, his face close to Fitz's. "You realize that? You guys didn't have to *do anything*." When he spoke the corners of his lips pulled back and we could see a lipstick smear of something red on his teeth. "You didn't have to kill her," he said.

"Coop!" AJ cried. Nate had his arms around Coop's waist, and AJ was trying to pry is fingers free. "Let him go! He can't breathe!"

At AJ's cracking voice, Coop snapped out of it. He let go, his blood searing his fingers from white back to red. He took a woozy step backward. Fitz doubled over, gulping loudly at the air.

Coop cursed. "You guys don't get it," he said.

"Don't get what?" Nate asked.

But Coop couldn't bring his eyes to meet us. "It's just, I don't know. Different for you," he said. "For you guys, it's a game—a way to beat tests and win games and get girls. For me—for me it's a *skill*. I get better and better at controlling it every time, and now I can really steer it, I can really see what I *want* to see. And yesterday I finally was able to steer it back. For the first time. Into the past. Into stuff that already happened."

He looked up at us now, his sunken eyes wheeling between us. And just like that we knew what he meant. We knew what he was trying to see.

"But, Coop," AJ said quietly, "those are just memories."

Coop looked at him for a long time. Then he set his jaw, shook his head.

"Fuck it," he said. "Bury the thing."

. . .

It was midnight, the day before Christmas Eve. We had arranged a sleepover at Nate's. The plan was to sneak out the back door and raid his parents' utility shed. We'd have two shovels, a four-gallon tank of gas, and a book of kitchen matches. We'd have a dead cat in a cooler in a backpack.

But Coop didn't show. As we walked to the frozen baseball field, we discussed different theories for how we could best help him. Fitz spitballed about going to his house, giving him the cat after all. "I know, I know," he said, "but the thing's pretty much busted by now. He can't get any more out of it and this way he gets his own time to . . . grieve, or something."

But Nate and AJ were unmoved. "It's gotta be burned," AJ said. "I was reading on the Internet about some stuff like this"—Nate waved both his hands in surrender; he'd already made it very clear that if he was going to be cursed for life he'd rather not know too much about it—"Okay, fine. But we gotta burn it. All of it."

So in a white shaft of moonlight we dug and dug. The snow had melted and refrozen, so it was slick and packed heavy. It took a half hour just to make it down to the dirt, two of us digging, the third man standing watch at the top of the crater, squinting at the parking lot for incoming headlights.

We layered the bottom of the hole with Coop's filthy towels, dropped the backpack on top of them. There was a soft *phoomph* as a lank pile of fur tumbled out. Finally, with a gloved hand, Nate opened the cooler and shook what was left of Toby Peterson's cat into the hole. Then he glugged on the gasoline, shaking the whole tank dry, a shine coming over the pile at the bottom. And then we took one last look around for signs of our imminent damnation.

But there was nothing. The wind grew and scuttled a soda can over the ice.

Honestly, we felt sort of gypped. This was it? As far as we could tell the sky wasn't about to be rent open. No cackling demon was materializing to scorch us with hellfire. And worse than all that, there was nobody burning rubber into the parking lot—there was no sign of Coop. He was letting us do it. What did that mean? What did all of it mean?

Nothing. Probably it meant nothing. Probably Coop was trying to get the sleep he'd neglected since that first day at the Petersons'. Or maybe his dad had finally come home. Maybe he was just mad.

But still—there was this moment, this one achingly long moment, after the blazing match fell from AJ's hand and before the pyre lit, where we couldn't help but wonder if it meant something else. We'd all seen it, right? We'd all been warped to the future? Seen our own destinies? Tasted the dead blood magic in our mouths? Suddenly we were dying to ask each other one more time—to grab each other by the shoulders and shake, our eyes bugging out, saying, *Fucking promise me that this was all real!* Because without Coop there, it felt like it had been *him* we'd thrown into the bottom of that hole. It was us—AJ, Nate, and Fitz—and we were thinking: How do we go on like we don't know what's coming? How do we forget what we already know?

Then the match hit the cooler. A dry, tinkling sound. Toby Peterson's cat went up in a fat geyser of flame, so bright and hot we had to jump back from the hole—and we wondered, for a moment, if that scorched-cat reek might hang over the town for years. If the oily crater we'd burned into center field might be permanent. But there was no way to know. We'd have to wait and see.

Michael Burkard

HELLO MR. ESSAY

forgiveness for what?
you are my complete arc.

a dog barks with a
crayon

a car brakes because
of a global agreement
happiest when "doing"
undone art

the completer he realized
he completed her songs
with radar
pronouns

fractions
claims

LATER 13

One witness denies that the nuclear waste was
dumped in a liquid form directly into the canyon.
One witness is distracted by his id. My parents
have entered the slow burn telling a story about what
a visit to England in the truest way possible can
do to you—or not do, or midday—or not midday.
A single not-even-petal did not go down the drain
during recess, so the white of it—very small—
is drying or dying on a green sheet of paper. One
witness says I do not recall the shape of the can-
yon but I recall the shape of the liquid from a dream
I had, and I can tell you this is a kind of double
emptiness, a drink you could order, I'll have a double,
no, make that a double emptiness. It's hot so I am
dragging as many people to AA meetings as I can she
says, and then I see this liquid dream and I know I
have been breathing these toxins and so have my children
and all these trees and woods for at least ten years.

NERVE

why did I buy the house
i'm in where i hardly
ever live it is as if it
is an expensive studio for
my drawings and perhaps could
become an expensive studio
to paint in if i can ever
work up the nerve to paint—
i say "nerve" because i
am afraid that i will either
be a real lousy painter
or afraid once i start
painting there will be no
turning back—one possibility
does not necessarily negate
the other—i.e., i could
become a nonstop lousy
painter and delude myself.
Delusions, Etc. is a book
by John Berryman i enjoyed
but can no longer find my
copy. one poem i think
was entitled "Trakl," after the
German poet—the last phrase
read ". . . and overdose & go."

FICTION

TROJAN WHORES HATE YOU BACK

ERIC PUCHNER

They reached the top of the Grapevine and then puttered over Tejon Pass, beginning their roller-coaster descent into Los Angeles, that vast sedimentary basin where everything comes to rest. You couldn't coast down the 5 without feeling like you were heading down its drain. Even so, Alistair felt the old loop-the-loop of excitement. He gripped the steering wheel with one hand, trying to ignore the bursitis in his shoulder. He shouldn't have been driving, but it was his van—his MasterCard, in fact, was bankrolling the whole reunion tour—so he could endanger his bandmates if he felt like it. And wasn't pissing on danger what Trojan Whores were all about?

A food truck drifted into his lane, straddling the dotted line so that Alistair couldn't pass. He could not lift his arm enough to honk. "Frozen shoulder," his doctor called it, which did nothing to describe the pain.

"Get out of the way, Pussy Kitchen!"

"Did you just say 'Pussy Kitchen'?" Glenn asked. He was slumped in the passenger seat, noodling on the unplugged Jaguar in his lap.

"Maybe."

Glenn nodded in approval. "I smell a hit."

He improvised a riff on the Jag, a Cramps-y bit of staccato picking. The guy still had it. He was some kind of genius—could pull riffs out of the air like he was picking cherries. Alistair grinned but couldn't help thinking, as he had for the past two weeks, that his old friend's heart wasn't in it. Sometimes he glanced at Glenn's face and kind of, you know, wondered where he'd gone. His eyes bulged slightly, and his head looked sort of oblong without his old snowdrift of a pompadour, and there was the vague sense that he was making a face at you even when he wasn't. Somehow he'd gone from being the heartthrob poster boy of Trojan

Whores to someone you might avoid sitting next to on the bus. Behind him, in the backseat, Vladimir was perched on his hemorrhoid pillow, an inflatable blue donut he carried around with him wherever he went. He'd developed one of those things on his eyelid that old people get, like the stalk of a miniature third eye. And what was he wearing? A windbreaker? Blue linen shorts? If you saw him cruising the links in a golf cart, you wouldn't blink.

At least Andy, zonked against the opposite window, still looked like himself: a bit pickled around the eyes, but more or less the same Andy he'd been in 1982. Maybe the secret was sleep. The guy was basically a plant. Once, back in the day, Alistair had had to carry him into a photo shoot and use himself as a trellis, twining Andy's arm around his shoulders. The only thing that could truly rouse him was a drum kit.

Alistair focused on the road, trying to ignore the smell of rat shit stinking up the van and wondering if the scratching sounds coming from the back were real or imaginary. The rats were for Vladimir's pet python, Stew. He'd insisted on bringing it along on the road. No doubt he'd had some trouble finding a snake sitter. Watching Stew eat a live rat was one of those life-altering experiences Alistair had not known to avoid until it was too late. The thing was fed once a week, which meant it was supposed to be fed today—as Vladimir kept reminding them from the backseat. They'd been in too much of a hurry this morning to do it.

"I'm not playing any new songs," Vladimir said now from atop his donut. He looked, in the rearview mirror, like he was riding on a booster seat.

"Vlad the Complainer speaks," Alistair said.

"I'm not a complainer. I'm simply protecting our brand."

Glenn stopped playing his guitar, mid-riff. "Did you hear that? He just called the Whores a 'brand.'"

"Cut the horseshit," Vladimir said. "You need the money as much as I do. I've got a thirty-year mortgage and two kids going to college. Not to mention medical expenses."

"Funny he doesn't mention his weed habit."

> **He'd developed one of those things on his eyelid that old people get, like the stalk of a miniature third eye.**

"Like I said: medical expenses." Vladimir fished his vaporizer from the pocket of his windbreaker and took a hit, then cracked his window to blow out the mist. He was the only person Alistair knew with a medical marijuana prescription for hemorrhoids. "Poor Stew. Can't you drive any faster? He strikes at me if he's hungry."

"What a pity," Glenn said.

"Physic?" Vladimir said sweetly, offering his vaporizer to Glenn.

"I'm stoned on God."

Vladimir laughed. Alistair wanted to defend Glenn and his God trip, but the truth was he didn't understand it himself. How could anyone belt out the chorus to "Immaculate Cuntception" every night and then unwind with the Holy Bible before bed? As far as Alistair could tell, Glenn had been on Genesis 13 since Texas. He knew this because he and Glenn had been sharing hotel rooms. If he wasn't kicking it with the Word, the guy was reading a book of Chinese proverbs his sponsor had given him, trying to access his inner wisdom. Last night, Alistair had watched him poring over some proverbs in the next bed, lips moving the way they used to when he was writing a song, and felt inexplicably jealous. He wanted to ask Glenn about it—about the proverbs, the Bible business, what killer drug God was dealing to make him so *fulfilled*— but was afraid he'd take it the wrong way.

> **He stayed that way, blinking at the stereo. Never had they heard a song of theirs on the radio.**

"Does Naya know we're playing the Wiltern?" Glenn asked. He'd given up on "Pussy Kitchen" and was strumming along to the radio: Patti Smith's "Free Money." At least a few lonely college stations were still carrying the torch.

"She listens to Nina Simone. It doesn't mean anything to her," Alistair said. "Anyway, she's leaving me."

"You don't know that."

"Well, she did say that being married to me was like being married to one of those frogs that eats its own skin."

"What does that mean?"

Alistair shrugged. "I guess it's a metaphor."

"There's an old Chinese proverb: 'If I keep a green bough in my heart, the singing bird will come.'"

154   ERIC PUCHNER

"Also, she's looking for an apartment," Alistair said.

Something lurched in his chest, admitting this. If his heart were a bird, it was very sick. A motorcycle—a Ninja, or a Samurai, or some other Asiatic warrior—swerved into the next lane. The guy on the motorcycle was dressed up like a clown, red afro billowing from the bottom of his helmet. He had the gigantic bow tie and everything. The motorcycle shot ahead, slaloming through traffic.

"Did you see that clown?"

Glenn glanced up from his guitar. "Judge not," he said judgmentally, "that you be not judged."

They passed the Magic Mountain tower, poking from the earth like a great red nail, and entered the fathomless outskirts of LA. Then something miraculous happened. A Trojan Whores song came on the radio. "Trash Appeal." Alistair turned it up, and for a moment none of them spoke, listening to the strange yet familiar sounds rattling the speakers. Vladimir shook Andy awake. He stayed that way, blinking at the stereo. Never had they heard a song of theirs on the radio. There'd been rumors, of course, passed along by fans—but they'd never been able to confirm them. Glenn, proverb-less, let his guitar slide to his lap. Alistair chose to believe he was moved. He was a stranger to him, this person he'd once been in an orgy with. *Several*, if you wanted to be ultraprecise. The DJ came on and gave them a shout—"Last chance to see Trojan Whores, tomorrow night at the Wiltern"—and Alistair's eyes fogged up. The whole thing was supposed to be a lark, a prank: two kids out for blood and pussy. How had it become the most important thing that had ever happened to him?

In the city, Alistair parked in front of an inauspicious building—Lamebrain Productions, it said on the front—and tried to calm his nerves. He wished their gig at the Wiltern was tonight. He'd come to think of it, dangerously, as the passport to their future. For years, Alistair had been opposed to getting the Whores back together. He didn't particularly want to die before he got old—just didn't want to have to sing songs with names like "Immaculate Cuntception" in public. But then something had happened. He'd been walking to the BART station on his way to work one morning when he saw an enormous brown hawk swoop down and grab a squirrel that was high-wiring across a power line. One moment the squirrel was there, its long tail contrailing behind it; the next it was gone. It was a gorgeous day, the sun painting the windows of the Victorians on

Twenty-Fourth and making the noises around him seem like the soundtrack to a different street. Commuters whizzed by on their bikes or strode down the sidewalk with their eyes glued to their cell phones, thumbs dancing like flames. Alistair turned around and went home. He tracked down Glenn's number and found him in LA, living in a friend's garage, out of rehab and hoofing it to NA meetings twice a week, so broke he had one of those disposable Walmart phones. It was for Glenn, Alistair told his wife, that he quit his job and proposed getting the Whores back together. Glenn, who if he'd only died young would be as famous as Sid Vicious, but was a burned-out fatso without a penny to his name or any discernable vocational skills besides finding veins.

Burned out, but not forgotten. Improbably, the reissue of *Trojan Whores Hate You Back* had found a tribe of *Pitchfork* readers who hadn't been born the first time around. Three nights ago, at the Crescent Ballroom in Phoenix, Alistair had been amazed to look up and see two teenage girls in the front row, shouting along to "Sex Is Boring." They knew the words better than he did. According to Glenn, who still had some connections, Merge was interested in a new album. ("Intrigued by the idea," was how they'd put it on the phone.) Mac himself was coming to the show tomorrow night, to find out how intrigued they should be.

"We're doing a talk show in a mini-mall?" Vladimir asked from the backseat.

"It's a Web thing," Glenn said. "Our chance to go viral."

He smiled at them, as if the Whores' future were in his pocket. He'd insisted they didn't need a manager—that he could DIY a tour better than some "corporate douche"—and maybe he was right: Trojan Whores were on the radio. And yet there was something about his enthusiasm that seemed, well, *contractual*, as if he were freeing himself of a debt.

Alistair had some trouble getting out of the van unassisted. Meaning: he couldn't. His shoulder, while not actually frozen, was definitely experiencing a wintry mix. Glenn came over and hugged him to the ground.

"Shit!" Vladimir said, unloading the van. The sleeves of his windbreaker were pushed above his elbows.

"What's the matter?"

"Stew! He's not in his cage!" He turned on them savagely. "Who forgot to fucking pin the top back on?"

"Wasn't me," Glenn said, in a way that made it clear that it was. He'd been poking the snake while Vladimir was in the Conoco bathroom, trying to get it to come out of its hide box. Vladimir began throwing drum stands and distortion pedals into the street. Alistair put his good arm around Glenn, watching their bass player freak. It was like old times.

"You mean there's a fucking python loose in the van?" he said happily.

Glenn whistled into the open doors as if Stew were a dog, calling him by name, which made Alistair laugh. He had not put his arm around Glenn in thirty years. Of course, there'd been a time—say, in '85 or '86, after Trojan Whores had been at it for five years—when a loose python in the van would have seemed like one more stop on the Tragical Misery Tour, as Vladimir had dubbed their life. Rubberneckers started coming to the shows and waiting for them to implode. Once, for a reason he could not afterward recall, Alistair snapped in the middle of one of Glenn's strung-out solos and attacked him with the mic, beating him in the face and screaming, "I'll shrink your fucking head!" over and over, until it achieved a kind of contrapuntal rhythm to the drums. At night, sleeping on some crazy addict's couch, Alistair would dream of his childhood bed in Claremont, California, where he and Glenn had grown up. People went jogging there and listened to Springsteen and had trampolines on their lawns.

Alistair had some trouble getting out of the van unassisted. Meaning: he couldn't.

And so he'd left one day without telling Glenn: moved out of their apartment in East Hollywood, taking nothing but his records and whatever clothes he could fit into his dad's old army duffel. It had felt like an emergency. *I want a normal life*, he'd written, skewering the note on the turntable, where he knew Glenn would see it whenever he woke up from his drunken coma. And that's what he'd found. He'd moved to San Francisco, framed buildings for a while, then took some computer classes and got a job designing fire sprinkler systems. The job bored him, in a not-unpleasant way, and the smart-ass camaraderie of the other designers reminded him a bit of being in a band. He bought a tiny house in the Mission, before Silicon Valley colonized it. He dated a chain of women—volatile weather systems, given to dark silent prayers to the self—and wondered if he was destined to die alone. Then he met Naya. She had a master's degree and worked as a therapist for at-risk youth. Even her name sounded healthy, like a karate chop. She'd grown up in Georgia and had an enchanting disregard for syllables. ("CoC-ola," she ordered on their first date, and he was smitten.) They went to museums and fed the ducks at the park and crossed the Golden Gate Bridge to where the fog feathered into wisps, winding their way into the mountains, where they hiked through trees as old as cathedrals. They were ambivalent enough about kids that after trying for a year they decided to stop. Even after sixteen years of marriage, they had regular, loving, secret-universe sex. He was happy enough, lost in the moment—but Happiness eluded him. He couldn't help feeling like there was something else he needed to do. It reminded him of that old Stephen Wright joke: *I bought some powdered water at the store, but I don't know what to add.*

And so he found himself missing Glenn, those first years after they'd moved to Hollywood, fresh out of high school and pissed off at anything that wasn't a guitar. The world was an enemy country, so they could do whatever they wanted. Once, Alistair had put his head through a pane of glass. One of those miraculous trucks with sheets of glass strapped all around it, just sitting there by the curb at 3:00 AM, pulsing with the lights of the Strip, pink and purple and fuck knows what else—the city was full of such things, dreams masquerading as objects. Back then a truck or a lost shoe could break your heart. Glenn had dared him to do it, half jokingly—*If you're so fucking punk, then stick your head through that piece of glass*—and he closed his eyes and ran at it like a football player and rammed his head through without a scratch, the thing crashing wavelike over his back. If not for his leather jacket, he might have ended up in the ER. The truth was he'd expected to die, but was too happy to care. It was the first he'd ever heard of it—trying to commit suicide out of joy.

> **The trick was to keep the fear out of his face. Because this was it. Do or die.**

That's what he'd wanted in getting the Whores back together. That feeling of possibility, that his heart was an open perch.

Alistair popped enough Advil to ulcerate his stomach and rang the door of Lamebrain Productions. A chick in a Black Flag T-shirt greeted him at the entrance. She couldn't have been more than nineteen, betrayed by a pimple on her forehead. Her concealer had turned it into a beige growth. Did these beautiful girls really listen to Black Flag, charmed by the lyrics to "Slip It In"?

"Can I help you, sir?" she said to Alistair.

The "sir" lanced his heart. She squinted at the minivan, where Vladimir was standing among the rubble of Andy's drum kit, looking like he might cry. Glenn smiled at her, lifting a Jamba Juice cup.

"Are you with the Trojan Whores?"

"Just Trojan Whores," Alistair said importantly. "There's no 'the.'"

In the studio, which was decorated to look like a fifteen-year-old boy's room, complete with a lava lamp and Che Guevara poster, four wheelchairs awaited them. The idea was that they'd pretend to be decrepit during the interview and then wheel themselves onstage, leaping out of the chairs when it was time to launch into "Trash Appeal." Alistair wasn't crazy about the idea, but a talk show was a talk show. In their prime, the Whores had been interviewed exactly once, on a college radio show called *Sniffing Glue on KPYU*.

Instinctively, Alistair glanced at the ceiling, counting the tiles between sprinkler heads: the spacing was completely fucked, alternating between light and ordinary hazard. Clearly, they hadn't pulled a permit. He went into the bathroom and spent some time in front of the mirror, doing his best to become a Whore, fine-tuning his sneer so that it had the right pinch of irony. The trick was to keep the fear out of his face. Because this was it. Do or die. Or more accurately: Do *and* die. The music biz was kaput. The best you could hope for was to sell your song to Volkswagen. Alistair knew this; he wasn't naïve. Still, if the Whores actually went *viral*, they could blow up: Jimmy Kimmel, European tour, the main-stage festival circuit. They could squeeze in a last few years of fame.

The host of the show—a guy with a Cockney accent and a leopard print vest, circa 1978— helped them set up their gear. He looked ridiculous. Maybe he was new to the country. For the interview, Alistair positioned his wheelchair between Glenn and Vladimir, who looked ill at ease without his inflatable donut. He was staring at Glenn as if he wanted to separate him from his head. Andy slouched in the wheelchair beside Vladimir's, his eyes at half-mast.

"Can he talk?" the host asked.

"No," Andy said.

"He needs fifteen hours of sleep," Glenn explained. "It's like a disability."

"Love it," the host said in an American accent. "We can get a shot of him zonked out."

"At least he's not a snake killer!" Vladimir said. "He doesn't release juvenile pythons into the streets!"

The host giggled. He turned to Alistair. "Can you, like, act fucked up too?"

"What do you mean?"

"Pretend you're wasted. It'll be funnier."

Alistair blinked. So it was a joke. The guy in the leopard print vest was playing a part. The name of the show, *Famouser Than You*, made sense to him now: this was a show that made fun of talk shows, or perhaps even a show that made fun of shows that made fun of talk shows. It was hard to be sure. The cameras started to roll, and the host slipped back into his persona, a washed-up "punk rocker" with delusions of grandeur. He claimed to be in a band called the Bottomless Assholes. Alistair felt his cheeks go warm, but both Glenn and Andy were cracking up.

"Was you ever on tour wif me mates, the Clash?"

"No," Alistair said.

"Wuzzabout the Vibrators?"

"We're from the San Gabriel Valley," Alistair said, making everyone on the set laugh.

Then the host introduced them, Trojan Whores, and they wheeled themselves toward the stage to take up their instruments. All Alistair had to do was get to the microphone. But he couldn't. His bursitis, fulfilling its imperialist dreams, had colonized his entire arm. It felt like someone had nailed it to the chair with a stake. He couldn't wheel himself at all. The host, thinking Alistair was playing along, pushed his wheelchair up to the microphone and handed it to him.

Andy, fully awake now, tapped his drumsticks together, and Glenn crashed into the first three-chord riff of "Trash Appeal." Around him, Alistair's bandmates leaped from their chairs, healed by the power of song. Alistair grit his teeth, summoning all his strength, but he couldn't do it. The pain was too great. The mic smelled the way mics always smell, like a stereo that's been on all day—a faint whiff of singed cat—but this lovely smell didn't help him. He had no choice but to sing from the chair. He closed his eyes and imagined Naya watching him sometime in the future, once his humiliation had gone viral, kicking back in her new apartment with a computer on her lap. He pictured her reaction, the guilty trace of schadenfreude on her face. Except the face wasn't Naya's. It was a clown's. The one he'd seen on the motorcycle. The clown, in his enormous bow tie, watching him sing.

"They were laughing at us!" Alistair blurted on the way to their motel. His face was still warm; it was like a sunburn, only on the inside of his cheeks. Glenn, steering the van with two hands, bumped painfully over a pothole.

"It's always been a joke, right?" he said. "A laugh. *Mate*, we named ourselves Trojan Whores."

"I know! But we were the ones playing the joke on *them*!"

"Now the world is punk," Glenn said. "No one takes anything straight."

He was right, of course, which pissed Alistair off further. "I knew we should have hired a manager."

They stopped for dinner at a Mexican place, where Glenn spent the entire time reading his Bible, the same page he'd been on for days. Alistair's phone buzzed in his pocket, but he was too upset to answer it. He wanted the old Glenn back, the guy who read *Flipside* instead of the New Testament and wrote songs with him till dawn, transmuting Alistair's dumb frantic longing into music.

"Read the part where Jesus mounts someone's ass," Vladimir said. He was still fuming about Stew. Andy, uncharacteristically, was sitting upright with his eyes open, sawing at his burrito with a plastic knife.

"You might at least try to converse," Alistair said to Glenn. "Be a part of the band."

Glenn sighed and closed his Bible, as if he were doing Alistair a favor. He hadn't once thanked him for saving his life. Who'd jump-started the whole tour and rescued him from a fucking garage?

"This whole reunion thing is for your benefit, you know."

Glenn met his eye for the first time. "*My* benefit? What are you talking about?"

"Look, we could all use a second chance. I'm not saying it wasn't my idea."

"You called me seven times in two days."

"I did not," Alistair said.

Glenn looked at Andy, who was air-drumming with his knife and fork. "Andy, how many times did Al get in touch with you? About getting back together?"

"Counting e-mails?"

Later, in the motel room they were sharing, Alistair watched Glenn gargle with warm water, something he'd done since he was a teenager. The Chateau Marmont it was not: hot and windowless and as narrow as a hallway, two beds crammed into it as if they'd snagged there during a flood. It smelled like a hospital ward. Adding to this impression was Glenn's sleep apnea machine. The mask was terrible, as large as a fighter pilot's, the tube hanging down like an elephant's trunk. Alistair had bought the thing for him because Glenn didn't have insurance. It had sounded like a blast, sharing motel rooms with his old partner in crime—maybe even gallantly helping him stay clean—but Alistair had failed to account for the Darth Vader sounds scoring his dreams from the next bed.

Alistair plucked out his contacts and dunked them in their miniature dunking booths. He thought about the first hotel room they'd ever shared, after the Whores had played Bob's Tiki Lounge in Sacramento. One of their first big gigs, opening for the Plugz. They'd dropped acid after the show and Alistair ended up at some runaway's campground, so wacked he spent an hour shouting into people's tents, weeping because he couldn't find Glenn. When he finally got back to the hotel and collapsed next to him, he saw a handwritten note taped to the ceiling over the bed. TAKE OUT YOUR CONTACTS, it said in enormous letters. Glenn knew he'd forget and wake up with them cemented to his eyeballs.

> He'd made a terrible mistake, pushing her away.

Alistair slipped on his glasses and checked his phone, to see who'd called him in the restaurant. He'd been hoping it was Naya, a wish like an egg, one that would hatch into being if he let it incubate long enough. But it was a number from Kansas: a telemarketer. He walked out into the hall and called Naya anyway. She did not sound thrilled to hear from him, though neither did she sound appalled.

"They played us on the radio," Alistair said.

"Congratulations," she said sincerely. After two weeks of being on the road, her voice sounded exotic again. "Which song?"

"'Trash Appeal.'"

"The one you wrote about Glenn?"

"It's not about Glenn."

"Really? The lyrics seem so . . . *biographical*."

"It's about, like, the whole SoCal scene."

"*Pall Mall in his strings / More pills than a med cart / Shoot him up good / Into your dead heart?*"

"Everyone smoked Pall Malls," Alistair said, blushing. He was touched, frankly, that she knew the words.

"Did the two of you do that thing while you're driving?" Naya asked.

"What thing?"

"That thing you're always talking about. On tour. Where y'all switch drivers, going a hundred, so you won't have to get off the freeway."

"I'm practically a cripple," Alistair said.

Naya laughed. "I know. I was being mean."

He deserved this. It had infuriated him that he could suffer from something so clichéd as a midlife crisis, so he'd taken it out on the person who'd failed to save him from it. Once, after the housekeeper had come, Naya said, "God, I love it when the house is clean!" and he realized he'd known she would say this, that she said the same thing every week in the exact same way, annotating it with an ironic cluck of the tongue meant to disguise the fact that it *really fucking pleased her*. To Alistair, it was the sound of their souls dying. What he hadn't admitted at the time—even to himself—was that he loved it when the house was clean too. He wanted a sparkling house and somebody to blame for it at the same time.

"I miss you," Alistair said.

"Of course you do," she said. Then, more quietly: "Which part?"

"What?"

"Which part do you miss?"

Alistair listened to the distance between them, a seashell-y roar. He'd made a terrible mistake, pushing her away. She was lovely, extraordinary in a thousand ways he took for granted, the only person he'd ever met who could use the word *weltschmerz* in conversation and also change the oil in a car. But he couldn't stop thinking of that squirrel on the power line, the sun-painted street after it was snatched away. He could hear her waiting for him to answer.

"The skylight's leaking again," Naya said sadly, giving up. "Can you hear the drips? I had to put the Dutch oven in the bedroom."

"Call Jim."

"Who?"

"The roof guy? Who you always call."

She sighed. "You have no idea what his name is, do you? What are you going to do when I'm gone?"

Glenn and Alistair drove out to Claremont the next day. It was Alistair's idea. He'd asked Glenn to drive, not wanting to tax his shoulder before the show even though it felt fine. (Such was the nature of his body, unpredictable foe.) Sound check wasn't until five, and he felt like seeing his father's grave—at least, that's what he told Glenn—but the truth was Alistair had no great longing to see the headstone. He'd just wanted to go out there. With Glenn. He'd been envisioning it for days.

God knows what he'd hoped for, but the suburban streets and their tidy, Spanish revival homes did not provide it. Hard to believe he and Glenn had grown up here, or that they'd been so desperate to get out, sweating around in the blazing sun with icicles hanging from their hearts. What was it that had made them so angry? They stopped at Alistair's old house, which looked much the same, except that the yard had been landscaped into a cactus garden, primly pebbled, like a diorama of the Sonoran Desert. They got out to look at it. The driveway was empty, and Alistair walked into the garden and stopped at a cactus with a single white flower blooming from the top of it like a bowl balanced on someone's head. It smelled atrociously pleasant. Beside the cactus, painted to look like stone, was a statue of a fairy riding a butterfly. Alistair picked it up and brought it to Glenn, thinking they could smash it onstage—maybe give it to Vladimir as a joke—but Glenn glanced down the block and returned it to the garden.

Alistair made him drive by the record store where they used to buy LPs, which had become a gourmet cheese shop. He got out of the van and peered into the window, as if Twig, the owner, might still be inside, blasting the latest Pere Ubu album. They used to ride their bikes here every Friday afternoon, jackets caped out behind them, to spend their allowances on records they'd never heard. The Weirdos, the Flesh Eaters, the Angry Samoans. The smell of new vinyl! The midnight-movie names! The first lovely crackle of the needle, as if the record were on fire: it was like the fuse before the song exploded. Even much later, when the Whores were falling apart, Glenn and Alistair bought records in Hollywood every weekend and then rushed home together, slitting the shrink-wrap with a fingernail because they were too impatient to find scissors. They'd listen to the album straight through sometimes, watching each other's faces, then start it again if it made them envious. There was the Sonic Youth LP—*EVOL*, was it?—where the last track on side B had an ∞ next to it. It played forever: there was no groove to send the needle off the record.

Back in the van, Glenn was reading his Bible again, the same inescapable page. Was he memorizing it? Humbling himself like a retard? *Pay silent communion to page nine, and page ten shall deliver you from page nine, and henceforth onto eleven.*

"You could at least fucking *react*," Alistair said.

Glenn laid the Bible on the dashboard. He didn't seem to give a shit about Twig's Records.

"What's that stupid page about anyway?" Alistair asked.

"You really want to know?"

"Yes!"

Glenn looked at him shyly. "It's the story of Lot. It's about how bad choices are cumulative—you know, how one leads to the next. First Lot *looks* at Sodom, then *moves his tents* near there, then *dwells* there, then in the end he's *sitting in the gate* of Sodom, a city official."

"I thought Lot's wife turned to salt."

"She does," Glenn said logically. "First he loses his home. Then his wife. Then his daughters get him trashed and seduce him."

"They date-rape him?" Alistair said, laughing.

"Basically." Glenn watched him laugh without cracking a smile. "My sponsor told me to read it every day."

"To remind you not to fuck your daughters?"

"To remind me that our choices have consequences."

Alistair looked out the windshield. He did not believe that bad choices always had consequences. It was a fantasy that adults had cooked up, to make them feel better about their boring lives. In fact, you could do everything right and still die miserable, just as you could do idiotic things—like smash your head through a pane of glass—and get off scot-free. It might even be the highlight of your life. Thus says the Lord of Punk. Alistair watched an elderly couple in Birkenstocks enter the cheese shop, which was named Gouda Vibrations. His old friend must have noticed something in his face, because he mustered a look of charitable nostalgia.

"How'd the phone thing go this morning?" Glenn asked.

"What?"

"The interview I set up! With *LA Weekly*."

Alistair frowned. He put on his seat belt. "They asked what makes the perfect Whores song."

"What'd you say?"

"You wouldn't be interested," he said.

> **He did not believe that bad choices always had consequences.**

On the way home, Alistair stared out the window, where a gibbous moon hung in the blue sky, faint as a fingerprint. What was it about LA, that you could see the moon in the daytime so often? He felt strangely desperate.

"Remember how we used to switch places while we were driving, so we wouldn't have to get off the freeway?"

"Of course," Glenn said, unable to resist a smile. Inside of it was the old Glenn, glimmering like a prize.

"Let's try it."

"Ha ha."

"I'm serious," Alistair said. It seemed like a great and urgent thing. He unpopped his seat belt.

Glenn stopped smiling. "Don't be stupid. What about your shoulder?"

"Fuck my shoulder," he said.

"We're on the 210," Glenn explained. "You want a twelve-car pileup?" He pointed at the SUV in front of them. "Not to mention that. BABY ON BOARD."

The ghastly phrase, coming from Glenn's mouth, broke Alistair's heart. "You wrote a song called 'Infanticide.' Remember?"

Glenn looked at him in amazement. "Are you saying you actually want to kill babies?"

"How'd you get so fucking . . . *sensible?*"

Glenn shrugged, though Alistair could tell he'd gotten to him a bit. It was there in his eyes, as if he'd been pricked with a needle. "There are worse things to be," he said. "Like dead. As the Chinese say: *Fear the wolf in front, and the tiger behind.*"

Alistair slid over till they were leg to leg and grabbed the steering wheel with one hand. They were going about fifty. Glenn looked at him with something like anger, then resignation, then a faint sparkle of excitement that narrowed his eyes into the old fuck-it-all squint of his youth. All of this in a one-second glance. He undid his seat belt, shaking his head, and Alistair stretched his left leg down to the gas pedal so that their Chuck Taylors touched. He could feel the toe of his old friend's sneaker. The trick was to transfer the pressure of their feet as gradually as possible so that their speed remained constant, steady as a yacht's. This required a kind of telepathic footometry. And they had it, Glenn and Alistair—it had served them many times, crossing the Badlands or the Mojave or the Great Plains of Texas.

Glenn lifted his foot, very slowly, Alistair stretching his leg like a ballet dancer in order to keep his toes firmly on the gas. The speedometer dipped, but not too much. Then Alistair began to scootch over Glenn's lap, blocking his view of the road, doing his best to keep the van on a true and steady course while he squeezed between Glenn and the steering wheel. The problem was Glenn's belly. It was as large as a basketball and just as inflexible. Alistair tried to wriggle past but only wedged himself against the wheel, so close that he was basically humping it, sounding the horn now with his chest. When he tried to shove himself free, the van swerved wildly to the right. Glenn screamed. Alistair yanked at the wheel, righting it as best he could, still pinned against the horn—this was the end, the Great Hawk coming to pluck him from the wire—but then Glenn popped out from under him, freeing himself in the nick of time and leaving Alistair half sprawled in the driver's seat, unable to see the road, hanging from the wheel as if it were a trapeze, so that he hit the brakes without thinking and sent them fishtailing across two lanes before they jounced to a stop on the shoulder, trailing an explosion of honks.

Alistair sat there catching his breath, his heart flopping like a fish. His hands still gripped the wheel; he was afraid to ungrip them.

"Whoooo!" he said, though his voice came out small and hoarse. It sounded far away, even to himself. "Talk about stoned on God, hey?"

Glenn hit him in the face. A full-handed slap. Alistair touched his cheek, rubbing it so Glenn wouldn't see that his hand was shaking. The van smelled like burnt carpet.

Glenn retrieved his Bible from the floor, where it had fallen off the dash. "Why did you move out that day without even telling me? You stole half our records."

"I only took the records I'd paid for myself," Alistair said. "It wasn't stealing."

"I didn't know we were keeping track."

"I was unhappy," Alistair said gravely.

"So? When were you ever happy?"

That night at the Wiltern, they killed. If a few people were sitting, it was only from exhaustion. The songs were like holy water, the crowd begging to be sprinkled on. "Trash Appeal" had them pogoing in their All Stars. "Sex Is Boring" mined new layers of infernal sludge. "Traffic Report" had everyone shouting, "Northbound off-ramp is completely fucked!" as if it were their own song and the Whores were merely backup singers. For the encore, they did a cover of the Brains' "Money Ruins Everything." The crowd wouldn't stop chanting their name. Even Vladimir was smiling. Drenched in sweat, Alistair squinted into the lights. The place was far from full but still looked crowded: a pond of faces if not a sea, the biggest they'd ever played to.

"Epic," the singer from the opening band said afterward, wearing a Trojan Whores T-shirt two sizes too small. The kid had cut the sleeves off, just as Alistair had done to his own shirt in the picture. "You guys kicked ass up there."

It was true, they'd kicked ass—so why did Alistair feel miserable? He heard the ringing in his ears, loud and merciless, like something that would follow him to the grave. His shoulder throbbed, and there was a new pain in his lower back, flaring when he walked. Vladimir and Glenn and Andy were breaking down the gear, still glowing with triumph. Mac from Merge had just asked them to sign an original pressing of *Trojan Whores Hate You Back*, gushing to them about the show and telling Glenn to be sure to call him on Monday. Alistair grabbed a Diet Coke from the cooler backstage and then went out to the van and climbed into the back. He rooted around the stray cords and boxes, looking for Vladimir's python. He had the vague idea he might wrap it around his neck. But the snake was still nowhere to be found.

He sat on the back bumper, then took out his cell phone and called Naya. She answered before it rang, which made her voice seem to spring from his own head. It was two o'clock in the morning.

"We brought down the Wiltern tonight," Alistair said. "They couldn't get enough. It was like 1983 in there."

Silence for a moment. "Was it everything you dreamed of?"

"No," he said. "I mean, it was exactly like it used to be, but nothing like the way I remembered it."

He wondered if he was shouting. His ears were ringing that badly. He'd called her, he realized, because she was the only one who'd understand him. Across the street, a boy with a blue Mohawk climbed into a Prius and blasted some hip-hop through the open sunroof. Another boy and a girl got into the car, laughing.

"Please don't leave me," Alistair said, beginning to cry.

"Because *I'm* the answer to your problems."

"Remember how we used to walk across the city, just make a day of it, from the Haight to Coit Tower, and we'd dream up the worst movies we could think of? That one about the pickle heiress and the small-town little league coach who fall in love, even though she's planning on selling the company and making lots of hardworking Americans lose their jobs. What was it called?"

"*A Pretty Pickle*," Naya said. "God. Ha. That was an awful one."

"Anyway, that's one of the things I miss."

Naya made a sound he couldn't decipher. Somehow the sound—the sob, or whatever it was—contained the whole intimate failure of their marriage.

"So now you're starting to get nostalgic about us," she said.

She hung up on him. Alistair sat there for a while, listening to the hip-hop booming from the Prius. This was punk, its true meaning and incarnation: fury and menace and a swagger to match God's. *Fuck you and your Hampton house / I'll fuck your Hampton spouse / Came on her Hampton blouse / And in her Hampton mouth.* It made Trojan Whores sound like the Wiggles. Alistair saw the boy with the Mohawk rise through the top of the Prius and stand on the roof, rapping along to the music. His face was bleeding and exultant. The hands of the damned yanked at his legs.

"That's one fucked-up teenager," Glenn said, appearing from nowhere. He glugged from a bottle of Jim Beam.

"Fuck are you doing?" Alistair said, grabbing the bottle from him. "You're not supposed to have that!"

"Too late."

The bottle was half-gone. Glenn sat on the edge of the van, already drunk. Alistair felt a sadness in his bones, like a weight.

"Fucking hell," he said. "Who gave it to you?"

"Some punk reenactor. A creative anachronist."

"What about being 'stoned on God'?"

"It was a great show," Glenn said grimly. His Dead Kennedys shirt was drizzled with blood, like old times. It was too late for Glenn—too late for keeping him sober, tonight and the next night and the next; too late,

> It was true, they'd kicked ass—so why did Alistair feel miserable?

Alistair saw, for the whole carsick revival of their friendship. He'd convinced Glenn to get the band back together—*It'll be good for you!*—and he'd made his life worse. And Alistair saw his own life, the only one he would ever live, as an incurable thing, hopelessly yoyo-ing between freedom and companionship. It was rock 'n' roll's fault, for pretending you could have both at once. He took a swig from the bottle himself.

"Give it here," Glenn said, grabbing the bottle back. He seemed angry and besotted with it at the same time. He swigged from it again, then farmer-blew one nostril onto the street. Graced by the old Glenn at last, Alistair found him much less appealing.

"So what did you tell that reporter? About what makes the perfect Whores song."

"I don't know," Alistair said. "The usual BS."

Glenn looked at him fiercely, his eyes narrowed into cracks. "Tell me," he demanded.

Alistair cleared his throat. He felt strangely inadequate. "The song has to be short. Under two minutes."

"What else?"

"It's simple. Three chords. Anyone can play it."

> **Sure enough, Stew was lying in his terrarium, coiled around a dead rat.**

Glenn nodded, hugging the bottle to his chest as if he were slow dancing with it. "It has some mistakes in it. Don't forget the fucking mistakes!"

"That's what makes it good," Alistair said.

"Fuck good," Glenn said. "It has to feel unstoppable."

"That's what makes it feel unstoppable."

Glenn snapped his fingers. "And then it's over. Just like that. Before you even expect it."

Later, Vladimir drove the four of them to the motel, bouncing on his hemorrhoid pillow every time he stopped at a red light. Alistair helped Glenn up to their room, then deposited him on one of the beds and went to brush his teeth. Emerging from the bathroom, Alistair was confronted with Glenn's naked body. He'd removed all his clothes but had failed to get himself under the covers. Amazing, how time seemed to stop in the presence of a naked body, no matter what condition it was in. Glenn was flat on his back and yet his belly still looked large, weirdly autonomous, perched on top of him like a sleeping pet. His breasts, if that's what they were called, sagged to either side of him. His toenails were topographical: thick and yellow and rippled like clamshells. His pubic hair had turned gray. Alistair sat on his own bed but couldn't take his eyes off Glenn. Alistair's pubic hair was still brown. Maybe it was the bourbon sogging up his brain, but the white wisp of hair on Glenn's balls moved him deeply.

Glenn seemed to stop breathing for a moment, turning strange and red-faced, before gasping back to life. He'd forgotten his sleep apnea machine. Alistair got the mask from the bedside table and untangled the elastic straps. It smelled a tiny bit rank, like the sourdough starter his mother used to keep in the fridge. The hose was misted up inside from Glenn's breath. You could see the actual beads of mist. Kneeling by the bed, Alistair lifted Glenn's head with one hand and fit the mask over his face, snugly, and turned on the air.

In the morning, amazingly, Glenn was still there. Alistair had assumed, once he'd sobered up, that he'd go out at the crack of dawn and try to score. But he was lying nakedly on top of the covers, snoring inside his mask.

Alistair got out of bed, nursing a hangover, and shivered into his jeans, careful not to wake Glenn. His shoulder throbbed. He went out to the van to look for his Advil. It was gray and foggy out, the marine layer carrying a whiff of salt. Vladimir, awake already and grinning like a maniac, was sitting on the rear scuff plate of the van, holding Stew's terrarium in his lap. His hands were black with grime.

"I found him!" he said, beaming.

Sure enough, Stew was lying in his terrarium, coiled around a dead rat. He was beginning to swallow the rat's head, which was several times larger than his own. Alistair kept his distance.

"He was hiding under the floor panel," Vladimir said.

"Didn't you look there already?"

"He was coiled under the spare. Happy as can be. Had to take the whole fucking tire out."

Alistair stared at the python, which as far as he could tell seemed no happier or sadder than before. How could you even tell the difference? Vladimir scooted over and patted the space beside him. Alistair sat down. Obligingly, without making a sound, Stew tipped his head back and began to eat the rat whole, shaking it painstakingly down his throat, hind legs sliding into his mouth until all you could see was the rat's tail sticking out like a demonic pink tongue.

The sun, shining weakly through the fog, warmed Alistair's head. He'd been appalled the other time he'd seen Stew eat a rat, but sitting there with Vladimir, watching the snake, he felt a strange hush of relief. Nothing was expected of him—not even enjoyment. Stew choked down the rat's tail, bit by bit, as if he were eating his own tongue. He seemed unaware that there was an audience at all. Vladimir offered Alistair a hit from his vaporizer, then looked surprised when he said yes. It felt like a breath of sunlight. The snake didn't move for a long time, an inch of tail sticking out of his mouth like a toothpick. Alistair wondered if the performance was over, feeling suddenly ashamed, but of course it wasn't a performance. It was just his life.

Per Aage Brandt
translated by Thom Satterlee

100

I once wrote a little song
on the sunrise, for a political
rock band, and I seem to recall
the sun's rising being a meaningful
occurrence in the historical perspective,
deserving of a song; the sheet music fell
out of a moving box recently and is
now somewhere behind the piano;
concerning the sun, it still rises
every once in a while

From *Elegi. Poesi*

99

no it's not quite as easy as
you might think at first to
regain your breath when the
black nothingness sinks its
claws into people you carry
inside yourself including heart
lungs sexual parts brain and
all organs of sensation also
their sorrow rain wind fire
earth fire sorrow wind light

98

spring started today, according to my calendar,
and what would we do without it, when big
decisions have to be made, like spring, we must
know what the day is called, and what it should
be used for, whose name it bears, and which
deity we should praise, worship, and celebrate,
whether it's found on other people's calendars
and here, naming the same heavenly names; time
is the principle of our principles, the feast dwells here
and thought, everything we share; tomorrow: spring

97

while the presidents smash away at those stubborn cities,
the ladies take bubble baths in their rosy pink apartments,
and life goes on, people give speeches in the squares,
if the electricity allows for it, or play cards on the sidewalk,
if the snipers allow for it, otherwise in the basements,
whose rats know nothing about the conditions affecting our
species, these cannot be recommended, the problem is
water and food supplies, corpses in the street, the problem is
dread, including the one that turns young human bodies
into the president's dazed killers, who haven't got a clue

He would have let it be—the elk calf hunkered in the shadow of the fallen pine, motionless but for its frightened eyes—if, a hundred yards farther on, he hadn't found its mother. Her eyes were gone: red holes opened to the sun. Her belly, too: bowels spilling a mess of wet green grass. It was late enough in spring that the aspens in the lower elevations had burst into new leaf, filled the valleys with sudden sweeps of viridescent clouds, but up here they were still white stripes against dark pines, gray branches barely showing buds. He'd been on his morning walk, cutting through the woods beside his pasture, climbing over a half-rotted trunk, when he stumbled on the calf—stepped on it, actually: sudden soft life beneath his boot. It squeaked. How strange that a noise he'd never heard before should seem so familiar, that something in him— his whole body had jerked back—should so immediately know the sound.

Now he listened for it through the silence of the trees. No breeze, the morning still too shivery for flies. And how long had it been hiding? How hungry might it be? Could it have survived the night, the cold, coyotes? Something had tugged out the elk cow's entrails, eaten a hole in the chest, but the blood was pooled freshly in there, the meat of the haunches and neck untouched. A few hours, he thought; the calf might not even know yet. Then he thought of the hours to come, the day getting hot, the night bringing the cold, whatever had brought the mother down coming back.

Returning up the hill, he stirred a crow; it clattered away through the branches. Maybe it was that, or maybe some carcass smell clung to him, but when he reached the calf again it panicked, pushing itself up, its legs unfolding, all thinness and length, wobbling on bulging knees beneath a body that seemed somehow to become smaller as it rose. It faced him straight on, shaking.

"You okay?" he said.

Its squeak was like some child's squeeze toy. It couldn't weigh much more than a toddler. He didn't know till right then why he had come back.

"You're okay," he said, reaching for it.

But when he touched it he heard his son—Hal, in his first year, still too small to stand—squeezing; he could feel his son's hands squeezing. His chest pooled with blood. He drew his own hands back.

The calf's eyes were on him, huge and black.

"You'll be okay," he told it, looking away.

A year ago, when he'd moved out here, fifty miles from any supermarket, almost a hundred to the hospital, a thousand from the home he and Janet had sold, when he had bought the old ranch house nearly nine thousand feet up in mountains that climbed another four thousand all around, everyone who heard he'd come—which was everyone, which wasn't many—told him he'd want a dog—for company, they said, or to keep the coyotes at bay—or, once word got around about who he was, just came by with puppies in their trucks, got out presenting them like gifts. But he didn't want a dog. Or a cat. Or a horse. Or sheep. The old couple who'd sold him the hundred-plus acres had wanted him to buy their livestock, too; then, when he'd agreed to take the house still full of furniture, they offered to throw the animals in for free. But he'd refused. Said he wouldn't know what to do, didn't want the hassle. He thought the woman looked at him with pity, preferred the glance her husband gave him: How busy did he think that he—out here, alone, already retired and barely over fifty—could be?

> **How busy did he think that he—out here, alone, already retired and barely over fifty—could be?**

There were the fence lines: he inspected them weekly, walking the perimeter of his empty acreage, the pasture already clumping with sage, nothing moving in the wide open around his home but wheatgrass in the wind, the occasional startled hare sprinting away from him. In June the real ranch down the dirt road moved its herd onto the Forest Service land and by July the far side of the barbed wire would be grazed down, looking more lived on, cared for, than his. Which it was. He'd listen to the cattle lowing to each other, watch the bull calves play, tell himself, each time he fixed a section of the fence, that he should simply let it fall, tell the neighbors they could let their livestock in, would one day soon. But each day there were the geraniums to water; Janet had brought them—the only plant in the house—the one time she'd come out. There were the swallows' nests to knock down from the eaves; he went around with a long pole breaking up their mud homes before they could complete them. Last year, he'd waited too long—*fleas*, the mail woman had told him, handing him his package, standing in the doorway of the low log house—and the first he'd struck had crumbled over his head, tiny speckled eggs smashing to the ground around him. He'd stood there, the splattered bits of half-formed things still twitching at his feet, his eyes shut tight, shaking. He'd started taking photographs again. Lugging his old 4x5 box camera on hard-breathing, chest-hurting climbs, sometimes all the way up to the snow. By late September it would be falling on his home. And then there'd be the work that came with winter—shoveling, splitting—though he had gas heat, paid a plowman and, the truth was, what he'd done most of the months he'd lived here was read.

> **What was the first time he'd seen his son stirred by a book, by something true in it?**

When they'd moved—Janet into a two-bedroom in Santa Barbara, him to here—he'd taken so little from their sold home he wouldn't have needed the U-Haul if it hadn't been for Hal's books. Eleven heavy boxes. Half of them what Hal had brought back from Berkeley before going overseas, but, still, how had he read so much in just twenty-three years? Sixteen, really, since he started reading to himself. Maybe a dozen since stepping up from Hardy Boys to . . . What was the first time he'd seen his son stirred by a book, by something true in it? The basement: he'd found the boy—nine? ten?—sobbing. His son had made himself a nest out of old Jackson's bed, stored unwashed since the dog had died some months before, surrounded by his dad's old darkroom equipment, the trays stacked with books, the enlarger used for light, the red lamp meant to, in Hal's words, *do the mood*. Open on his lap: *Where the Red Fern Grows*. Though maybe his son had been moved by another first. *Island of the Blue Dolphins. Sing Down the Moon.* He had found them both on the shelves in Hal's room, the small boy's shaky handwriting inside: *Ex Líbra: Henry*. Each time he opened one of the books now and saw that small error—"bra" where there should have been "bris," his son's library become, instead, a sign in the stars—it made him smile. And when, sometime in his teenage years, the boy had discovered his mistake, started writing *Ex Libris* instead. And when, sometime after Hal became a man, he began—he could see his son smiling while he uncapped his pen—writing *Ex Libra* again. A dozen years, or sixteen, or twenty-three: What did it matter? It was all so unfathomably, horribly, short.

He started at the end, reading the books his son had bought in the year before he left. *The Q'ran Interpreted, From Beirut to Jerusalem*. He read a book by a journalist who'd been held hostage and survived, another about a photographer who didn't. After one, he couldn't sleep; after the other, he didn't want to. The nightmares woke him sheetless and sweaty, his breath short, his heart frantic. He would turn on the lamp the old couple had left, amber beads rattling when he pushed the switch, reach to the floor to draw their heavy quilt back over him, open up another book, and begin to read. In the morning he sat in the green vinyl glider, or outside on a section of split-rail fence that hadn't yet collapsed. He read everything Hal had saved from his year of J-school, then backward through his four at Kenyon, all but the Arabic language books: those he read in order, along with the workbooks Hal had hung onto, laying clean pieces of copy paper over each, tracing his son's ح and ل, his penciled sentences of flowing script, learning less the language than how his son's fingers moved, until by winter he had become fluent in Hal's handwriting. هال. Hal. He had chosen the name for himself, come home one day in second grade and simply requested over after-school snack that they call him that instead of Henry. Harder to know exactly when he'd read which novels, what books he'd picked up for pleasure in what part of his life, but they were all there, some clearly from college, others from summers spent reading about barnstormers, bomber crews, a time before then—it must have lasted longer than the others—when newly christened Hal had read nothing but stories of trappers and herders, histories of Indian chiefs and cavalry campaigns. But before then? Back when he'd still been Henry? Henry, who, for a while, had loved only books about dogs.

Next time, Janet said the last time she'd called—the last time she'd called that he'd answered—*you'll be reading Curious George. Or Goodnight Moon.*

Goodnight, wife, he said.

Frank, she said, *sooner or later you're going to get down to his board books, start chewing corners.*

But she was wrong. He was on Jack London now—these dog Westerns that only this week he'd realized must have been the bridge—and he could already feel it ending in him, that soon he would have to begin something else. *Something that will make him proud of you*, Janet had said, *when he comes back.*

Now he couldn't even get through a single page. *The Call of the Wild*. It would have made him laugh if he wasn't wondering how many hours an elk calf could survive without its mother's milk. At the computer, he checked the weather: thirty-two tonight. He tried to think of what he might search for to find out if the scent of the mother would cover the scent of the calf. He typed in *carcass*. His fingers hovered.

In the barn, he searched among the rubber trays and plastic bins, trash cans shut tight around half-empty feed sacks. He hadn't been in there since the first days after the old couple had gone, when, sorting through the things they'd left, he found a box full of what looked like babies' bottles. And, inside one of the bins, a bag of something labeled *Sav-A-lam*.

This time he took the truck. Forest Service gravel to a two-track that branched off into the brushy grass, his windows down and the tires rumbling and the smells of pine and sage and sweet warm milk. Whisking the powder into the hot water, he had wanted to drink it, it smelled so good. And getting out of the truck into the still chill midday air, the warmth of the bottle felt good in his hand. The slope dropped away, rocks and dry lichen tumbling down into a swale of bright green grass and brighter dandelion blooms and on the other side rose again into the thin woods of high-country pines. Above them, buzzards circled. The raspy, nasal *kaks* of magpies. The mother's carcass had been dragged a little farther out of the trees.

Climbing through the entanglement of saplings and downed trunks he startled something large, a swatch of gray breaking away, becoming fur before it disappeared from where he'd last seen the calf. But when he got there it was alive, curled beneath the limbs of a log, its pale-speckled back rising and falling with quick breaths.

"Hey there." Crouching, he held the bottle out. "You want some?" He lowered the rubber teat through a gap in the broken branches. "Milk." It stared at him and he told himself to stop talking, eased the bottle closer. The calf watched the red tip like it was some carrion bird's beak. He nudged the nipple against its lips. It jerked its head away. The bottle was warm in his hand, but plastic, hard, so different, he thought, from the soft flesh of its mother's udder. *The boob*, Janet had called it. *The boob cometh*, she would tell their baby when he was hungry. She would lift her shirt and say, as if her sole role in life was to present her breasts, *Behold the boob!* The tiny being would latch on, eyes staring into hers, small hand softly pawing her chest. Sometimes he'd wished he had something like that to give his son. *Take them*, Janet had said. *I'll swap them to you every night.* He would have. Even with the waking, the night nursing, the lack of sleep. Janet wouldn't let him use a bottle, didn't want to get their baby used to its unnatural ease. Watching the calf turn its head back and forth to escape the nipple, he thought, *ease*, and, before a smile could take shape, the missing her swept over him so hard he had to shut his eyes. When he opened them he saw a thread of milk was dribbling onto the calf's forehead, the fur there dark and wet. He lifted the bottle away, sat back. Above, the pine tops shifted, clouds rolling in, some bird circling. The far-off sound of a high-up plane. He found its jet trail. What was he doing here? What gave him the right? He shut his eyes. The contrail cut its way across the inside of his lids, the bird circled, circled. His son was dead. For over a year now he had known it, said it, silently, to himself, *My son is dead.* And then, out here, no one to hear but him, he had said it aloud: *He's dead.* While standing over the red slits of the toaster. *He's dead.*

> **He thought he would now leave nature alone. Let it take its course.**

While watching the moon through the window at one or two or three in the morning. *He's dead, he's dead, he's dead.*

"Well," he said to the calf. Pushed himself up. The pine needles had pressed red creases into his palm; in his other the bottle was barely warm. *Unnatural*, he thought. He thought he would now leave nature alone. Let it take its course. He thought he would tell the calf he was sorry, but when he started to crouch again the trembling thing let out one of its little squeaks and he had to turn away.

He was halfway across the swale when a gust brought the elk cow's smell. He could see it at the ravine's edge, the carcass now opened to glints of ribs, the hole in the belly eaten back to the hips, and that was what stopped him: the memory of how lightly mauled it had been that morning. Surely a bear would have eaten more; a lion would have ripped up the neck. Coyotes would have dragged it down in a pack. And wouldn't a pack have done more damage?

Standing over it, he looked for signs of mange, or of a disease the rancher down the road simply called *wasting*. But its haunch was muscled, its neck fur full. He wondered if it could have died giving birth, but then why would the calf not be beside it? In the cow's neck there was a puncture from a tooth.

Except, crouching closer, he couldn't find a second hole. And wouldn't there be two? Unless—he watched a fly find the wound, dip its forelegs into the darkness there—it was from a bullet. He didn't own a gun, had never shot one, didn't know whether the hole was too big or small, but he knew that if it had entered the throat on this side it would have had to leave out the other. The stench was too strong; he had to stand up again. He walked away as much to breathe as to break off a dead branch, returned with his windbreaker collar cinched over his nose, the stick in his hand. But the neck was too heavy to move. He tried prying the underside up enough to see, knelt down, his face too close to what had spilled on the ground, then, finally, wishing he'd brought a pair of gloves, he threw the stick aside, shoved up his sleeves, and straining at the neck with one hand, with the other felt beneath. The cold, congealed gunk of the fur, the weight of muscle that had once held itself, the sudden dip of his fingertip into a wet spot of sucking nothing—he jerked his arm free, snatched his hand back, stood.

> **They had made two videos, the men who killed his son.**

A female. A female in spring. Inside the windbreaker collar, his breath came warm and thick. In calving season. The fabric crackled, clung to his mouth, crackled. And whoever it had been hadn't even wanted the meat. Had just wanted to shoot something. He took another step away, yanked the windbreaker off his face. What part of nature was that?

His hand was sticky with blood. He stood looking for somewhere to wipe it and then he backed into the thicker grass and crouched and put his hands in it and he was pulling at it, ripping, crushing dandelion heads in his fists, a man on his hands and knees surrounded by a thousand yellow blooms, the air swirling with seed puffs released around him.

They had made two videos, the men who killed his son. The first four years ago: it was how he and Janet found out Hal had been taken. Their boy looked into the camera with his eyes the brown of his mother's and the shape of his father's and said their names, and then said other things Frank had thought he had not been able to hear but found afterward he could repeat verbatim—every word about this country and that religion and their demands—in his head. For almost a year. Until the second video. In that one, Hal was wearing a blindfold. Beside him: another boy, blindfolded too. This time only the man with the knife talked. He walked back and forth behind the two boys kneeling before him, grabbing first one by the hair, then the other, letting one's chin fall while he switched to stretch the other's neck. Hal had grown a beard. He had never seen his son with a beard. It was blond. The man yanked Hal's head back and he had seen the small curls like gold shavings on his son's throat and then the man dropped Hal's head and wrenched the other boy's and, holding that boy's neck skin taut, sawed. When he was done he took Hal's blindfold off and, with his bloody hands in their son's blond beard, turned his face to make him see the body. Then he said, to the camera, *This one is next*. He said things after that, too, but this time those words were all that Frank remembered. He had not watched the video again. Except in his mind, his nightmares, where he could not stop seeing what seeing that had done to his son's soft, brown eyes.

The bottle had half fallen from his jacket pocket: it tilted, nipple bent against the ground, slowly flooding the grass. He could feel the milk, cooled now, reach his hand. Sitting back, he looked at his fingers, his palm. The blood was still there, though it was mixed now with dirt and grass and the downy seedpods and the milk. The milk that smelled so sweet. Stronger even than the blood. The milk—he could feel his heart still beating unnaturally fast—that he had leaked onto the elk calf.

By the time he reached it, his breath was coming hard from the quickness of the climb, but his heart had slowed. He waited for his breathing to calm, too. Then he reached down and slid his arms beneath its trembling body and lifted.

"You what?" Janet said.

"It wasn't heavy," he told her, "just hard to hold."

Every few steps it had struggled, its legs flailing, his arms so worn out from gripping it against his chest that by the time he reached the truck he wasn't sure if, back home, he'd be able to lift it out again, though he did, and got it into the barn, and shut the door, and came in here and called his wife.

"I wasn't asking *how*," she said.

Standing by the phone, wrapping the old corkscrew cord around his free hand, he knew she wasn't asking *what* either. They used to understand each other. Could tell from a glance at the other's eyes what sort of mood their teenage son, come home from rehearsal, or a meet, or a date, was in. Could tell, waking beside the other's sleepless stirring, whether to reach for reading lamp and book or restless hand and bare thigh. In grad school he would start setting up a shot before she'd finished describing it; in the editing room, she'd lean over his shoulder and comment on some detail of lighting or composition he'd thought no one would ever see. Even after she found her path producing documentaries and he took the safer one of teaching, they had still understood those parts of each other's lives that they no longer lived together. Still did. So long as it was anything that didn't have to do with Hal. Which was nothing.

"I just thought . . ." he started. But what had he thought? That, together, they would figure out what to do? The way they used to? The two of them who now couldn't figure out how to move their lives ahead together, how to stay living together, how to *live*? She wouldn't have sold their home if he hadn't needed to; she wouldn't have changed anything. When she moved into her new place she moved everything—the too-soft couch, the rusty weight bench; she reconstructed Hal's room almost exactly. Down to the bookshelves Frank had emptied. Her new place was half the size. When he'd last been there—months ago, January, the week Hal would have turned twenty-five—it had been as if the walls of their old home had shifted inward, the space between all their old things shrunk; he couldn't take a step, turn around, *move*, without brushing up against what their life had been.

"I mean," she said now, "what are you going to *do* with a baby elk?"

"I'm not going to keep it," he told her.

"Then—"

"That's why I called you."

"You want to raise it?"

"No."

"Then what?" In the background he could hear music. "Make steaks?"

When was the last time he had listened to music? He couldn't remember. He couldn't remember ever having listened to music in this house.

Maybe she sensed his thought—it wouldn't have surprised him—because, in her house, she shut the music off.

"Oh, Frank," she said, her voice quieter, the silence after it quieter. "Am I the only person you've talked to?"

"This month?"

"Frank," she said again, "you need to talk to someone."

"That's what I'm—"

"Someone there. Someone who *knows*." She took a drink of something. "I mean, is it even supposed to have milk?" A beer, he thought. "The same milk as a lamb?" A Lebanese Pale Ale. "And what about disease?" The summer

Hal came home from Beirut he'd brought them bottles of the spiced beer—za'atar, sumac, chamomile, mint—poured it over cracking ice, couldn't contain his pleasure when, despite their skepticism, his parents loved it. "Something it could give you?" That summer he'd been twenty-one and they'd driven three hours to Fresno, in a heat wave, to the only Middle Eastern store that stocked the beer, and cleaned it out, and drank LPAs over ice each afternoon for two weeks straight. "Or you might give it?" And then taken Hal back to the Oakland airport, their suddenly grown son who'd become the one introducing them to new things. "Or, I mean"—their son, who, that afternoon standing curbside at departures, they had held for the last time—"what if it's already eating grass and maybe it's old enough it could have survived on its own and you—"

"Is that a beer?" he asked.

She took another sip. "Sweetie," she said, "it's not your fault, but you don't really know anything, here."

"Well—"

"I mean, you can't be certain, you can't be *sure*, of anything."

"Well, what would you have done?"

> **He couldn't remember ever having listened to music in this house.**

In her silence he could hear her thinking: *stayed here, kept hoping, not given up*. But he had had to. That was the one thing—the everything—she could not understand. Three years since the second video. Though there had been a third a few months later, without their son in it, with only the same man saying the same things to the same people, except somewhere in there also saying that Hal had been killed. Frank hadn't seen it, hadn't needed to, had listened to the woman from the State Department say *not yet verified* and *unconfirmed* and understood what was beneath the words. What became inescapable as the months passed, and then a year, and then another. Though not for Janet. She did watch the video. Then she watched all the others the group had made. Over the months that he was coming to grips with never seeing his son again, she was watching and reading and researching everything about the men who she still hoped were holding Hal, who he had come to know were not, to know in his soul, to *need* to know it, so that he could begin to grieve. So when she had begun to make a movie of it—her search, her struggle—to record on film her endless efforts to find their son, on clips she posted to the website she maintained, he understood it was a call for help, a plea to the rest of the world not to forget, he understood, but could not live with it.

The Elk-Calf

Over on the edge of the Pacific Ocean, she swallowed, swallowed again. A clink. "*Was* a beer," she said. Then: "Did you get my message?"

"Which one?"

"Oh any of them. All of them."

Maybe he had not listened to music here, but he had drunk beer. He wished he had a bottle in front of him now. He wished he had three. "Sure," he said.

"The last one?" she asked. "The one about reports of an unknown—"

"In Afghanistan," he said. Hal had been captured by a group that had since joined another group, which had since been disbanded, or defeated, or whatever it was, was gone, which had all happened in Yemen and Syria and the Sinai and now he asked her, his voice tired as if he *had* drunk three beers, "Why, would he be in Afghanistan?"

"I told you," she said.

And she had. In the last message. Which he had deleted before hearing most of it. The way he had deleted the others that she had left in the months since they'd last talked, since he'd asked her not to call again, or send him e-mails, or contact him at all unless she wanted to talk about *her*, about *them. About when we'll have a fucking funeral*, he'd said, *a fucking memorial service*, and she'd hung up.

> **He had wrapped the cord around his hand so tightly his fingers had gone numb.**

He had wrapped the cord around his hand so tightly his fingers had gone numb. "Do we really have to do this?" he said, and spent the whole time it took to unwind the cord waiting for her to decide.

"Is that the wind?" she said.

He told her it was.

"Are you doing any photography?"

He told her he was. Landscapes. Mountains, valleys, that sort of thing. The sort of thing he used to think was dull. Maybe it still was. Maybe that was just what he wanted now.

"Good," she said. "It's about time. You're too good to stop shooting forever."

He didn't tell her he hadn't set up the darkroom. That the enlarger and bins and reels and tanks were all still in boxes. That the freezer was full of negatives he hadn't even developed yet.

"And you?" he said, because he had to.

There was the sound of traffic. Standing in the ranch house with the wind rattling the windows and whistling through some faulty chinking in the logs, the sounds of traffic seemed like something from a different world, a different life.

"Call a vet," she told him. "Or isn't there a ranger or something?"

"I'll ask Ron," he said.

"Who?"

"The rancher who lives down the road."

She laughed.

"What?" he said.

But when she spoke her voice was as full of sadness as he felt. "Sometimes I forget you're actually out there."

"I'm here," he said.

"Sometimes it's like you *can't* be in Colorado, you *can't* be not coming home."

"I love you," he said. She was breathing in a way that didn't seem to let her say anything back. "Janet?"

He could tell—amazing, wasn't it?—that she was nodding. "Send me a picture," she said before she hung up.

Outside, the day had changed, fast, the way he had grown used to up here, the snow-bright peaks of the distant massif set sharp against dark cloudbanks of a northward-lunging sky. With each gust a loose strip of tin banged at the barn roof. He crossed the yard toward it, windbreaker hood whipping behind his head, a fresh bottle of milk replacer in his hand. By the time he ducked inside, the mountains had disappeared behind a sheeting rain; he heard it hit: a blast of hail battering the roof. Well, he thought, shucking his hood, she couldn't tell him it wasn't good he'd gotten the calf in out of this. She couldn't tell him he couldn't be sure of that. It was warmer in the stall, the wind a thing that roved and roared behind the walls, the floor old straw and droppings decomposed halfway to dust, and he wondered if it still held horse smell and what the calf must think of that and then—there it was in the shadow against the far wall—what it must think of him. For a while, long enough the battering of the hail softened to a rumbling rain, they stood there watching each other. Then the elk calf took a step. Toward him. Another.

"Hey, girl," he said—it seemed to him it was a she, thank God—and, holding out the fingers of his free hand, he stood still and let it come. Its muzzle was soft on his knuckles; its breath tickled. The fur of its neck was fuzzy and when it cocked its ears toward him he could see they were as white inside as milkweed pods. On its forehead, where he'd spilled the replacer, its hair had clumped. Slowly, gently, he brushed it free with his fingertips. For a second, the calf seemed to consider whether that should make it shrink back, and then, instead, it pressed its head into his hand. He let his palm slip over its forehead, down its neck, along the darker hair ridging its spine, all the way to its tiny fluff of tail. Which twitched. Before the calf leaned all its small weight against him.

This was why nature made them like this, these newborn things, so that you had no choice but to want to help them. He could still remember the first time he'd held Hal, the wonder of it; why should he have loved so much something that he'd known so little? Why should it not stay that way? His son had grown and his love had grown with him and why had nature made it so that it wasn't the same with everything? So that this calf when it became a cow wouldn't stir him even more strongly? So that his baby when he became a man wouldn't stir other men in such a way that they could not bear to harm him?

He sat in the straw. The elk calf sniffed at his face, licked his cheeks. Sometimes he couldn't believe he was still here, either. Sometimes he couldn't believe he wasn't going home. If only she hadn't shown Hal how she hunted out the truth in documentaries; if she hadn't glowed so when their son told them he'd been inspired to do the same abroad; if she hadn't used her connections to help him get there: he knew it wasn't her fault, he knew it, but the truth was, the reason he was here, the reason he couldn't go back to her, had as much to do with his inability to let go as hers.

The rain quieted. And then there was just the wind. And him, sitting in old straw and dung, holding on to the elk calf as if it could somehow help him.

At first it wouldn't take the bottle. It tried to turn away, and when he tried to turn its face back, it struggled free and, slowly, he followed it around the stall, until, cornering it, gripping its muzzle in one hand, keeping his fingers clear of its small teeth, he managed to wedge the nipple into its mouth, squeeze out a little. Not much—it pulled away, shook its head, spattered him with drops—but some. That was how it went, then, until he'd gotten enough into it he thought it would at least have the energy to stay warm. With the pitchfork he gathered hay, pushed it into a corner. Then, cupping his arms under the calf, he picked it up and nested it into the pile—from where it rose immediately and, wobbling on its long legs, chose its own corner of bare dirt.

While he stared at it the light that came through the old barn window slowly brightened, the weather changing again, the fringe around the calf's ears, the wet gleam of its nose, the white spots on its back, beginning to glow.

He was crossing the kitchen to get his camera when he heard the beep of the answering machine. He looked at it—little flashing light—then turned back to the Hasselblad, lifted it off the table. Passing the phone again he said to it, "*You* wanted a picture." The machine chirped back at him. He told it, "I'm only doing what you asked," turned the handle to the mudroom door. That beep. "Shit," he said.

In the message, her voice was tight—"So I looked on the Internet"—somehow too sharp for this house—"and"—she took a quick breath—"it turns out that mother elks, in the morning, when they go off to graze, they don't take their calves with them."

He could still remember the first time he'd held Hal, the wonder of it.

He set the camera on the counter.

"It turns out," her voice said while he reached to the dish rack for a glass, "they leave them. Hiding."

He held the glass under the faucet.

"They're born with almost no smell," the machine went on, "and those spots for camouflage. So they can hide all day. Where their mother left them."

Carrying the glass into the dining room, he tipped it over the geranium pot—"Until she returns at dusk," he heard, "to retrieve them"—and only then realized he had never filled it, never turned the faucet on.

"So," Janet's voice said into his empty house, over him holding the empty glass, "what if that wasn't its mother? What if it was just a dead elk? I mean . . ."

The phone rang.

". . . what if you took it and now . . ."

And rang.

". . . when its mother comes back . . ."

He snatched the receiver.

". . . she can't . . ."

The Elk-Calf

"Janet—" he said.

"...find him."

In the silence, his wife said, "Frank..." But it was from the message. On the line there was a man's voice: "Frank?"

He shut the answering machine off.

"Frank Hayes?" the man said.

"Sorry," Frank said. "I thought..."

"That's all right."

Frank looked at the empty glass still in his hand. "Who is this?"

"Cliff Rutland," the man said. "Parks and Wildlife." The glass, when Frank set it down, seemed to clink too loud. "District manager. Your wife—"

"Did Janet call you?"

"Well she called Doc Carter. He told her to call the sheriff. Gene called me."

Frank could hear the man waiting for him to say something. "Is Doc Carter a vet?"

"Sure, Doc Carter," the man said. Then he said, "Do I understand right that you've got a elk calf in your barn?"

Frank turned back to the geranium, the window, the barn out there framed in it.

"Mr. Hayes," the wildlife manager said, "you're gonna have to trust me a little here, all right?"

He was going to have to put the calf back. The manager said it was the only thing to do. He said it was better off out where its mother might come get it, or the herd might take care of it. He said it took training to raise a wild creature so it could be returned to its natural state and the rehab centers weren't taking elk for fear of wasting disease and, anyway, it was illegal—"a violation of the law," the man said—for Frank to keep it.

A hummingbird had come to the window. It hovered there, in front of the geranium, a couple inches from the bright red blossoms.

"I wasn't going to keep it," Frank said.

A couple inches and a pane of glass.

The manager said he understood about the bullet hole, the carcass, why Frank had done it. He said he'd come by early in the morning and they could go out there together and he'd inspect the dead cow and see if he could find a bullet or some brass up on the road and if the calf was still there he'd take it and try to find a place for it.

> **The manager said he understood about the bullet hole, the carcass, why Frank had done it.**

"And if you can't?" Frank asked.

"The important thing," the manager said, "is that you get it back there before dusk. So the herd has a chance—"

"So you think the carcass is its mother?"

"Might be."

"And the herd, if it finds it, it'll take care of it?"

"Might."

"And if not? It'll survive the night? I mean the cold?"

"Well . . ." the man said.

"The coyotes?"

". . . I'll come out in the morning and we'll see."

The hummingbird was still there, drawn from bloom to bloom to bloom, darting at and away from the glass.

"And if I don't take it back?" Frank said.

"Yeah"—the man sighed like he'd been waiting the whole conversation for that—"then I'll come out in the morning, anyway."

When they were done, Frank set down the phone and carried the water glass to the sink and filled it and drank it empty. Some brass, the man had said, up on the road. Bullet casings. Left by whoever had shot the mother. From the road, the warden guessed, from inside some truck, just rolled down the window. Must have missed the jugular. The cow must have fled, her lungs filling with blood, run almost all the way back to where, that morning, she'd left her calf. Where, now, he was supposed to leave it again. He thought about the morning, what he and the warden would find: an eagle feasting on its entrails, a crow fishing with its beak inside the hole of its eye, or maybe it was so small it would be dragged and scattered and they would find nothing. It would not survive the night—of that he was sure—and he could not help but see the fear come into its eyes, feel its trembling, hear the squeaking beneath the snarling of coyotes closing in. And if it did somehow survive? If it didn't die from cold? The warden would take it, take it far enough away that Frank wouldn't hear when he lifted it out of his truck again and put his pistol to its skull and shot it. He thought about how he was already breaking the law, how he could try to hide the calf in the barn, or take it back but lead the warden to a different spot, thought about the absence, then, of the mother's carcass, and, staring down into last night's dishes, the remnants of a life that had not yet contained the calf, the dirty plate and soaking pan and carving knife, he thought that maybe that would be the kindest thing: no long hours alone in the dark, no coyote pack pulling limb from limb, just him holding it on his lap out in the dry hay of the warm barn while he slit its throat.

He backed away from the sink. Over by the geranium, the hummingbird was gone. Through the window, the barn was still there. On the phone, the message light glowed red, the rest of his wife's words trapped unheard inside it.

Back in the stall, staring through the viewfinder at the calf, he knew he could never have done it. The window light lit the thin skin of its nostrils so they seemed to glow from inside, the sun sculpting the fine bones of its face, the high dome of its forehead and delicate bridge of its nose and the brittle crescents above its eyes. He was wrong about its eyes: they weren't all pupil, all black. In them, now, he could see the thinnest ring of deep, warm brown. He could not even take the picture. His wife would just have to live with what her mind imagined.

Instead, back in the kitchen, he did the dishes while the milk was warming. When it reached a hundred degrees he poured it into the bottle again. By clamping an arm around the narrow neck, using that hand to grip the muzzle, working his thumb and fingers in—the teeth little more than ridges of gum, the tongue a warm worrying against his skin—he managed to wedge the rubber teat into the side of the elk calf's mouth. He watched the soft fur of its throat. Swallow by swallow, he got the milk in. Each time it took a little more he told it how good it was, how well it was doing. In between attempts, when they were both resting, he whispered to it about how much strength the milk would give it, how strong it would need to be. He sat, holding it against its struggling, stroking it when it was calm, until half of the milk was gone. The window light deepened. Through the panes he could see the streaks of swallows starting to flit into the sky.

It was an hour before the sun would set when he drove the elk calf back. The swale was in shadow now, the grass dark, the dandelions scattered like so many stars. As he made his way down, his arms clenched around the calf, it struggled so much that by the time he crossed the bottom and started up the other side, his forearms were aching, his biceps feeling about to rip, a good pain: the calf stronger, it seemed, suddenly full of life. He took it as far toward where he'd found it as he could manage, then, when his arms at last gave out, set it down, let it stand, stepped back. He thought it would turn to watch him, worried it might try to follow when he went, but it just started up the hillside, picking its way over branches and scrub, working toward the place where, that morning, or the night before, its mother had let it know to wait.

Breaking back out into the meadow above where its mother now lay, he caught a movement—some winged thing rising—and stopped. At the edge of the woods the carcass looked smaller than he'd remembered. Maybe it had just been eaten away, but, standing there, it seemed to him it might not even have been a full-grown female. He tried to remember if he had seen an udder, any sign of nursing teats. The stomach had been too torn up to tell. Suddenly, the evening air cool around him, he felt sure it wasn't the mother. All along the hillside there had been elk scat, the duff churned with hoofprints: the herd would come back, her probably with it. He turned to look at the slope behind him, stared for a long time, saw no sign of the calf. Just the last light catching the branches of the aspens near the top. Up there, where they got more sun, they were beginning to leaf out, a green that seemed almost too bright for nature. But there it was, aglow against the dusking sky.

> **He was wrong about its eyes: they weren't all pupil, all black.**

The summer before Hal started first grade they had taken a road trip to see the Rockies, left right on the last day of kindergarten, found the mountains still filled with spring. Driving up into them was like rewinding time and when they came around a curve into a valley at nine thousand feet the sun was hitting the new-leafed aspens just like now. But there were thousands of them, acres, all aglow. Hal had been so thrilled they had to pull to the side of the road. As soon as they stopped, he burst out, ran breathlessly toward the rise from where he could see the widest view. It was one of the few times Frank had filmed his son: a six-year-old boy backed by a field of impossibly bright green, leaping with joy. How many times had he watched it in the past four years? Looking up at the last light on the trees, he watched it again. He could hear a far-off voice shouting—*Dad*, it said, *Dad, come see!*—and, listening, he knew that it would be all right, that in the morning they would find no sign of struggle, no sign at all, except, perhaps, a faint depression in the leaves where, for a time, a patch of earth had felt the presence of a slight weight.

That night he woke to the crying of coyotes. The moon was up and through his window he could see its light on the snow of the distant mountains, on the small straight scratches of the fence posts, the tin roof of the barn gleaming. He lay in his bed listening. Sharp barks built into howls, pinched yips slid into wavering, broke apart in frantic bursts, so many crowding upon each other they seemed shards of the same sound. He shut his eyes. They were feeding. If he held his eyes closed tight enough he could see them snarled over the old cow's carcass, far down at the edge of the dandelion swale, far away from the fallen tree on the upper reaches of that aspen-covered slope. He squeezed his lids harder, pressed the heels of his hands to his eyes, tried—arms aching, chest cramping, a terrible tightness clamping his throat—to convince himself that he could know.

Anna Journey

SUMMER OF CHOOSING THE DRESS

There can't be a right one
for this occasion. Not racy
chiffon, not crepe, not plain
cotton. My mother's best
friend, Donna, is dying. Her liver
has mutinied, has begun
to throw her overboard. Soon
she must choose a pattern, a color,
a cut. Once, I watched
my lover's roommate—a soldier
back from Iraq—leap screaming
from a couch to buzz
a bald stripe down the orange
spine of an alley cat
that had peed on his pillowcase. He
switched off the electric
razor, asked me, if I had to choose
fire or drowning, which
would be the best
way to go. I said probably
water. He said, *No.
Too slow*. I don't know why
he kept squirrel meat stacked
in the freezer next to the bags
of snow peas as if they belonged
together. I don't know what to do

except mark the weeks
by her chemo, wonder which
dress she'll pick. There isn't a best
choice, so I'll keep
her options open. Black cocktail
or a peach neckline low
as her alto. Calico climbing
her chest, her liver, entwined
as if all those
twisted roses could hold.

VICTORIAN CHAMBER POT MY MOTHER USED AS A PLANTER FOR CLIMBING IVY

Why I'd imagine phantom asses
floating over the television as a child:
that cast porcelain bowl sat on top
of the TV in the den for decades—
its fat ivory base, flared lip, and ear-
shaped handle. It looked
like a giant white teacup spilling
devil's ivy up the walls. The vine climbed
all the way to the ceiling's corner
before doubling back to the carpet. Before
I was born, my mother bought
the chamber pot for five bucks
at a flea market near Ottawa. At a cocktail
party that night she told a doctor
she was thinking of using it
as a soup tureen and he gagged
on his brandy, said the uric
acid could still be lodged
in the pot's hairline cracks. So, no gumbo
ever simmered in the antique
piss of Victorians, no molecular secret
fumed from my lips or escaped
the flawed glaze. I once waitressed
at a café in Richmond

that served its buffet brunch
from a claw-foot bathtub
the owner had found in an alley
and enthroned on a long table
in the center of the restaurant. He hung
the plexiglass sneeze guard on brass chains
over its mouth like a budget
chandelier. Each Sunday, I'd fill the tub
with ice cubes, line the hump with raw kale,
place bowls of lox, rye toast, scrambled
eggs, and cantaloupe in the kinked
green foliage. After church
rouged ladies would scoop
breakfast from the bathtub
onto their plates with metal tongs
while I brewed coffee and pictured
the naked genitals of bathers rising
slick from the porcelain,
shivered and blue-tipped
from the ice. Halfway through
my shift the lox would disappear, leaving
its bowl slick. A pink strip of it always
caught on the tub's edge, bent,
almost raised, like a finger.

FICTION

Visitation

Sean Ennis

The background here is that my son, Jake, and his friends signed a pretty lucrative recording contract two years ago. Some articles I read speculated it was worth seven figures, but I'm sure once the checks were actually cut, my son and his bandmates were not millionaires. Still, he lived well for a while, it seems, renting a space in Brooklyn, not calling home for money. He was twenty-three. He dated a Victoria's Secret model for a bit, if the pictures on the web can be interpreted. Good for him. Jake and his bandmates all graduated from NYU with degrees in finance and philosophy and theoretical physics. His friends always frightened me, the way geniuses can.

Also, after twenty-seven years of marriage, Colleen and I split up. The divorce was amicable. No one had made any major mistakes in the relationship, but once we felt that Jake had been properly deployed, I think we realized we were sick of each other, our evolutionary duty complete.

I was not interested in other women, had good reason to doubt their interest in me, and really just valued time by myself. I'd like to say that my time was spent revisiting classic books or building a necessary work shed or volunteering for others less fortunate. I did none of these things. I had another interest.

Colleen kept the house in Silver Springs, Maryland, and I moved to my late parents' house in Water Valley, Mississippi, which had been empty and unsellable during the housing crisis. My parents were both Southerners by birth, then worked for the federal government in DC, and moved back to the Deep South after their retirement.

They chose to move back to that particular town because of a *New York Times* article that dubbed the place "genuinely quaint." Housing was cheap;

there was a coffee shop and an art gallery and an old-time grocery store that they could walk to. Still, they complained incessantly about the heat, their childhood memories of it romanticized, I guess. And the politics, assuming that being so close to a university, they'd find the familiar liberalism of DC. And the food, which was delicious but monotonously deep fried, they said. They were aliens in that place, and I think it broke their hearts a bit. About a year after they moved to Mississippi, they were both killed in a car accident while trying to pass a tractor on a backcountry road. The irony being that both had navigated the treacherous Capital Beltway for decades.

After I'd been living in my parents' house for a year, Jake called me in tears. In the space of a week, the band had broken up, re-formed without him, and signed a new, more lucrative recording contract, he explained. Clearly, he was the problem. His money was gone, and he was too ashamed to call his mother. His lease was up and I guess his Victoria's Secret girlfriend wasn't offering help.

> "I'll get you a ticket to Memphis," I said. "Pack your shit. Pull it together."

"I'll get you a ticket to Memphis," I said. "Pack your shit. Pull it together."

"Thanks, Pop," he said. "I'm so sorry."

"Love you," I said. "We'll figure it out."

At the Memphis airport, we dragged two enormous pieces of expensive luggage off the carousel. Jake shrugged.

"It's everything I have left," he said. "It was pretty tough getting them here by myself."

As we walked to the car, I inspected my son. He was thin, but he'd always been thin. He was nervous, but he'd always been a nervous kid, and that felt like an appropriate emotion right now. He smoked a cigarette in the parking garage and I didn't fuss. I waited on him.

It was about an hour and a half drive back to Water Valley, much of which was on the same sort of road that killed his grandparents. Once we got off Highway 55, it was incredibly dark. There was only the occasional farmhouse light, or the glare of oncoming traffic, or the reflective eye of a stray dog. This was not Brooklyn. This wasn't even Silver Springs.

"We're going to have to tell Mom eventually, you know?" I said. "She'll want to know where you are."

"When?" he said.

"Tomorrow, I'd think," I said.

"What are you going to tell her?" he said.

"What are *you*?" I said. "I didn't screw up here."

Of course, I'd screwed up plenty. Colleen could attest to this. Beyond my lack of interest in laundry or dishes or vacuuming, I'd gotten interested in something that makes people uncomfortable. Maybe I neglected my wife because of it. Maybe I allowed my son to get involved in business deals he didn't understand when maybe he could have used my help.

> **I wasn't ashamed of my work—I saw *something*—but I felt outed a bit at his appearance.**

I saw the Black Triangle three years ago. I was driving back to our home in Silver Springs after work, when three red lights forming a perfect equilateral triangle flew overhead slowly and soundlessly. There was a lack of stars inside the triangle, suggesting one large structure as it moved across the sky. It took nearly fifteen minutes to pass out of view.

There is another detail that is more difficult to describe. There was something distinctly *alien* about this sighting. The hair on my neck rose; my heart raced. I was frightened in a reptilian way, a way that three simple lights in the sky should not induce.

I told Colleen about what I'd seen when I got home and she rattled off the usual explanations. Airplanes in formation or some other experimental craft (we lived in a suburb of DC after all). Those balloons people put candles in for breast cancer awareness or some other good cause. My own exhaustion, maybe—work had been brutal. None of these solutions felt right, though. To her credit, Colleen never mocked me, but was comfortable ending the conversation with "Pretty weird."

I had never heard of this phenomenon, and felt both justified and terrified when I learned that others had similar experiences. While Colleen slept that night, I did a Google search for "UFO triangle" and found a whole community of people debating what this was. There were videos and photographs, crackpot theories and semiprofessional documentaries.

There was some variation in the accounts, but for the most part, they agreed with mine. If I was crazy, I was not alone.

Jake slept late his first morning at my Mississippi house. This didn't trouble me. No doubt, he was exhausted, and probably not looking forward to whatever talk he expected we'd have. I had no interest in pouncing on him. I made a pot of coffee and put the English muffins and butter and jam in plain view for when he got up.

When I moved into my late parents' house, I turned one of the three bedrooms into an office, though I was no longer working. I had cashed out my retirement plan, but also had the money that was left with my parents' estate, and I figured if I was smart about it, I wouldn't have to work again. Colleen had no interest in arguing about money during the divorce. She had a great job in the attorney general's office, and the house in Silver Springs was paid for. Occasionally, she even appeared on CNN as a commentator about legal issues. She was fine. I think she just wanted to date with a clear conscience. It was fine.

The office was where I did my Black Triangle research. I'd started an Internet forum about the topic and had a decent community of serious followers. There were a few small pictures of Black Triangles on the walls of the office, as well as a map of the world with thumbtacks where sightings had been reported. It did not have the appearance of the den of a delusional person. I made a point of that, though I had few visitors.

At eleven o'clock, Jake appeared at the office door holding a cup of coffee.

"What's all this?" he said.

"Just some research I've been doing to keep myself busy," I said. I had never told him about seeing the Black Triangle. He had already been out of the house, living in Brooklyn, performing and recording. I wasn't ashamed of my work—I saw *something*—but I felt outed a bit at his appearance. On some level, I must have wanted to be caught. I could have locked the door. I could have taken the pictures and the map off the wall.

He scrutinized one of the pictures. It was a photo of the Phoenix skyline at night, with three lights forming a triangle above the skyscrapers.

"It's a stealth bomber?" he said. In many ways, he was a lot like his mother.

"I don't think so," I said. "Too big."

"What is it then?" he said. "A UFO?"

"Technically speaking, yes, that's exactly what it is," I said. "Unidentified."

"You're researching aliens, Pop?" he said.

"I have no idea what is piloting that craft," I said.

He laughed. "Cool," he said. "I guess we need to have a talk, huh?"

"Whenever you're ready," I said. "And then we need to call your mother."

Jake took his coffee onto the back deck and lit a cigarette. I watched him from the window in the office above; he didn't seem to be suffering from some sort of serious withdrawal. He was steady on his feet. We'd call Colleen after lunch, I decided.

I turned back to the computer. There was a new Black Triangle video on YouTube that needed my assessment. There were multiple witnesses. Birmingham, England. I put another thumbtack on the map, and went down to the kitchen.

Jake was buttering an English muffin. I refilled my coffee cup and sat with him at the table.

"So, I have a few questions," I said. "To clear the air. I'd appreciate your honesty."

Jake sighed and said, "Shoot."

"Heroin?" I said.

"No."

"Cocaine?" I said.

"Barely," he said. "I didn't like it. Some of the other guys did though."

"Booze?"

"Sure," he said. "Everyone drinks in that business."

"That's why you're here?" I said. "You were drinking too much?"

"I don't think so," he said. "My lawyer told me to say 'creative differences.'"

"I'm your father," I said. "Why are you here?"

He crunched into his English muffin. "They kicked me out of the group. They said I couldn't really sing. I was just yelling. The rest of the guys are *musicians*."

Jake was right. His friends were all talented at their instruments, and he was the voice of the group. The band's songs were often without a chorus, and he wrote strange lyrics that reminded me of my most confused moments in literature classes in college. Colleen and I had never pressed the music angle with him. He banged a tambourine and babbled into the microphone.

"What are you going to tell Mom?" I said.

"I don't know," he said. "The truth?"

"I'm going to ask again," I said. "Heroin?"

Jake got up from the table, slapped me on the back, and put his plate in the dishwasher. "You can't believe everything you read on the Internet, Pop."

I had good reasons for these questions. The bloggers announced him as an addict when they talked about the breakup of his band, but there was little proof. They linked to YouTube shorts in which my son seemed to be some sort of charismatic gorilla with a microphone. Falling off the stage. Crashing back into the drum kit. Strange mumbles between songs. Did that really mean heroin? Could it not be showmanship? Artistic intensity? Genuine weirdness?

I decided to give Jake his privacy while he called his mother. I paused on the stairs as he made the call, I heard him say, "I'm at Dad's," and, "Yeah, Mississippi," and then I went back up to my office.

I pulled up the Birmingham video again, and then applied the filters. Nothing strange about the footage. It looked legit. I posted my initial assessment that this seemed like more evidence of the Black Triangle phenomenon. I e-mailed the source of the video to get further confirmation of authenticity.

People are always asking me what I think these Black Triangles are, but I'm too cowardly to speculate.

Since I run a site like this, people are always asking me what I think these Black Triangles are, but I'm too cowardly to speculate. Maybe they are piloted by beings a lot like us, inspecting the earth out of pure curiosity. Maybe this is some sort of cosmic dare to see if we'll defend ourselves properly. Maybe they are as apathetic to our dramas as observers of ants are in their backyard. Maybe the gigantic crafts are funded by all our tax dollars and driven by humans with security clearance to soon float above NASCAR and the Super Bowl.

To be honest, a final explanation would have ruined my interest. As much as I was collecting data, the great fear was a definitive answer. I hoped the glut of information might preclude that, confuse that. My marriage had fallen apart; my son's life was falling apart. I could barely say why, but, please, don't tell me it's my fault. Please don't tell me a mysterious object in the sky is more intelligible than my own inscrutable family.

Jake appeared again at my office door. "She wants to talk to you."

As always, our conversation was congenial. Colleen was upset that Jake hadn't called her first, or at least right after he called me, but she understood. She wondered out loud if Mississippi was the best place for either of us. I let her talk because this was all news to her.

"It's not drugs, is it?" she said. "The Internet says it's drugs."

"He looked me in the eye and said no," I said. "You can't believe everything you read on the Internet. He says they kicked him out because he can't sing."

Colleen scoffed. "I never understood it, the music they made."

The Black Triangle hovering huge in broad daylight with plenty of witnesses.

"We're getting old, I guess," I said.

"Well, what are you two going to do?" she said. "What's the plan?"

Jake and I drove into Oxford that night to see a local blues singer play. The Longshot Bar was dingy and awkwardly shaped, but they had good music and decent food. The act that night was Blind and Deaf Calvin, an ancient man with both his sight and his hearing intact, but a local legend nonetheless. Forty years ago, he had played with many of the greats in the Delta juke joints—Muddy Waters, John Lee Hooker, BB King—but he never got the crucial invite to Chicago. Instead, he spent some time in jail for a stabbing, and had to wait for this college town to once again be interested in blues music. His original songs were catastrophes, like "She's a Dick" and "I'd Knife You Again."

Still, once his set got going, there was no doubt he was compelling. Sorority girls from Ole Miss were feeding him shots of Jack Daniel's, and as Jake and I kept drinking, Calvin was sounding better and better. It was difficult to say whether he was good as a guitar player, since the volume was turned so loud. Distortion and feedback ruled the performance, but the crowd loved it. He ended with a ten-minute-long cover of "Rollin' Stone" that brought everyone into a frenzy. We all wished we were catfish for a minute and it was joyous.

Then they flashed the lights on, and we were pushed out onto the square. I pulled my keys out of my pocket, and had to close one eye to find which was for the car.

"Give me those," Jake said and laughed. "You're drunk."

I handed them over. "I'm sorry I'm not fit to pilot this vehicle," I said.

"It's fine," he said. "My guess is that you don't get to have many nights out like this. It was fun."

When he pulled onto the dark road that killed his grandparents, I said, "That man can't sing. What makes him so special?"

"Yeah," Jake said. "But he's doing something right."

Highway 7 gets darker and darker as you make your way from Oxford toward Water Valley. I craned my neck in the passenger seat to see the sky. Nothing moving, nothing shocking. I knew from my map in the office that the Black Triangle rarely appeared in Mississippi, but I thought it might be the best way to end such a night.

"I never told you what I saw," I said. "Those pictures in the office. I saw one back in Silver Springs. A Black Triangle."

Jake nodded, lit a cigarette, and cracked his window. "I figured as much, Pop."

"Think I'm crazy?" I said.

"I'm not sure yet, to be honest," he said. "But it's a hard thing to disagree with your father. Why would you lie about it?"

"As an excuse for why my marriage failed?" I said. "As a reason why you're going through what you are? I wonder about these things all the time."

"No offense," Jake said, "But your opinions about aliens have little to do with the way I'm evaluating my situation right now."

I was drunk and this made me angry. "You think, like your mother, that I am a fool. And I never said 'aliens.'"

"I didn't mean to say it didn't matter," Jake said. "Just that I'm not exactly in the position to judge people."

The dream is always the same. The Black Triangle hovering huge in broad daylight with plenty of witnesses. Sometimes Colleen is there. It's a bit menacing, but obvious, and what it means isn't important in the logic of the dream. We're all cheering, as it passes overhead, then disappears behind an anonymous skyline or mountain ridge. There is this overwhelming sense that something is about to change. It's not difficult to interpret.

But the worst part of the dream, which also repeats without fail, is that I always turn to someone and say, "This is just like my dreams. But here it is. *Real.*" It's at that point I always wake up, the logic of the fantasy glitching, not knowing how to proceed.

I had this dream again the night after Jake and I went to Oxford, and I woke up, as usual, covered in sweat. I hadn't been hungover in years, but I recognized the symptoms. The deep, dull ache in my head. The wretched taste in my mouth. The unnamable guilt.

I staggered down the hall toward the coffeemaker and saw Jake in his bedroom with the contents of his luggage strewn across the room. He was sitting on the floor, crying.

He looked up when I knocked on the door and he did not try to hide his distress.

"What am I going to do?" he said. "What am I going to do with all of these ridiculous clothes?" Empty beer bottles were scattered around the room and it was clear that Jake hadn't gone to sleep the night before.

But he was right. There was a pair of white leather pants with red stitching. There was a button-up shirt that looked as though it had been made out of a scorched American flag. There was a pair of green boots with the toes curled up like some kind of medieval bard's. So many sparkling scarves. And on and on, probably thousands of dollars' worth of clothes, unwearable, except onstage.

"It's all right," I said. "We can go to Walmart."

"I'm a clown," he said. "*Was* a clown. A talentless clown, apparently."

I told him I was proud of him, which was true. I told him I knew it wasn't easy to admit that things had gone bad—just look at me and his mother. I told him we could do whatever he wanted with those clothes. I told him to look in my closet. Nothing too great in there either. We could bombard Goodwill with bizarre clothes and start from scratch. He smiled for a second.

Jake paced around the men's clothing section of Walmart shaking his head. He'd occasionally pull something off the rack and hold it against himself, then he'd put it back. Mississippi was an infamously obese state, so the Walmart didn't stock many jeans with a twenty-eight-inch waist. I watched from the aisle, trying to give him some space. When he was a kid, Colleen and I would often have to put his socks on five or six times in the morning until he finally said they "felt right." I hoped something like that was happening here.

"Why do all the pants have six pockets?" Jake said. "What the hell am I supposed to be carrying around?"

"Whatever you want, I guess," I said. "Cargo. No need for a purse."

He didn't like the joke, and stepped back among the racks. This shopping trip was a bad idea. Why hadn't I taken him to the fancy mall in Memphis? Why not just give him my credit card and let him shop online?

In the end, he bought a pair of Wranglers and a pair of Dickies, a package of Hanes white undershirts, and an Ole Miss sweatshirt. A whole wardrobe for about $100. The look on his face at the checkout was pure disgust.

We drove across the Walmart parking lot to the Chili's.

"I'm not much of a chef," I said. "Is this okay?"

The restaurant was huge, but still packed. They gave us one of those machines that vibrate and flash when your table is ready. Jake was chuckling and shaking his head. I got it.

"Not like waiting for a table at a hip restaurant in Brooklyn, huh?" I said. "At least they have the game on." There were eight televisions in the bar, each with some obscure contest, and I knew Jake could care less about sports. Neither did I.

"You know, when you order one beer here, they bring you two," I said. "That's part of the deal."

"That seems inefficient," he said. "Bringing things people didn't order."

"It's just the way they do it," I said. "Part of the charm of the place."

"The charm . . ." Jake said. "If I wanted two beers, why wouldn't I order that? I don't understand why a person would want two beers at once."

"You're right," I said. "And they probably just pour one beer into two glasses. The bastards!"

The machine in my hand would not flash or vibrate. Jake was getting more and more agitated. After twenty minutes of waiting, he excused himself to the parking lot to smoke and talk on his phone as he hovered around my car. It wasn't clear to me who he was talking to. He hadn't mentioned anyone.

I knew that Chili's was a ridiculous restaurant, but when he was younger, he preferred places like this. Salads drowning in dressing, burgers unnecessarily elaborate, french fries "improved" by something other than salt. The cheap decadence. I thought we'd create some nostalgia.

When we finally were seated, Jake ordered salmon. Chili's was not known for its fresh fish. He ordered one beer, got two, and drank both in

The look on his face at the checkout was pure disgust.

Visitation 211

frantic, shaky gulps. When his food arrived he pushed it around the plate like a child. In his defense, the pink flesh of the salmon did look more like something that had been experimented on rather than cooked. So I quit my bacon cheeseburger, paid the bill, and we left.

Back at the house, Jake took his Walmart bags to his room, then came back downstairs wearing his ill-fitting Dickies and a white undershirt.

"I think I need to go back to Silver Springs," he said. "Being here is not helping."

"Well," I said. "You'll need to talk to Mom about that. You've only been here a few days."

"I appreciate how you've been about all this, Pop, I really do," he said. "But I don't think I'm cut out for Mississippi."

I said, "You're welcome to stay as long as you want, and I appreciate the company, the time spent with you. You'll have to talk to Mom."

I wasn't shocked that Jake wouldn't thrive in Mississippi. But it was my home now, and I'd seen how the place was mocked and reviled in the national media. It wasn't Brooklyn or Silver Springs but it was the way normal people lived. What did it mean not to be "cut out" for it?

He cried a little again, and I told him I'd give him a minute. I went back to the office, and found eight e-mails about a new Black Triangle sighting. Tucson, Arizona. When I clicked on the video, it was clearly a fake. It was taken in broad daylight, but the craft didn't interact well with the clouds and looked splotchy as it passed behind and reappeared on the other side of tall buildings. Such an obvious, real sighting would have been international news. This was some asshole playing with a computer graphics program.

I'd seen plenty of fakes before. It always astonished me how many people were working on these sorts of things. As obvious as they were to identify, they still clearly took a lot of time to create. What was the point? I hoped the creators were young artists, honing their craft, aiming for some special-effects job. My fear was that they were just fucking liars.

Colleen agreed to take Jake in. I don't know exactly what was said between them, but I wasn't surprised. I drove him back to the Memphis airport the

> **Would aliens be so unoriginal and clueless as to think I could help them?**

next day, his mother paying the exorbitant last-minute one-way fare. He had winnowed his luggage down to just one bag, but his ticket was a red flag. He'd be pulled out of line for sure for inspection and interrogation. If they Googled his name, it might get worse.

But he was wearing his Wranglers and Ole Miss sweatshirt in the terminal like every other goof in the Memphis airport. I suddenly felt compelled to yell, "Don't you know who this is? He's a famous singer!" But this was Elvis's town, and I really had no idea just how famous my son was.

"I love you, Pop," he said at the gate. "Thanks for everything."

"You're my son," I said. "What the hell else could I do? Let me know when you get into Dulles."

He got in line for security and I walked back to the parking garage, the snarl of jets overhead, the dark drive home looming yet again.

What I never told Colleen, or Jake, or any of my Internet colleagues, or anyone at all, was that something else happened that night I saw the Black Triangle in Silver Springs. I was taken, I think. I was transported somewhere and lost what felt like several days. Mainly, I lay on a table and was submitted to all kinds of medical inspections. There was a crowd, a theater like in those paintings of the first operations. I was the star of the show.

But I've watched a lot of dumb movies and TV. And I've always had an active dream life. Maybe it was nothing. Would aliens be so unoriginal and clueless as to think I could help them? Imagine traveling millions of light-years to meet me.

Still, there is a scar on my inner thigh that I have no explanation for. The occasional ache in my groin. The nightmares.

These impressions came back to me over time, too. I don't remember leaving or being returned to my car. I didn't arrive home late that night. Colleen didn't seem to think I was acting strange, besides reporting about the lights.

Jake called to say he'd landed in DC safely. His mother eventually called to say Jake looked okay, but she'd bought a home drug test to administer regardless. She didn't want to take any chances, especially since he had come home to her to be taken care of. She needed to "clear her conscience," she said.

I went back to the Longshot Bar to see Blind and Deaf Calvin. Again, I drank too much, just kind of marveling at the spectacle from my stool. All these rich sorority girls going nuts for Calvin's songs about poverty, heartache, and violence. And me, the geezer taking up space at the bar. Who was the real alien here?

On the one-eyed drive home, I got a text message from Colleen. It read, "*HEROIN!!!*" as if it were some sort of victory. Further proof that I had screwed this up. I decided that I'd call her in the morning because more than likely she had locked him in his room, strapped him to his bed, and howled questions he couldn't answer at him.

When I called Colleen the next morning, I could hear the smile on her face.

"He's been using this whole time," she said. "I knew it. The Internet knew it. How did you not?"

I was groggy and heartbroken. "He was only here a few days," I said. "We had a good time. He looked me in the eye about it. Where is Jake?"

"I'm not going to say," she said. "I don't want you showing up with more of your great, worthless advice. He's somewhere safe."

"I need to tell you about something," I said. "The night that I saw that triangle—"

"Don't start with that shit," Colleen said. "That's some kind of weird alibi you've adopted about your family. Jake will *die* if this goes on any longer and you were allowing it to happen."

I crawled back to my office. There were three more sightings posted. Two were clearly fakes, making use of technology Hollywood used in the nineties. Delete. Delete. No need to comment. The next one was hauntingly familiar. Watching the video on YouTube, I got chills, the sense of just being a creature looking up at something incomprehensible. You can hear it in the voices on the recording. It is genuine shock and terror at the lights overhead. Then they are whispering. I clicked the thumbs-up button, typed nothing.

But I reject the idea that Jake was using heroin while he was here. He was not under my observation the entire time, but he exhibited no odd behavior given his circumstances, met with no one strange. The Longshot Bar has its shady elements, I suppose, but nothing so insidious as heroin, right? I'd have to talk to an expert about how long heroin stays in a person's system, the validity of such over-the-counter tests, etc., and I plan to do so. As if I didn't have enough to do. He could have stashed it in his fancy luggage, I guess. He could have been high from the moment I picked him up at the airport.

If heroin weren't a deadly drug, I could care less about Jake using it. The regular world bores fast and needs some enhancement. I get it. Especially if you thought you'd live your life on some stage, in some sort of spotlight.

Two things terrify me now: The reappearance of that Black Triangle in the night sky, that gigantic, obvious thing that no one will believe me about, and that will probably just ignore me now too, an old man. It would coast past, been-there-done-that. And it's too complicated to say what I'd really want to happen. To be the center of its attention is terrifying too. Best to never see the craft again, shut down the site, and call Jake every day.

Or there is what I consider to be the very real possibility that my dreams are something more, that I'm not delusional, that I'm not shifting blame, or desperate for alibis. That I was actually taken away from my family, judged to be genuinely useless except for my ability to produce sperm, and discarded without the benefit of explanation or spectacle. And that I could have, on some other world, yet another son I couldn't possibly understand.

CONTRIBUTORS

John Ashbery's most recent collection of poetry is *Breezeway*.

Anthea Bell, OBE, is an award-winning literary translator. Her best-known translations include works by Hans Christian Andersen, Cornelia Funke, and W. G. Sebald.

Per Aage Brandt is a Danish poet, semiotician, and jazz musician. He was born in 1944 in Buenos Aires and currently lives in Villeneuve-sur-Yonne, France.

Michael Braunschweig was born in 1976 in Meuselwitz and lives in Berlin. "The Tsuchinoko" appears in his forthcoming collection *Other Species*.

Michael Burkard is an American poet.

Sarah Bridgins lives in Brooklyn, New York. You can find more of her work at sbridgins.tumblr.com.

Amanda DeMarco is a translator living in Berlin.

Michael Dickman was born and raised in the Pacific Northwest. His most recent book of poems is called *Green Migraine*.

Joel Drucker's work has appeared in such places as Huffington Post, Salon, HBO, and Tennis Channel. He wrote the book *Jimmy Connors Saved My Life*.

Sean Ennis is the author of the story collection *Chase Us*. He teaches at the University of Mississippi.

Nathan Gauer is the author of *Songs to Make the Desert Bear Fruit*. He currently lives in Paraguay with his wife and son.

Edward Gauvin's translations have been honored by PEN America, the NEA, and the Lannan Foundation. He has translated over 200 graphic novels and 60 short stories.

Misha Hoekstra taught creative writing and literature at Deep Springs College before fleeing to Denmark in 1997. He writes and performs songs as Minka Hoist.

Anna Journey is a poet and essayist. Her third collection of poetry, *The Atheist Wore Goat Silk*, is forthcoming.

Dorianne Laux's most recent collections are *Facts about the Moon* and *The Book of Men*. She teaches poetry in North Carolina State University's MFA program.

Joseph Millar's fourth book of poems, *Kingdom*, is forthcoming in 2017. He is founding faculty and teaches poetry in

Pacific University's Low Residency MFA Program.

Dorthe Nors is one of the most original voices in contemporary Danish letters. Her works include the celebrated short story collection *Karate Chop*.

Whitney Otto is the author of, most recently, *Eight Girls Taking Pictures*.

Alexandra Pechman is a writer living in New York.

Eric Puchner is the author of two books. His new story collection, *Last Day on Earth*, will be published this spring.

Sam Riviere is the author of the poetry collections *81 Austerities*, *Standard Twin Fantasy*, and *Kim Kardashian's Marriage*.

Marin Sardy is an essayist whose work has appeared or is forthcoming in *Missouri Review*, *Fourth Genre*, *Post Road*, and elsewhere.

Thom Satterlee is a novelist, poet, and translator. He lives in Marion, Indiana.

Alexis M. Smith is the author of the novels *Glaciers* and *Marrow Island*. She lives in Portland, Oregon with her wife and son.

Saša Stanišić won acclaim with his debut novel *How the Soldier Repairs the Gramophone*. *Before the Feast*, his second novel, won the 2014 Leipzig Book Fair Prize.

Jackson Tobin is a graduate of the MFA program at the University of Wisconsin-Madison. He is at work on his first short story collection.

Jean-Philippe Toussaint is a Belgian writer and filmmaker whose books have been translated into more than twenty languages.

Deb Olin Unferth's next book, a collection of stories, is forthcoming in spring 2017.

Josh Weil is the author of the novel *The Great Glass Sea* and the novella collection *The New Valley*. He lives in the Sierra Nevadas.

Malerie Willens's stories have appeared in *Best American Nonrequired Reading*, *AGNI*, *Electric Literature*, *Open City* and *Canteen*. She lives in New York City.

FRONT COVER:

Delicate Garden: The Bear, acrylic on canvas, 48″ x 42″, 2015. © Kevin Sloan. www.kevinsloan.com.

MIDWESTERN GOTHIC
A LITERARY JOURNAL

FICTION AND POETRY BY
FRANK BILL | BONNIE JO CAMPBELL | ROXANE GAY
AMOREK HUEY | LINDSAY HUNTER | JEFF VANDE ZANDE
AND MANY MORE

DISCOVER A REGION WITH A VOICE ALL ITS OWN
MIDWESTGOTHIC.COM

The BAFFLER

Baffling the consensus since 1988, the magazine abrasive ridicules respectable business leaders, laughs at popular consumer brands as souvenirs of the cultural industry, and debunks the ideology of free-market nincompoops in the media and on the campuses. Issues contain art and criticism from some of the best writers, artists, and poets in the country.

Commodify your dissent for just $20–25 a year.

thebaffler.com & mitpressjournals.org/baffler

"In phantasmagoric, almost delirious prose, Steven Sherrill writes from a distinctly southern perspective, from a landscape that is rendered credulous and incredulous at once, as parody and earnest rendering, a psychic road map of contemporary dystopic America. Happily, there's still a place for skewed prophetic voices the likes of Sherrill in American letters. A singular voice; there's no one else like him on the literary landscape."

—Robin Hemley, author of *Reply All*

Yellow Shoe Fiction | Michael Griffith, Series Editor
$22.50 paper

Available in bookstores and online at www.lsupress.org

IR
INDIANA REVIEW

Fiction
Poetry
Nonfiction
Artwork

SINCE 1976

indianareview.org
inreview@indiana.edu

MASTER OF ARTS/MASTER OF FINE ARTS IN
Creative Writing

- Work closely with faculty through workshops and individual mentoring.
- Take advantage of the best features of residential and low-residency programs.
- Choose from specializations in fiction, creative nonfiction and poetry.
- Refine your writing skills in convenient evening courses in Chicago and Evanston.

RECENT AND CONTINUING FACULTY INCLUDE

Chris Abani	Goldie Goodbloom	Naeem Murr
Eula Biss	Miles Harvey	Ed Roberson
Stuart Dybek	Cristina Henríquez	Megan Stielstra
Reginald Gibbons	Simone Muench	S. L. Wisenberg

The fall quarter application deadline is July 15.
sps.northwestern.edu/cw • 312-503-2579

Northwestern | SCHOOL OF PROFESSIONAL STUDIES

ABOUT THE COVER

KEVIN SLOAN's allegorical paintings tell of the intersection of natural and man-made worlds. He aims to convey the darkness in this conflict and to create a sense of hope, illustrating a transitional world where, he says, "some things will be lost and others will continue on." His art comes from "the tension between loss and the [remaining beauty]."

This issue's cover art, *Delicate Garden: The Bear*, is part of Sloan's Delicate Garden series, in which he depicts animals as porcelain objects. His creatures are positioned as if they are still lifes and marred with cracks. Like the natural world they are "alive, sentient, and very fragile." They are, at once, wild and manufactured. Nature persists as flora grows through broken spaces. Our ursine cover model exudes a relaxed air, his expression pleasant, as he sits on a pile of littered clocks—evidence of humanity's intrusion.

Sloan's influences range from the landscape of his home state of Colorado to the visual narratives found in advertising. While he uses photos as starting points, he follows an organic process. He begins with soft charcoal and reworks the structure of each painting until he has a strong foundation. From there, he adds acrylic washes, switching back to charcoal or chalk when necessary. "Eventually," he says, "the painting starts to need me less and less, until it has reached some sort of equilibrium. It's almost like a perfect tone, not too sharp or flat, just right."

You can see more of his art at www.kevinsloan.com.

Written by *Tin House* designer Jakob Vala, based on an interview with the artist.